TEST OF TYRANTS

VEILBLOOD ACADEMY

BOOK TWO

CLARA WILS

Gryphon's Gate Publishing

Test of Tyrants

Copyright © 2026 Clara Wils

All rights reserved. No part of this book may be reproduced in any form or by any means without written consent, excepting brief quotes used in reviews.

This is a work of fiction. Names, places, characters, and events are entirely the product of the author's imagination or are used fictitiously, and any resemblance to persons, living or dead, actual locals, events, or organizations is coincidental.

Gryphon's Gate Publishing
550 King St. N.
PO Box 42088 Conestoga
Waterloo, ON
N2L 6K5

Print ISBN: 978-1-990587-73-3

IZZY

I HATED FAINTING. IT MADE ME FEEL WEAK, LIKE SOME delicate damsel in distress, which I wasn't. I'd fainted twice in the past. Once when I'd been a child and I'd learned my foster mother, Beatrice Moonie had died. Then again, after my first shift at the bar. I'd been out of work for a while and hadn't eaten much in days, then I'd worked myself to the bone that night, fainting at the end of my shift.

And now...

Well, to be fair, it had been a difficult few days. I'd arrived in a strange new world, with magic and dragons and demons and angels. I'd been beaten and bullied by an insane princess, while stretching myself to my limits trying to understand and learn magic.

In the last two days, my room had been incinerated, I'd had my first threesome, I'd brought an angel back from the brink of death, had a rather stunning quickie with that angel, then fallen out with the two guys I'd had the threesome with, because of that quickie with the angel. Then... as if that hadn't been enough of a roller-coaster of emotions,

Saldrea — the aforementioned insane princess — had found me, roughed me up, and ripped away some binding magic, which I'd had all my life, forcibly changing my form. At which point a dragon I'd thought wanted to kill me, helped me escape and I'd gone into hiding. And to top it all off, it turned out I was a *true princess*, and my real name was Isolde.

So yeah, I may have been a teensy-weensy bit overwhelmed and had good reason for blacking out.

"Izzy?" Myel sounded worried. His voice drifted to me. It wasn't the first time he'd said my name, but this one sounded closer. I became aware of lying in someone's arms. Given the sense of ease and comfort filling me, I guessed it was Myel's. The two of us had been magically bonded, our souls linked and our bodies craving each other — yes, sexually — practically *all* the time. The upside was, when I was close to him, I got the best high, serene and relaxed.

Someone else was holding my hand, and from that connection came an influx of warmth, like summer's heat with a hint of humidity and the faint smell of rain after a storm. That would be Vyns. He too was connected to me, but in spirit. I had no clue how that link worked. It was still relatively new. Yet the soothing warmth he sent me helped me recover.

I sighed heavily as I came to.

Time to face the music.

I blinked my eyes open. I was indeed in Myel's arms, looking up at his beautiful pale face. Vyns knelt next to us.

Three others stood nearby.

Rook was tall, dark, and sexy, with eyes like smoldering embers and flame-red hair. The two of us had a complicated relationship, if you could even call it that. We had sex, and as an incubus he'd rocked my world more than once, but he was also the reason I'd been brought to this strange world. I'd thought we'd mostly reconciled that betrayal of his, and were *maybe* friends? I didn't know anymore, he'd been distant when we'd last spoke, and even now, he stood farthest away, arms crossed over his chest, looking a little worried, but mostly confused and put out.

Then there was the dragon — I still didn't know his name — who'd served princess Saldrea right up until a few minutes ago. I had no clue if I could even trust him but he *had* helped me get away from the princess and her goons, taking attacks meant for me. Then, he'd bowed before me offering me his allegiance. If that didn't deserve a *what-the-fuck*, I didn't know what did.

He'd also been naked, having shifted into a dragon and back, but now he was covered with a bed sheet. And when I say covered, I mean it was wrapped around his waist, revealing his thick torso, beefy chest, and heavy arms, all of which were covered in *a lot* of scars. Nobody in this world had it easy it seemed, not even dragons. Waves of silvery hair framed a hard-featured face with eyes of glowing gold under a strong brow and the perfect scruff of a beard on a square jaw.

He wasn't quite as handsome as he could be, though, not with that nasty, weeping wound marring the left side of his face, which looked painful as hell. If I had to guess, that would be Saldrea's handy work.

The sheet around the dragon's waist was from the bed belonging to the last man in the room, because this was his room. He was new, older. Myel had brought us to him. He'd been the one to tell me my name.

Isolde.

Fucking hell.

Isolde? Really? Could you get more archaic and out of date? I mean, sure I was glad I wasn't an Isabella, I'd never been fond of that name, but still...

"Hey," I said weakly, attempting a smile for everyone.

Myel smiled softly, relief flooding his features. "Hey." Myel was all my teen goth-girl fantasies made manifest. He had thick black hair falling over his face, sable eyes filled with soulful angst, and a tall, lean body covered in scars, because this world treated shifters like shit.

I sat up slowly, my head still spinning, brain a little fuzzy. Though whatever Vyns was doing with his spirit was quickly dispelling that fog.

Ah... Vyns, my literal angel: beautiful, built, blond and blue perfection, like a Hemsworth, but with stunning white and gold wings!

"So..." I drew out the word. "Someone want to explain... *everything*?"

Several people began talking at once, Myel and the dragon and the old man.

Yeah, that wasn't going to work for me.

"Stop!" I yelled. The effort made my head throb, and I had to close my eyes and take a few deep breaths to get back to a non-pained state.

First thing's first.

I pointed at the dragon. "What's your name?" I couldn't keep referring to him as *the dragon*.

"Koarthandris, Your Highness. Most people call me Koar."

That was simple enough.

I shifted my pointing hand to the old man. "What's your name and who are you?"

"Safir, Your Majesty," he said with a deep bow. "I am a

tiger shifter, who served your parents and have been working for some time to bring you to the throne."

There was a lot packed into that sentence.

My parents? He knew my parents! That was huge!

And he'd been working *for some time* to bring me to the throne? Like... how long? As much as my curiosity clawed at me to ask more about my parents, I had to know...

"How long...?" I asked, jaw tight, voice strained. "How long have you known all this? How long have you kept me in the dark about who I am?" It came out as a growl. To say I was upset was a vast understatement. Had this man known who I was my whole life and never bothered to find me and tell me?

"Told you she'd be pissed," Myel muttered under his breath.

Oh, I was, and at Myel too. He'd known who I was as well. But for now, my wrath was focused on the old man: Safir.

"Your whole life," he said, voice soft, breathy. He knelt, head bowed. "I am sorry, Your Majesty. I... I failed you in so many ways. I should have protected you as a child, should have raised you... but I... lost you."

Lost me?

What the fuck?

How do you lose a child?

I mean, I'd heard of parents losing their kids in crowded places, but still...!

"It's a long story,' Safir hedged, perhaps sensing my mounting fury.

"I think we have a few minutes!" I growled.

Safir sighed. "Yes, Your Majesty."

"And stop calling me that!" I snapped. "My name is

Izzy!" Okay, fine, actually my name was Isolde, but I wasn't ready to accept that yet.

Myel helped me up and got me to a chair. I sat heavily as Myel and Vyns hovered nearby. Koar and Rook leaned on the walls. The dragon seemed wary, glancing about, worried. The incubus looked bored, head back against the wall, looking at the ceiling.

Safir sat on his bed.

"Should I start at the beginning?" he asked.

"That's usually the best place," I fumed, still worked up.

He nodded.

"I served your father," he said, voice even, looking away, gaze distant. "Well, my father served your father first, but I took on my father's duties when he passed."

Again... everyone in this world seemed to have a master, working for someone. It irked me to no end. If I *was* a princess, I'd do my damnedest to make sure everyone in this world was free and didn't have to serve anyone!

"By then, we were all in the human realm. Your parents had been banished from our realm because of your parents' love. An elf and a nymph... together... Your grandmother did all she could to shelter them, but when they insisted on getting married, she had to exile them."

Had to?

Wouldn't my grandmother have been the queen? Women ruled this world, not men — which was nice — but if so, why couldn't *the queen* have changed the laws if she didn't like them?

Fuck, this world was messed up! Exiled because of love? Sheesh!

"I was not your protector immediately, but... when assassins came for your parents—?"

"Assassins?" I cut in. "Human assassins?"

"No, Your Maj— Isolde... Izzy." Safir stumbled over the words. I didn't quite understand why it was so hard for him to say my name. "Assassins from *this* realm, sent by Valnea most likely, though I've never been able to confirm that fact."

Valnea was the current queen regent and Saldrea's mother. Viciousness ran in their family, it seemed.

"Why?" I burst out. "They were already exiled! Why send assassins?"

"Because even as exiles they were a threat to Valnea's power. She couldn't leave any true royal alive. If your mother had chosen to renounce her husband and reclaim the throne..." Safir shrugged.

I simmered with rage, but I didn't know who I was most angry at: Safir, Valnea, this whole damned world! With no outlet, I let my fury boil, which made it hard to concentrate on Safir's story.

I tried more deep breaths.

Didn't help.

Safir went on, "When the assassins came, your parents tried to fight them off. Your mother was incredibly strong with earth magic and tore through dozens of them... but more came. So, your parents gave you over into my custody. I was charged with getting you to safety. And I did."

Safir sighed heavily. "And that's when... I chose... poorly. I felt duty bound to return and protect my master, your father, and your mother as well." His head fell, ashamed. "Once I'd found a safe place to hide you... I returned to your parents to help them, but by the time I got back, they... had... perished. I immediately returned to where I'd left you... but you... were gone."

Wait... "How old was I?"

I'd been first adopted when I was two. Though no one had been sure of my exact age since I'd had no records.

"A few weeks past your second birthday."

"You left a two-year-old *alone*?" I scolded him, in shock. I'd known enough two-year-olds to know you can't just leave them. They walked well enough and rarely had enough sense to stay in one place: too curious and absent-minded for their own good.

"It was... a mistake." And the instant he said it he knew those words had also been... a mistake.

"A mistake!" I erupted, standing. "Your little *mistake*... ruined my whole life!" I shouted. I shouldn't raise my voice. We were supposed to be hiding, but I couldn't help it. "Don't you have some shifter sense which could have found me?" Everyone here seemed to be able to smell the weirdest things. As a tiger... couldn't he have tracked me down somehow? "What happened?"

"I don't know, Your Majest— Izzy." Safir was clearly flustered.

At any other time the word majestizzy would have made me laugh, but not today.

"I followed your scent, but whoever found you must have put you in a car or something, since your trail just... stopped. After that, I searched for years... but I could never find you. I suspect your mother did more than bind you into human form but also made it difficult for people to track you."

My mother had put that binding on me? The one Saldrea had undone? The one which had kept me looking human for most of my life? When in truth... I'd been something else entirely.

God! There was so much I didn't know... and this man did.

And he could have explained it all to me years ago, if he hadn't left a two-year-old alone!

I couldn't even look at him. One glance and I'd see red and explode. I focused on my hands, balled into fists, as I sat back down, still fuming, furious. My body vibrated with a righteous rage.

Myel knelt next to me, holding my hand. And it said something about the extent of my anger that the contact barely soothed me.

"And how much did *you* know?" I accused my bonded.

"Not the details, but I've known you were royalty for some time. I argued that we should tell you, but Safir overruled me."

"And you can't think for yourself? Make your own choices?"

My words hit home. Myel flinched. A part of me cheered in victory that I'd won that little fight, but another part felt his shame and self-loathing and impotence.

He averted his gaze, looking down.

Fuck. I'd kicked a puppy.

"Sorry," I said, though even to my own ears I didn't sound apologetic. "I'm a little *enraged* right now. I don't know what your situation was. Thank you... for *wanting* to tell me?" It didn't sound like a good apology, but Myel looked up with a sad smile and nodded.

God, this man... always so damned understanding. That puppy-dog analogy was really on point. I'd kicked him and he'd come bounding back, loyal to a fault.

I sighed heavily, but it did nothing to relieve my fury, nor the frenetic tension bouncing around like some crazed rubber ball inside me.

"Anyone else have any surprises they want to spring on

me?" I asked with an edge to my voice. "Might as well do it now so I don't have to get angry again later."

"If Saldrea finds out about *any* of this, she'll kill you," Koar rumbled, voice hushed.

Yeah, because that's what I needed to hear right now.

Fuck!

Well, let's add that to the pile of deadly shit I'd stepped in when I'd come to this world.

IZZY

"Did she suspect anything when she undid the binding on you?" Koar asked.

"I don't know..." I said, honestly. "She didn't have a lot of time to take it in, before I escaped. She seemed more upset and disgusted that I was a half-breed."

"So... she may not know you're a royal... not yet anyway," Safir mused.

"I don't think we can rely on that," Vyns offered.

Thank you Vyns.

"Why *did* she undo the binding?" Rook asked, sounding like he didn't want to be involved in this at all. "How did she even *know* about it?"

"As an elf, she might have sensed it," Safir said, but Koar spoke over him.

"It was luck or fate, call it what you will. She wished to torture Izzy, wanted to have Neyalim turn her into a frog so she could pluck off her limbs, then heal them, over and over again."

"Sick fuck," I murmured.

"Indeed," Koar agreed. "But when Neyalim tried to

transmute Izzy, she couldn't. That's when Saldrea found out there was a binding keeping Izzy's form as it was. After that, she sought to break it."

"While we're on the topic, why are you even here? How did you find out about Izzy's royalty?" Safir asked Koar.

"Her handwriting," the dragon said stoically. "I saw some of Izzy's handwriting in her notebook when Saldrea and the others trashed her room. Something seemed familiar about it, so I compared a sample to old written records. Turns out, she has a lot of the same writing inflection as her mother, even her grandmother. After that... I suspected, but I didn't *know*, till you confirmed it just now."

"Wait," I said, interrupting. "You rescued me, took those attacks for me, and you didn't even know for certain I was a princess?"

Also... wow, I did not give the big man enough credit. I'd thought him a relatively mindless thug, but he'd done all that research and meticulous study.

Koar shrugged his massive shoulders. The sheet hanging off him swayed and I caught a glimpse of thick thighs, but nothing more. Did I want to see more? I mean... right now a distraction wouldn't go amiss, and that huge man's dong would be one hell of a distraction. Still, not what I should be focusing on right now.

"I knew Saldrea *wasn't* what a princess should be... and I had hope," Koar replied evenly.

Wow.

Hope.

He'd been going on hope alone?

"We can't trust him," Safir said, an edge to his voice.

Koar nodded. "That's fair. But consider: I could easily bash through this wall and go tell someone about this illicit meeting. There's not a single one of you who could stop me, except maybe Izzy, but she's still new to her power." He looked at me. And I couldn't say what exactly was in that look, except for maybe some of that hope he'd spoken about. "And Vyns knows me, knows I serve the true crown to a fault. Up till recently, that *fault* was following Saldrea, but I'm done with her. I serve *you* now, Izzy."

And something about how he said it made me want to believe him. And something in the rumbling admission also made me want to climb that sexy AF body of his and find out how dedicated he was.

Wow, girl, slow your roll. You barely know him!

That's how we like our men, remember, unknown, I reminded myself.

True. But he was also threatening you just last week. We can't trust him... yet.

We rarely trust any guy we fuck. Trust is for relationships, which I don't do... or didn't... until recently. That had all changed in the last few days, now I was bonded to two men and had a third fuck-buddy on the side.

Fair. Where were we?

Got me?

I listened to see where the conversation had headed while I'd been chatting with myself.

"Maybe you're waiting to hear our plans, *then* you'll report us to Saldrea," Safir accused Koar.

Koar sighed. "Why would I wait to hear your plans? What purpose would that serve when Hana can rip them from your minds?"

"He's right about that," Vyns added. "He has no reason not to report us if he's working for Saldrea. There's no point to a long con here, that would only make Saldrea mad."

That sounded like the truth to me.

Time to end this argument.

"Safir!" My stern tone got the shifter to turn toward me. Looking at him still made me see red, but not as much as it had a moment ago, more like a deep rose, not quite crimson blood, enough that I could speak to him without exploding.

"I don't trust him either, but Vyns does and Vyns is bound to me and that's good enough for me. That means it's good enough for you, if you serve me. Got it?"

Safir nodded. His disgruntled expression told me he didn't like it, but he didn't argue.

And since I could look at him without combusting, perhaps it was time to find out more.

"Why did you wait to tell me who I am? I've been in this world for several days now, which admittedly isn't too long, but still... you knew exactly where I was. Why couldn't you tell me who I was?"

Safir met my gaze with an intensity I was staring to understand was at the very core of the old man.

"For your own safety." His tone was level, unemotional.

That irked me even more. I hated the tired male trope of using "protecting women" as an excuse for not being honest with them. Also... how could he be so calm at a time like this?

"Please explain how me not knowing made me safer?" I said.

"I don't doubt you could have kept the secret, but it's inevitable: knowing things changes people. Others may have sensed a difference in you and if Saldrea's mind-reading sylph companion had caught one glimpse of your thoughts..."

Ah, yeah. Hana, that damned sylph and her mind-reading. And if Saldrea knew who I was... I'd be dead, plain and simple.

Safir finished with, "The fewer people who knew the truth the better."

Well fuck. That made a lot of sense. Still, others were playing games with my life and that royally pissed me off.

Royally... ha!

I sighed heavily. "Okay yeah, fine. But I'm still mad at you."

"Understood Your Maj— Izzy."

Again, under different circumstances *Majizzy* would have been hilarious, but not right now.

"What does this mean?" I asked. "I have no clue how to be a princess... or an elf for that matter. Wait... do I have earth magic now?" Probably.

The nods from everyone else confirmed it.

"And... bindings?" I murmured. "I can do those?"

Myel tensed. I felt his trepidation, but I didn't know why. Did he think I'd bind him somehow?

"Yes," Safir confirmed. "Your mother was very strong in earth magic and you most likely are as well. The fact that you wore down your mother's binding — enough to start showing your true form — without *any* clue what you were doing, is proof enough of that."

Huh... I had done that, hadn't I?

And...

I shifted around a little, stretching and rolling my joints. I ignored the odd looks from the others as I confirmed... no pain.

My lingering body pain — from healing Vyns, who'd been on the brink of death a few hours ago — had vanished. It had dissipated the instant Saldrea had broken the binding on me. That seemed significant.

I worked it out slowly, talking it through. "Would that binding... would it have potentially caused me pain if I did anything which might have modified my form? Would a workout or strain, where the body usually grows... would the binding have resisted that?"

"That seems logical, yes," Safir confirmed. "If the binding was keeping you as a human, it may have resisted growth in that manner, causing pain."

"But then why didn't I remain a two-year-old, I did grow...?" There was so much I didn't know.

"Your mother was extremely proficient, as I mentioned," Safir said. "She would have accounted for regular growth, so she wouldn't have to constantly redo the binding on you every few weeks or months, especially when you were young."

That explained my chronic body pain every time I'd worked myself too hard: my muscles had been trying to grow and the binding had shut it down.

I looked at Safir. "Since we're stuck here and I'm not the least bit tired." Despite it being quite late at night. "You're going to tell me everything. Everything you know that I don't. Go."

He nodded. "As you wish, Izzy." He'd finally managed to say my name.

Safir told me everything he knew about my parents, which was a lot. Most of it, I probably could have read about in some history book, but the little details were fascinating. My mother's love of plants, nurturing them with her magic, helping them grow. She'd been a florist in the human world and done well for herself. My father's quiet and contemplative nature, which I had *not* inherited. How both had been truly beautiful people inside and out and how much I looked like them.

"Wait..." I stopped him. I rose quickly and went to the small mirror hung on the wall to one side of the room. I hadn't looked at myself since the binding had been broken.

Seeing my real form… took my breath away.

"Oh…" I sighed, lost for words.

My eyes were the same, at least the same color — that rich sea-green, with a ring of emerald around the iris and a circle of darker blue around the edges — but they were also a little larger. Wow. I didn't need makeup to make my eyes pop now! My nose was more refined, a bit smaller and sharper. My hair was no longer dirty blond, but a rich, deep golden blond and my ears were so much taller and very pointy, peeking up through my hair. Gone was my slightly tanned complexion, I was quite pale now. And I looked more like a model, my figure leaner and slimmer, which included my bust. Huh… I didn't know how I felt about that. Being chesty had been one of my prime attributes, even if it hadn't always been a blessing.

To distract myself, I moved my mouth, stunned at the plump fullness of my lips.

This new look was a little too freaky though, so I tried changing myself back to how I'd been before. As a half-nymph I could change my form, but it took a lot of concentration. I was able to fill out my body — back to being chesty and not model-thin — and returned my hair to dirty-blond. But I couldn't control my ears and eyes for some reason. Perhaps I didn't have enough practice for smaller things like that.

I breathed out slowly and let the changes go again, returning to my elven form.

This was going to take a lot of getting used to.

"I can't go out like this," I whispered.

"Saldrea already knows," Koar said from across the room.

"Yeah, but... still..." I traced my cheek and jawline, now much sharper, more defined.

"It will probably be best if you... don't return to your classes," Safir said stoic. "At least until you've learned to control your features, learned your powers."

"How long will that take?" I asked.

"Could take months," Safir said.

Oh, hell no. I couldn't abandon everything here for months! Though... what I was abandoning was learning about this world and my powers, and I *could* do that elsewhere, perhaps it wouldn't be so bad.

Still, what about my friends here? I didn't have many, but I had Tala and Professor Rheoran and Zora... It would be nice to be able to connect with a woman every now and then. The sausage-fest currently surrounding me was nice at times — especially the sexy times — but not *all the time.*

"However," Safir continued. "If you are as much your mother's daughter as I suspect, then you may learn quite quickly, with a good tutor."

I grimaced. "Yeah, but where are we going to find an elf to teach me?" Finding a nymph wasn't a problem, but elves...?

"Not all elves are evil," Safir said. At the same time Koar spoke over him,

"I may have some friends in the capital who could help."

The two glared at each other.

The hatred and distrust between those two alphas was going to be a problem.

"As for your nymph side, your grandmother would be your best resource," Safir said, turning back to me.

I spun from the mirror.

"Grandmother? I have a relative? A *living* relative? Why didn't you say so sooner?"

"I was getting to it, but you asked about your parents first."

I had.

"Your grandmother has been bankrolling this whole operation," Safir added. "She's... quite wealthy."

A rich grandmother. Okay things were starting to look up.

"Well, I guess that's one thing I have going for me," I muttered.

"And you have friends, people who care about you and want to help you," Myel added stepping over to slip his hand into mine, instantly soothing.

"Lots of friends," Vyns added with a smile.

"New friends," Koar added, once again getting down on one knee. "I cannot apologize enough for all the horrible things I did to you. I feel... disgusted with what I did in Saldrea's name. I seek only to serve the crown and now that I know you are the true princess, I will serve you with everything I have and everything I am. I know you will be a far better ruler than Saldrea could ever have been. I dedicate myself to you: body, mind, and soul."

Wow.

"And I accept any and all punishment you wish to give me for my past transgressions," he added.

Punishment?

An image flashed in my mind of me in a black leather catsuit with Koar naked, on his knees, bound and begging to serve me, pleasure me, please me, his towering erection... was *not* what I should be thinking about right now!

I breathed out slowly as that vision faded.

"He's a good man," Vyns whispered. "I trust him."

He'd misunderstood my hesitation.

"Ah... yeah... well, we'll see about all of that. No punishment yet, okay, so... get up."

Koar did.

"I can think of a few fitting punishments," Safir mumbled.

"Shut it, old man," I scolded.

Safir nodded solemnly.

Still, despite the support the guys had shown me — all except Rook — I was completely overwhelmed.

And why *hadn't* Rook said anything?

I asked him point blank, "What do *you* think about all this?"

He sighed heavily and shrugged, reluctantly meeting my gaze. "I'm just a sex demon," he said with a half-hearted grin. "Not really sure why I'm here."

Ouch.

Okay, so *not* friends then.

"Saldrea will soon know Izzy was staying in your room, if she doesn't already. That makes you an accomplice. She'll come for you," Koar said.

"Great," Rook muttered.

"You're a part of this, one way or another, incubus," Safir said, not sounding happy about it. Though, if I understood the old man — and that was still an uncertainty — he was more irritated that too many people knew *his* secret.

"What's gotten into you?" I asked Rook directly. "I thought you were my friend?"

"We have sex and I help you out a little, if that makes us friends, then sure." He shrugged and looked away.

I'd known since we first met, he wasn't into relationships, but wow, I'd thought we were more to each other than that.

I guessed not.

And I didn't know why that stung my soul so much. Rook wasn't bound to me, and I'd never been the type to get attached... so why did I want *him* to be more attached?

Was that selfish of me?

Probably.

Fuck it. I had too much to worry about without him being a dick. If this is what he wanted, then fine.

I turned to Safir. "So... what's the plan?"

VYNSIEL

What was the deal with that incubus? Was he an idiot? Couldn't he see Izzy was intelligent, beautiful and powerful? Why in hell would he push her away? Yet, that seemed to be exactly what he was doing.

I'd never understand demons.

Because to me, Izzy was perfect. Sure, I was biased, my spirit knew her to be my ideal mate, but it didn't affect my mind, didn't skew my thoughts. I could still see reason and the truth of the matter was... when Koar had told me Izzy was a royal, everything had clicked for me. She wasn't just perfect for me, she was perfect *for this world*, exactly what Seial needed.

I could see in her gorgeous, sea-green eyes that she didn't believe it yet, didn't see it in herself, but I did. She was pure and kind and smart. She didn't have a hair-trigger temper, like some *other* princesses. Izzy's anger was a righteous thing, meant to help the innocent and punish those who sought to oppress others. And even if she hadn't learned much magic yet, she was powerful. She'd healed me from the brink of death after having been here for less than a week, knowing so little of what she could do. When she came into her own, she'd be a force to be reckoned with.

That's why Izzy was perfect.

That and... a part of me still hoped that by serving her, being closer to her, loving her, she could wipe the filth from my soul and mend what had been torn asunder within me: the stain I'd acquired while being Saldrea's brute for far too long.

It no longer mattered to me that Izzy was mate-bonded to a shifter, or that she'd had intercourse with a demon. It was clear Myel loved her deeply and Rook, well he didn't seem to want her, which baffled me. I could share this wonderful woman, and if the demon didn't want her, that suited me just fine.

Because when I was close to her, I felt more like the man I wanted to be, the man I should be.

I would follow Izzy to the ends of the earth... but first I needed to go home to Elysial and make sure my family was safe. They may not care for me, other than as a tool to elevate their status. And I shouldn't care what happened to them after how they'd treated me my entire life, but I did. I hoped that was the "good man" in me coming out. Because no one — not even my petty, self-serving family — deserved to face Saldrea's wrath. And they would. Saldrea was furious at me for leaving her and would take it out on my family. I needed to warn them.

I'd ask Koar to take me home, it would be a quick journey for him. Hopefully he'd have time before whatever else these folks had planned.

Safir, the tiger shifter, finally responded to Izzy's question after mulling it over.

"I need to get you off campus, at least for now," he said, pacing the limited space. "You should be safe with your grandmother. And she may know of some elves willing to train you."

He spun and pinned Myel down with his intense gaze. "Can you shadow-step us directly to the sigil point, Izzy and myself?"

Shadow-step, is that what the shifter had done to get us in here? A puff of shadow-smoke and he'd transported me from outside into this room. A curious and powerful ability.

"Yes," Myel responded. "It won't be easy, but I can do it."

"And myself," Koar added.

Safir spun on him. "No, we can't trust you yet."

"I have old friends, contacts in the capital, good elves," The dragon pleaded. It was clear he wanted to stay close to Izzy.

I'd known Koar a while. We'd served Saldrea together these past half-dozen years. He was as loyal and dependable as they came. He'd just been... misguided... in thinking Saldrea was worthy of his respect.

Now that he'd set his sights on Izzy, he'd protect her to the very end.

"Still, you'd be too much for Myel to shadow-step all at once, and we can only make one trip before someone will know we're at the sigil point."

Koar growled, going all alpha on the tiger shifter. Safir growled right back, smaller, but no less fierce.

"Actually!" I broke in. It seemed my time to speak had come. "Koar, I need you to return me home, to Elysial. Could you do that quickly... before you rejoin Izzy and Safir in the capital?"

"He isn't going to the capital," Safir muttered.

"Wouldn't it be better to keep him close, keep an eye on him?" Izzy offered. "*Keep your enemies closer* and all that?"

Safir practically vibrated with frustration.

I was beginning to understand the old man. All his life he'd served Izzy's family and now wished to serve her in the same way. He wanted to be the primary protector and advisor in her life. But if so, he shouldn't have kept her in the dark for so long. She didn't know him, didn't trust him. Hell, she didn't know Koar either, but Koar had saved her life. Safir had done nothing to earn her trust yet.

"If that is what you wish," Safir said to Izzy.

"It is." She turned to Koar. "If you take Vyns home and return, can you find us in the capital?"

He nodded once. "I know your spirit, your scent. I could track you from half a world away."

Her eyes went wide at that. "Oh," she breathed.

"He meant that in a good way," I added. "He'll always find you so he can protect you."

She nodded. "Ah, yes, of course."

Safir grumbled something under his breath.

"Someone will get suspicious if I miss training," Myel said. "I can't be away for long."

"You're right, you can't, which is why you're not coming with us," Safir said, his tone stern. "You need to stay here and maintain your schedule so no one suspects anything."

Myel clearly deferred to Safir... but his back went ramrod straight at this. "I can't leave Izzy's side. I... our bond..."

"Can wait a few days," Safir said, dismissing the tall, lean man. "Just satisfy it before we leave and you'll survive. We hopefully won't be gone for too long."

Myel shimmered, a shift nearly taking him as his anger grew. I'd thought he and this elder shifter were friends, but several things were becoming clear to me. First, Safir was the boss and liked it that way. He'd bristled, clearly not liking it when others took control. That was going to be an issue, since Izzy didn't like being told what to do. Second, Myel looked up to the man, followed him... in most things. But when it came to Izzy, Myel clearly didn't like how Safir handled things.

"Safir!" Myel growled.

It was Safir's turn to shimmer, and his beast was *much* bigger. A tiger shifter's beast form was second in size only to a bear's.

"We don't have time to argue. This is the way it must be." He turned to Izzy. "Get your mate under control!"

Izzy slapped Safir hard enough to send the old man to the floor.

"I know Myel," she hissed. "I *don't know* you. Do *not* speak to me like that. Do not presume to know me or attempt to dictate how my life should be."

And there it was. The first of probably many confrontations between the two of them.

Safir shook off the hit and rose slowly. "Of course, Izzy."

"I don't think I like you using my name anymore. *Your Majesty* will do."

Ouch.

Safir bowed his head. "As you wish, Your Majesty."

She turned to Myel. "How long do you think we can hold out? Two days?" she asked him.

He nodded at that. "The bond is mostly settled now. If we sate it before you leave, two days should be doable."

She nodded. "Then you stay and maintain your schedule while we go to the capital. We'll be back in two days." That last bit was to Safir.

"Yes, Your Majesty."

"What about me?" Rook asked. "If I can't leave, am I stuck here?"

Izzy glared at him.

"No," Safir said, before Izzy could explode on the incubus. "You should be safe if you return to your master and stick close to him. Don't show your face in public though. If you lay low, Saldrea will probably forget about you eventually."

Rook raised a brow. "And what do *you* know of my master?"

"The dwarf, Svokol? I know him well," Safir said with a grin which spoke of secrets and his sense of superiority. "He's been working for me for some time."

I choked on my next breath and Rook sputtered.

A dwarf working for a shifter? That seemed highly unlikely.

"He doesn't know it, of course," Safir said, preening like a peacock. The man clearly loved controlling others. "Are you aware of a dryad named Elnori?" he asked Rook.

Rook nodded. "My master trusts her, a source of... ah... So you're *her* source of information, are you?"

Safir nodded. "She's with me. And we'll need your master with me fully before Izzy returns from the capital."

Izzy growled.

"Before *Her Majesty* returns from the capital," Safir corrected himself. "Work with Elnori to find a way to tell your master the truth about Izzy. Sway him to our side, or at least to remain neutral. He won't turn her in. He's a good man. But, if he joins us, that would be the first step in getting *other* dwarves to follow us."

Rook sighed heavily. "Fine. Sure. But let me be clear, I'm not doing this for you, I'm doing it for Izzy... my... friend."

Izzy scoffed.

Safir waited to see if there were any other objections, then nodded and turned to Myel. "Please relay to Zora what's happened here tonight. Our plans are changing rapidly. I'm hoping she'll have a new plan by the time Izzy and I return from the capital."

"Wait... Zora? My housekeeper?" Izzy interrupted.

Myel answered, "Yes, she's with us too. We wanted another friend close to you."

Izzy's eyes went wide. "That's why! When you two met in my room, she hid it well, but you *knew* her!"

Myel nodded. "Yes."

"Huh," Izzy mused.

"Are we done?" Safir asked.

No one said anything.

"Good, then Myel and Izzy, I do apologize, but we cannot leave to give you the privacy you require."

"Leave it to me," I said, indicating everyone else should join me at one side of the room. Then I raised a barrier of light, enough to block our view of Izzy and Myel.

"Thanks, Vyns, you're a lifesaver," Izzy's voice drifted over to me.

I smiled, heart warmed.

"Any way you can block sound too?" Rook grumped.

"We'll be quiet," Izzy said, though her tone sounded mocking, kidding.

Rook sighed, sliding down the wall to sit, head in hands. "Doesn't matter. I'm going to *feel* it anyway."

Huh... I supposed he would. That made me smile all the more.

Served him right for how he'd treated Izzy.

Koar tapped me on the shoulder.

"Izzy is... mate-bonded to the little shifter?" he whispered.

I nodded. "Makes things far more interesting, doesn't it?"

"It does," the big man said, mulling this over. He shook his head and sighed. "No matter... Once they're done. I'll take you home."

Home... right. Soon enough, I'd have to face the music... and my family.

IZZY

"WELL, THIS IS AWKWARD," I WHISPERED TO MYEL AS WE quickly undressed.

He gave a nervous laugh. "Yeah." Then he shook his head. "I'm sorry... for all of this."

"What did I tell you about apologizing for things you have no control over?" I reminded him.

"I know, but... this is just so... well, awkward, like you said. And I know it's not my fault, but it also sort of is, because this bond didn't come from you, it's a shifter thing."

I could see his point, but this wasn't the best foreplay talk.

Still half dressed, I dropped to my knees, took his now free and rock-hard cock in my hand and brought it to my mouth. "Do I look like I care about any of that?"

His reply was a strained grunt as I took him deep into my mouth and sucked hard, playing my tongue over him and tasting his strawberries and cream scent as I sucked him off.

Perhaps this tantalizing aroma was some strange effect of this world to encourage blowjobs, because all the guys here tasted fabulous. Well, I'd only gone down on Rook and Myel, but between Rook's s'more flavor and Myel's strawberry shortcake... why would any girl want to stop sucking on either of them?

His fingers combed through my hair as I bobbed my head working him hard, knowing this wasn't going to be a drawn out affair. With our need to hurry and three men waiting — and potentially listening — on the other side of this room, this was going to be quick and dirty, and Myel and I both knew it.

"Yes!" he hissed. He was close, straining not to come right then and there. Instead, he pulled my face away and knelt to give me a long kiss.

"Your turn," he breathed, nodding toward the bed. I sat and Myel tore my pants down, opening my legs to press his lips to my already drenched core. He didn't need to repay my oral favor. His arousal had transmitted to me through our bond, so I was more than ready to take his thickness, but this was Myel, always so giving.

He devoured my folds, licking my seam and sucking my clit, before slipping two fingers inside me to stroke my G-spot. And when I came — as quietly as I could, biting my lips and panting through desperate moans — he drew back and lifted me. I wrapped my legs around him as he pinned me to the wall, then he drove his thickness into me, thrusting hard.

Oh yeah.

There was something about a rough fuck with no pretense. Pure unadulterated sex.

We were both desperate, and neither of us were as quiet as we probably should have been, cutting off cries and trying to keep our moans to a dull roar, but it wasn't easy.

Then Myel exploded inside me as he let out a long groan, eyes wide.

I pulled back to watch him come. I loved his "O" face, so pure and exulted. All that dark hair tumbling over his deep, soulful eyes.

I gave a clipped cry as a second orgasm hit me, straining my body. Every muscle tightened, my legs around his waist clenched like a vise.

We stayed like that, frozen, statues in the throes of passion as we finished.

When Myel moved, easily carrying me, he turned toward a door, which I took to be an ensuite. I leaned down to whisper in his ear.

"No, put me on the bed."

"But—" he began.

I knew what he was going to say, how much of a mess he was going to make when he pulled out.

That's why I wanted him to put me on the bed. I wasn't the biggest fan of Safir right now. Let him deal with the aftermath of our ecstasy.

"I insist," I breathed into his ear. Hopefully, no one else would hear.

Myel hesitated, then shifted and took me to the bed, setting me down before pulling out and... yup, good luck cleaning those sheets.

Did I feel bad? Maybe a teensy bit. Though mostly I regretted that Safir wouldn't be sleeping any more tonight. We'd probably be leaving right away.

Myel brushed some sweat-damp hair from my neck and kissed my pulse.

"May I?" he asked, breathy.

Oh right, he needed to feed. Myel had a disease, which meant he needed blood to survive, and since we were bonded *my blood* was all he wanted. Apparently, I tasted great and everyone else was shit.

I nodded and he bit into me, humming with delight as he drank. He didn't take much, enough to last him the couple of days I'd be gone. Then he drew back and I healed myself with little effort.

Now it was my turn to ask for something.

"Hold me, for a bit."

Myel smiled softly and curled up behind me on the small bed. Time was short but snuggle time with Myel was nearly as good as sex. The bond ensured we both loved fucking, but it also made sure we wanted to be close. No drug could compare to the serene bliss of being in Myel's arms. Even with the world going to shit around me, I always felt so damned good being held by him.

So, I gave us a few minutes of cuddling, for me, and for him, and for the bond, before I sighed and wiped myself off with more of Safir's sheets, then got dressed.

Time to go.

"I love you," Myel whispered as he dressed in record time — must be a shifter thing — then hugged me again from behind.

I still hadn't said those words to Myel, and frankly, given the bond and our permanent attachment, I probably should, but when I opened my lips to speak, what came out was:

"I'll miss you."

He smiled when I turned to kiss him.

Did I *need* to say it? The bond ensured we both knew exactly how the other felt. So Myel knew my feelings... but still... Perhaps?

"I l—"

The wall of light came down.

"Are you ready to leave?" Safir asked, marching across the room.

I couldn't help the little smile on my face when he saw the mess on his bed and grimaced.

"I'm assuming I can't go back and get anything?" I asked. I'd be leaving behind everything I owned. Ever since I'd gotten here, I'd gone through cycles of having nothing, then buying things, then losing them. I didn't know what it said about me, that I was starting to get used to it.

"No," Safir said, gathering a few things of his own. "We can get you what you need in the capital. Let's go, before Saldrea locks down the Sigil Point."

Vyns came to me. "I won't be gone long. I'll ask Koar to come and get me in a day or two. Luckily, our spirit link doesn't need any more than this." And he kissed me softly. A warmth, like wet summer heat, filled me.

The kiss ended all too soon, then Vyns nodded to Koar, who put a large hand on the angel's shoulder. The two of them spiraled in on themselves and vanished. So *that's* what it looked like when a dragon moved between worlds.

It reminded me of my trip to this world, with Myel and Svokol and a dragon lady whose name I didn't know. We'd all had to touch, then the world had spiraled and dissolved around us, becoming a strange and twisted rainbow-filled darkness, like light on an oil spill.

I'd had no clue what had been happening at the time. Hell, I barely had any clue what was happening now. Everything moved way too fast.

Myel took my hand, drawing me from my reverie, and I smiled, soothed.

He took Safir's hand and in a puff of shadow-smoke, we were outside again.

Stars twinkled above us in an inky black sky. No moon.

"Love you," Myel whispered, then he was gone, swirling shadows barely visible where he'd been.

"Think of a city of pearl-white spires amidst vast towering trees," Safir whispered. "Then say the name: El'Anderyn on the count of three."

"Hey! You there! Stop!" some guard at the edge of the massive circular platform yelled at us.

"One... two... three, El'Anderyn," Safir whispered.

I said the word in sync with Safir, voice hushed. I expected the same psychedelic colors over darkness like moving between worlds, but instead there was a flash of blue-white light and a sense of being pulled...

Then we were back on a large circular platform... still in darkness... stars twinkling above... but we weren't on campus anymore.

Safir's description of the capital had left *a lot* to be desired. It was stunning!

There *were* tall, delicate, pearlescent towers. Yet what he hadn't mentioned was how — even with the lack of moonlight — they glowed in the night, filled with their own inner brilliance.

And yes, trees towered all through the city, but I hadn't expected them to be *that* big, nor that kind of tree. Back on earth, I'd heard of the great redwoods and giant sequoias, even if I'd never seen them myself. They were evergreens, tall but relatively narrow: pointy. The trees here weren't pointy. They had massive sprawling canopies which were not only hundreds of feet tall but spread-out hundreds of feet in all directions. Absolutely gigantic!

And yes, those were the first two things which caught the eye, but the rest of the city was a sparkling wonder in the night. Most of the buildings were made of the same glowy-white stone as those tall towers, setting the night alight with a pleasant opalescent aura. And other buildings were built into those massive trees and out on their wide branches.

I slowly turned to take it all in... then lost my breath entirely when I saw the palace. That was the only thing this massive structure could be, too beautiful and colossal and wonderous to be anything else. White stone intertwined with massive trees as if they were one thing. A high wall stretched between trees, which acted like towers. At the corners, stood trees larger than any others I'd seen. Delicate webs of arching stone connected the outer tree-towers to impossibly high peaks farther back, within the walls.

My mind couldn't comprehend how those white towers could be so narrow and delicate and tall. But then I remembered elves were masters of earth magic. If anyone could create stone minarets like these, it would be them.

"We must go," Safir said, tugging on my arm.

I followed in a daze, still awestruck by this place. Then it struck me: this place was beautiful on the outside, like the elves themselves, but it was probably as corrupt and ugly on the inside?

And the fantasy of this city vanished.

When it did, I became aware of a gnawing ache in my gut, which made me want to stop and puke. Was I travel sick? I didn't know how we'd travelled, but that seemed likely. Yet as we hurried onward through the capital, I came to realize this sensation was my connection to Myel, and it clearly didn't like being this far from him. Even though we'd *just* renewed our bond, being such a great distance from my bonded made me feel ill. It wasn't an overpowering sensation, just awkward and uncomfortable, but I had a feeling it would only get worse.

And running didn't help. I was forced to stop, yanking on Safir to halt him.

"Wait. I... need a moment," I huffed, hand on stomach. I put my other hand on a nearby wall and leaned forward. I tried a few dry heaves, but it didn't help. This wasn't a physical sickness, not yet. I was soul-sick, not stomach-sick. Still, I hoped maybe one good puke would make me feel better.

"What's wrong?" Safir asked, clearly upset. "We need to move. It won't take long for those at the academy to track where we went. And they may not know it was you, but if they did get a good look... well, we can't be near the sigil point when they arrive!"

"Give me a fucking minute for fucks sake!" I yelled at him. "I feel like I've been kicked in the stomach and it's your fault!"

"My fault? How? I had no clue you'd react to Shadecasting like that?"

"Shade-what?"

"Ley line travel," he muttered, rolling his eyes. "It's called Shadecasting or shading. Didn't they cover that in your magic class?"

"Must be next week's lesson. And that's *not* what's bothering me." I wanted to heave again but knew it wouldn't do any good. Instead, I drew in several long, deep breaths.

"This is because *you* took me so far from Myel."

"Preposterous," Safir snorted. "Your bond can't be that strong, you've only known him a few days."

Something became clear in that instant. Safir may have been a shifter and known — theoretically — about mating bonds, but he'd clearly never experienced one. He had no clue what I was feeling.

I forced myself to stand, turned Safir to face me — he'd been scanning the road ahead — and slapped him. I made sure to pull the strike. I'd surprised myself last time when I'd seen him crumple to the floor. I hadn't meant to do that, even if he'd been a jerk. Yet, with my elven nature no longer bound, I really didn't know my own strength.

He staggered to the wall and leaned on it.

"What in the name of the spirits...?"

"Don't you *ever* presume to know what I'm feeling. I have zero tolerance for men who think they know what's going on with other people, especially women. *I know* what I feel. *You don't*!" I gave him time to recover, so I could do the same.

"You told Myel he'd be fine, that *we'd* be fine away from each other, but you had no clue how we'd feel, no clue what you were talking about."

Safir glared at me. "We don't have time for this! Suck it up."

I slapped him again, a little harder. "*You* suck it up."

He growled and for a second a man-shaped-tiger-being took his place, shimmering in the night.

"Don't test me," he snarled.

"Don't test *me* either," I warned him. "I don't like you and you're not doing anything to change that.

He steadied himself with several deep breaths. "If you don't like the bond, break it. You can do that now. You're an elf. And if you can't, we'll find someone who can. Myel is unimportant and *he* knows it. *You're* the only one who doesn't. Better to break the bond now and be rid of him."

Wait... what?

Break the bond?

I could do that?

Yet, the shock of that realization was secondary to another much more significant revelation. Safir had no intention of returning to the academy as he'd told Myel. He meant to keep me here and force me — or someone — to break the bond which he saw as a burden.

The realization hit me so hard I staggered back, gasping for air, which wouldn't come.

My dislike for Safir turned into a raging hatred.

How could he do that to me? How could he do that to Myel, who clearly looked up to him?

"Now come on, we need to move!" Safir hissed, grabbing my arm while I was off balance and dragging me along behind him.

I let him, because he was right about one thing, we were in danger. But as soon as we were safe, he and I were going to have a long talk about lying to his princess, and bonds, and so much more.

It was time for Safir to learn he wasn't in charge anymore. And I very much looked forward to teaching him that lesson.

KOARTHANDRIS

It was easier travelling between the three fae realms than travelling to the human realm, but two such jaunts in quick succession meant I was winded as I arrived back in Seial. Nothing that would slow me down too much, though.

Having switched to my dragon form, I brought myself back to Seial in the skies outside of the capital of El'Anderyn. Other dragons patrolled the night sky and my presence was detected.

What is your business here, brother? The voice spoke into my mind. It was how we dragons communicated when in dragon form. I swung my large head around to see the shadow behind me. He was larger than me, but his spirit aura not as strong. I could take him if I needed to.

Business for Saldrea. Sent from Veilblood Academy.

Hopefully, that would get me access to the city. I prayed word of my betrayal of the false princess hadn't travelled this far yet.

Proceed, the other dragon said, indifferent.

It seemed I was safe for now. Though I'd not be able to

use my connection to Saldrea after this. That didn't bother me. I hated being associated with that hellion.

I zeroed in on Izzy's spirit aura. There were many strong auras below, this being the capital city of the elves, the strongest race in all three realms. Still, Izzy's was burned into my memory. I locked onto her aura almost instantly and glided down toward a sprawling estate outside of the city to the east.

If this was where Izzy's paternal grandmother lived, the woman must be very well off indeed. Especially for a nymph.

I circled the grounds, searching for a place to land. As I did, angling through the night sky, the glowing towers of the city flashed in the distance, a place of light and power, and above it all... was the palace.

The sight of *that place* put a sour taste in my mouth as I descended toward a large, clear swathe of lawn.

Returning to the capital was never easy for me. This was where I'd failed the royal family, where I'd disgraced myself. One critical moment of distraction and the master I'd served — the late queen's brother, Talmarion — and his entire family had perished.

One mistake that had ripped the world apart, for it had left no more royals in all of Seial.

My shame had become a weight upon my soul, one I'd have to live with for the rest of my life. Or so I'd thought. But now I had a chance to make up for my failure. As I landed, shifted, and strode toward the mansion, I swore I would never fail the royal family again: never fail *Izzy*. I'd never leave her side. I'd protect her with my life and die happy knowing I'd saved her. It was the least I could do after failing her great uncle and his family.

One of the doors at the back of the mansion opened and a silken voice drifted out to me.

"You must be the dragon we're waiting for. Come in." It wasn't Izzy's voice, but it was familiar. I'd heard that voice before, knew it well.

And it stopped me dead in my tracks.

Olinara.

Everything had happened so fast — discovering who Izzy was, then making our plans, and springing into action — that I hadn't made the connection as to *who* Izzy's paternal grandmother would be.

Izzy's father had been Sa Eofine Keomar, a Nymph. He'd been a friend of the royal family, close to them... *because* of his mother. Sa Eofine Olinara had been one of the Inamorati: Queen Leastrine's harem. Seven men and women of the utmost beauty and grace, vigor and intelligence. Seven who'd been like family to the royals, even if they hadn't been elves. Seven who were envied by elves, because they hadn't just shared the queen's bed, they'd been her most trusted advisors and confidantes. And Olinara had been the closest of them all, the *head* of the harem, the Inamora.

No wonder Olinara had an estate like this.

From what I recalled of the woman, she'd played the political game better than most, using her assets — both physical and mental, but mostly physical — to pry secrets from the lips of the queen's adversaries. Her capability for seduction was legendary.

And here she was.

I couldn't see her face, only her silhouetted form, the light from within outlining her figure in the doorway. She possessed an hour-glass figure, much like Izzy's, but even more pronounced and curvaceous. As a nymph, she'd maintained this image of lush beauty and youthfulness for hundreds of years.

I sighed as I drew near.

"Olinara," I said with respect.

She gave a soft purring laugh. "Koarthandris. It's been a long time." The invitation in her voice was clear. I took pride in the fact that I'd never indulged in her advances. That wouldn't change now.

As I reached her, she played with the collar of her robe, a silken thing, mostly transparent — like the woman wearing it — slowly pulling it across one breast. She made the gesture seem absentminded, but I was fairly sure it wasn't.

"I'm not interested," I stated, voice flat. "Please take me to Izzy."

"She's arguing with her shifter. She'll be a moment." Olinara bit her plump lip and pouted. She was over two-hundred-years-old but didn't look a day over nineteen. Her gaze raked over me. I was naked, a side effect of shifting into my dragon form and back. "I wouldn't need long."

No, she wouldn't.

But I wasn't interested.

"Take. Me. To. Izzy. Please." My tone brokered no argument.

She pouted more, then sighed and gathered her robe around her, before flouncing back inside. This was the enigma which was Olinara: she *could be* a distinguished woman, or she could be a petulant tease — as she was now — acting one tenth her age.

This was going to be a long visit.

As I followed her, my keen senses picked up raised voices. Well before I saw Izzy, I heard her.

"...and *when* we get back to Veilblood Academy — which

will be in two days, if not sooner — *you* will tell Myel that you'd planned to have someone break his bond with me and that you've never cared for him as much as he thinks you do!" Izzy's voice was adamant.

I sighed, recalling she was mate-bonded to the small shifter. That was a complication I hadn't foreseen. If Saldrea found out, she'd kill Myel in an instant, or worse, capture and torture him to death for fun, knowing it would hurt Izzy. And she would find out. Now that Saldrea was even more furious with Izzy, she'd be doing everything in her power to dig into Izzy's life. It wouldn't surprise me if she'd put out a sizable reward for any information on her nemesis. After that all it would take is one slip-up by Myel or Izzy and someone would know, someone who wished to receive that reward and please the tempestuous princess.

"You're being unreasonable," Safir said, voice more level, calm. Olinara and I were still a ways off and I barely heard him. What I did hear was the clap of flesh-on-flesh and a soft grunt.

"You must like being slapped," Izzy fumed. "*Maybe... someday...* in some *distant* future where you've *earned* the right to speak freely to me and advise me, I'll let you tell me I'm being unreasonable. But right now, unreasonable or not, you do *not* get to say anything of the sort! Do. You. Understand?"

The only reasonable response would be a quick yes.

"Your Majesty, I—"

I hadn't known Izzy long, but even I knew talking back was a bad idea.

"DO! YOU! UNDERSTAND!" The power in her voice radiated out to me and poured over me and through me. Wow... Izzy would far surpass Saldrea in potency and ability once she was fully trained. Her raw power now was... indescribable.

Olinara and I had come in sight of the two, and I watched as the dominance in Izzy's voice pushed Safir to his knees.

He bowed from there.

"Yes, Your Majesty."

Olinara and I stopped at the arched entrance to the vast living room in which Izzy and Safir fought or *had* fought. It was done now. Izzy was livid, flushed crimson with fury, arms straight with fists balled at her sides as she stared down at the shifter. Skies above! She was magnificent!

There was something about a powerful woman who could put people in their place without physical violence or bullying. And Izzy was exactly that. I didn't doubt that Safir had brought this tirade on himself. From everything I'd seen and heard about Izzy she wasn't a cruel person. She could have beaten the shifter to a pulp. Even without knowing her elven abilities, she'd still have elven strength, yet the only mark on the man was a red spot where she'd slapped him. Saldrea would have done so much worse.

My hand rose to touch the still weeping wound on my cheek where Saldrea had carved her mark into me and made it so it would never quite heal. *That* was brutality. Izzy's wrath was a righteous rage.

And that's when it hit me...

Izzy was perfect for me.

The thought struck me like an elven sucker punch. I didn't want it to be true, but it was. For the longest time, I'd had no interest in women because my ideal woman simply wasn't possible. I desired someone who was kind and gracious and witty, soft when she wished to be, but also hard and determined, strong in her convictions. That alone was hard enough to find, but my additional requirement was a woman who was physically sturdy enough to take my rather *aggressive* passion in bed. Something only a dragon or an elf could do. And no dragon or elf I knew had the requisite softness and graciousness and kindness.

But Izzy, raised in the human world, had all of that *and* was an elf, sturdy of form.

She was perfect.

Just like Mynrial.

Fuck.

All my desire and arousal drained away instantly, shredded by that comparison.

Mynrial had been the reason I'd failed the royals. My desire for her had been the distraction which had caused her and her family to perish.

I could never let that happen again.

As much as Izzy might be perfect for me, I could never let my desire distract me. I had to focus on protecting her above all else. Because as much as Izzy might be perfect for me, she was also perfect for this nation. She had the power to rule yet possessed none of the prejudices which had torn the fae realm a part. She was what a queen should be, what the royal line had been and could be again... only better. A half-blood on the throne would mean a fundamental shift for Seial, but it would be a change which this broken realm desperately needed.

I quelled my feelings for her, focusing on being the man she needed me to be: a protector and guardian, nothing more.

Izzy's wrath waned, and she realized she had an audience. She looked over at us and shook her head with a heavy sigh. What a pair Olinara and I must make, an overlusty, nearly-naked nymph — who happened to be Izzy's grandmother — and a completely naked dragon.

One glance at Olinara and Izzy rolled her eyes. When her gaze turned to me, it raked down my body. Her pupils dilated, her body giving a near-imperceptible shiver, as the bloom of arousal filled her scent of apples and cinnamon. She was aroused… by me?

I hadn't thought I was her type, not if she liked Myel and Vyns and Rook.

But I couldn't deny what my senses told me.

My cock twitched with hope, but I stilled it instantly, since that was a hope I couldn't allow myself to have.

"Still naked?" she chided, hiding her stimulation. "Put some clothes on!"

"At once, Your Highness," I said with a short bow.

"Upstairs, third room on the left, should be something that fits you," Olinara said with a wave of her hand, dismissing me. "And take your time… I need to have a long chat with my long lost granddaughter."

"Could you *look* a bit more *like* a grandmother?" Izzy said with scorn. "As opposed to a playboy bunny or porn star, young enough to be my little sister?"

"No, I cannot," Olinara said as I fled upstairs. "Get used to it."

I had to smile at that. The woman had an iron will… like Izzy.

I had a feeling the two of them were going to get along just fine… or tear each other's throats out.

One of the two.

IZZY

I couldn't quite reconcile the woman before me being my grandmother. As I'd said, she looked more like a *younger* sibling with a body straight off a porn set. It seemed she liked showing off her *in-bed-fooling-around* body — to quote my friend Tala — all the time. I should not be staring at my grandmother's chest. Yet it was hard not to... when she made Dolly Parton look like a willowy waif of a woman. And it wasn't just her porn star look which baffled me, but the whole vibe she gave off.

She came across like a wide-eyed, "innocent," ingenue sex-kitten, not a respectable grandmotherly woman. Her practically see-through robe and faux-blasé attitude toward near-nudity was hella confident. I applauded any woman who could pull that off. But it was distracting as hell and not fit for a grandmother. The cognitive dissonance broke my brain.

"I don't suppose you'd consider putting some clothes on too?" I said with a heavy sigh. It seemed like nothing was going right for me tonight.

"No," she replied as she crossed the room to me, then turned to Safir. "Shoo, shifter, the adults need to talk."

Safir nodded, bowed low, and left the room.

"I love how you shut him down, by the way," Grandma purred. "Very dominating. Do you like to dominate? Is that your thing?"

"Does everything revolve around sex for you?"

"Pretty much, yes," she said with a grin. Then her features hardened a little. "You're right, though, it's time I spoke to you as your grandmother, but I don't think you're going to like it?"

"Oh?" I didn't much like how anything was going in my life right now, so... *Lay it on me, Grandma.*

She slapped me. I barely felt it. Perhaps that was my new elven heritage kicking in, or she hadn't meant it to be hard, just a wake-up call.

"Get your act together, woman!" Grandma hissed. "You're all over the place. You can't keep your form stable. You know how to boss men around, great. Glad we've mastered that, but it's clear you haven't mastered yourself."

Huh, not what I'd expected, but not awful either. It felt a bit more grandmotherly to be scolded than it did for her to be flouncing around in next to nothing.

"I'm well aware of that fact. It's the entire reason I'm here to see you," I muttered. When we'd arrived, Safir had quickly outlined to Olinara what had happened and what we needed. Then she'd left while I'd scolded the shifter.

She sighed and motioned to a long divan.

I sat as she took a seat nearby.

"Last week, when Safir called to tell me you'd shown up in this world, I figured this day would come, but I didn't think it would be this soon. Trouble seems to follow you everywhere. But then... that's something you're going to have to get used to if you want to survive in this world."

"Your empathy is overwhelming," I snarked.

She raised a brow. "Suck it up, princess. From what you've told me, we don't have time for empathy, just action, correct?"

"Correct," I said with a sigh. "I need to get my act together and learn my powers... like yesterday. So please teach me all the nymphy things I need to know. Then I need to find an elven tutor we can trust to teach me about my elven side," I restated, clarifying the situation. "All within two days, then I have to get back."

"To your bonded shifter?" She shook her head. "That's asking for trouble, but I suppose you didn't have any say in it, did you?"

"Nope."

"Then let's get things started, no time like the present."

"Could it wait till after I've slept? I haven't been to bed yet tonight."

"No. I've got a trick which should help you with your form. If you learn it now, hopefully it will sink in while you rest."

I shrugged. "Sure, fine... though..." Something had been bothering me. "What should I call you?" I asked. "Grandma? Gram-gram? Olinara?"

"Oli will be fine," she said with a smile. "If you want to make me feel old, than Grandma Oli."

"And please call me Izzy," I said since Safir had introduced me as Isolde.

She nodded. "Izzy, sounds good." Her smile grew. She leaned forward and took my hands. I tried to ignore the shot of cleavage that gave me. "It's a pleasure to finally meet you. Sorry I didn't say that earlier."

"And to meet you as well," I said. "Now... what's this trick you mentioned?"

She squeezed my hands.

"Answer me this: who do you want to be?"

I blinked, brow furrowed. "I just want to be me, but right now I don't even know who I am anymore."

"Okay then, what *version* of you do you want to be? As a nymph, you can be whoever you want. You are an elf and you are a nymph. You could be either or both or neither. What do you want?"

I shrugged. "I want... I want to be human and normal and uninteresting." With everything that had happened over the last few days, that seemed safest, even if a part of me knew it wouldn't be practical.

"I never thought I'd hear a descendant of mine say they wished to be uninteresting. But if that's what you want, we can arrange it. However, you cannot be *human* here. Humans are rarely seen in the fae realms, you'd stand out even more as a human, far from uninteresting."

Fair point.

Oli sighed. "Perhaps I rushed in too quickly. Let's back up. Forget about who you want to be and tell me what you want... in general."

I sighed and told her about my dream for this world. I wanted to change things, to get rid of the institutionalized oppression and bring freedom and equality. As a nymph, I couldn't do it, but as an elf, maybe I could change things... and as a royal, my dream seemed even closer to reality.

Oli nodded. "Understood." But then she sighed heavily.

"You *could* be an elf," Oli continued. "But claiming you're a royal right away, might be problematic. People have been searching for residual royals for years and found none. You'd need proof. But even then, the people who've been looking for royals are mostly trying to kill them, so..." She grimaced.

I knew most of this, but I let her go on.

"And as a half-blood, most of the elves would shun you rather than accept you as their queen. So... here's what I suggest. For now, be a nymph, lay low, under the radar, and simply be yourself. Take time to gather followers before you make your claim on the throne."

Seemed reasonable.

"Learn what you can, as quickly as possible," she continued. "Bide your time. Wait for the right moment to rise up and fight the tyranny of the elves."

I nodded.

"But..." she hedged, "you can't do any of that... as no one special, as some uninteresting nymph or human."

Yeah... on some level, I'd known that.

"So... I guess I'll be a nymph for now," I said. "Someone who can be uninteresting and lay low, under the radar to those in power... but who can also inspire those around her."

Oli smiled. "Now we're getting somewhere. This should be simple."

Simple sounded good.

She stood and with our joined hands, drew me up with her.

"Calm your mind, get comfortable, shake out your body a little, relax."

Relaxing wasn't easy with everything going on, but I tried. She released my hands, and I shook out my arms and shoulders and took several long breaths.

"Good... now look at me," she coached. "Later, you can do this with just an image in your head, but to begin, it will help to have a model to work with." I stood there and took her in... even if it wasn't easy to see my grandmother this way.

As if reading my thoughts, she smiled and said, "If it's easier, don't think of me as your grandmother, just a model, a sexy model."

I smirked and raised a brow.

She shrugged with a grin.

I relented and nodded.

"I find it helps to start at the top and work down. Reach up and stroke your hair. You'll be able to make it longer or shorter, any color you like... eventually. For now, feel it in your hands." She mirrored me as I combed my hands through my hair, stroking my locks.

"As you do this, look at my hair, see its color, its texture, how full and bouncy or straight or whatever it is. Then, as you feel your own hair, make it the same."

Currently Oli's hair was a shimmering golden blond, falling in lustrous waves to mid-back. This wasn't too hard. The hair I'd grown up with had been similar enough to that. Having already done a little body-shifting with Tala, it didn't take too much effort to match my hair to Oli's. The shift was subtle, my hair extending while becoming more voluminous. When I lifted it up before me, I saw the shimmering golden hue.

Nice!

"Well done!" Grandma cheered. "Now your eyes. Touch your face, trace the socket and the brow and lids. Feel any lines or puffiness or bags, and all the while look at my eyes, the skin around them, the bridge of the nose, the color. Focus on me and match what you see."

Her eyes were a stunningly clear cobalt blue, and the skin around her eyes infuriatingly smooth. I moved my fingers over my face, feeling myself shift, skin tightening, growing taut and silky.

"Good," Oli purred. "You're a natural."

And in this manner, we slowly progressed over every part of my body: my ears and nose and cheeks and lips and chin. Then lower, elongating my neck a little, which felt super odd, but I did it. I'd already worked on my chest with Tala, but Grandma Oli had a way of making the work seem simple without turning it into a sexual thing, just... tactile and clinical. We rounded my shoulders a little, narrowed my waist, tightened my abs, streamlined my hips and lengthened my legs. And somehow, even though it felt damn weird, it didn't feel... unnatural.

And when I was done, she led me to a long mirror in her front hall and I marveled at the change. I'd become her twin. And what was even more stunning was... there were no fluctuations. I was solid, set.

"How...?" I breathed.

"It's all in the touch," Oli said next to me. She smoothed her hands over her massive bust and as she did, they shrunk to a much more manageable and reasonable size. Then she ran her hands back up over herself and the outrageous bust returned. "Just thinking yourself into a new body isn't easy at first. But you've touched yourself and others many times. Sometimes your fingers know forms better than your mind does. Working with the hands as you change helps to solidify the process. Given time, touch won't be necessary, but for now, as you change, touch yourself and it should help you keep your new form. Try it."

I did.

This time I closed my eyes and imagined the me I'd seen so many times in the mirror. I couldn't do it as quickly as Oli had, but I took the time to touch every part of me, picturing myself in my mind's eye and, when I opened my eyes, I nearly wept.

There I was. The me I'd always known. A human with dirty blond hair, sea-green eyes, round ears and chesty enough to stand out without getting back problems.

"Perfect," Oli whispered next to me. "Give me your phone and I'll send you some pictures I have of me in various forms. You can practice more tomorrow. Now... get some rest, granddaughter."

I nodded, still a little overwhelmed at being back in the form I'd grown up in, even if it felt... easy and known. And after Grandma had shown me to a luxuriously spacious room, I fell into the massive bed and slept like a log. Even if I didn't get that much sleep before I heard arguing in the hall outside my room sometime later.

"She needs her rest!" A raised voice... the dragon... what was his name again? Koar.

"We don't have time," Safir growled. "She needs to learn everything she can as soon as possible."

"Olinara and I have talked. We've worked it out. We have an elf in mind to help Izzy. Olinara is on her way to get them. So let her rest for now."

Okay, I'd known this dragon for less than twenty-four hours, but I already liked him. Anyone who argued for me to sleep in was a hero in my books.

"You and Olinara? When? Who?"

"Lower. Your. Voice. Now!" This, I barely heard, but the whisper held so much threat I shivered.

"I will not be commanded by the likes of—"

A crunching sound.

Someone hit the floor.

"Suck it up, shifter. Izzy's resting. We have a plan."

"You'll pay for that," Safir growled, sounding pained.

Yup, Koar had just proven himself to me. Not enough for me to trust him completely, I didn't trust anyone easily, but enough to certainly give him more of a chance than I'd be giving Safir.

I snuggled back up in the huge bed and fell asleep again.

"Izzy?" The soft voice woke me sometime later.

I hummed as I woke, feeling refreshed. This bed had been a wonder. I felt safe for the first time in a while. Though as soon as I blinked to awareness, the churning need in my gut to be closer to Myel made me squirm.

Oli sat on the edge of the bed with a soft smile on her face. Behind her, at the edge of the room was Koar, tall and proud. He wore one of those billowy, pirate-like shirts... only on him it wasn't so loose, tight over his chest and shoulders and biceps. Black pants clung to his hips and legs, also a little too tight. Beside Koar, Safir was stiff, clearly not happy. I'd have to have a conversation with him today. He was on my side, but he had to start giving up some control, which I guessed wasn't easy for him.

And there was a new person in the room.

"Izzy, this is El Siandalla Lhorine," Oli said introducing the woman. I'd seen a few "older" elves on campus, Dr. Pointy-Ears being one of them. Yet it still struck me as odd how young and fresh an adult elf looked. Though, when you lived for *thousands* of years, you probably didn't start looking old for quite a long time. Hence, it was hard to tell exactly how old Lhorine might be. She exuded grace and poise, standing tall, shoulders back. She was willowy and tall, slender and sleek, like most elves. In fact, there really wasn't much to set her apart from other elves... save for two things. Her hair was darker than most, a dark honey brown, and her amber eyes weren't filled with scorn and hatred, but a soft kindness.

"Hello, Izzy," Lhorine said with a bow of her head. "It's an honor to meet you." She smiled, like with genuine sincerity and softness. A smile like that was out of place on an elf's face.

"I want it on record that I had no say in this and haven't had time to vet this individual," Safir griped. I flashed him an annoyed glance and he shut up.

"Both Koar and I know Lhorine," Grandma said, voice reassuring. "She was an aid to the Queen's brother Talmarion. She can be trusted."

"I am no fan of Valnea, nor her daughter," Lhorine added. "And there are more like me, who do not like what has become of our people, though... we are not many."

She seemed honest, but my gut told me I couldn't trust her. However, if my grandmother vouched for her, I had to believe this woman was on my side. Still, I didn't know her and remained a teensy bit wary.

"Good to know," I said as I sat up in bed, sheets clutched to my chest. "So... when do we begin training?"

Grandma Oli answered. "Get dressed and eat something, then we'll begin."

BAYN

"You'll be my guard from now on," Saldrea declared, poking me in the chest. She was livid, pacing and ranting. I hadn't been here long, but I assumed she'd been up all night. I'd woken when I'd felt a massive surge of earth magic. When I'd investigated, I'd found the front of the library destroyed by giant stone spikes. It had to be Saldrea's work. She was the only one powerful enough in earth magic to create such raw destruction. I'd wondered what had caused her to go on such a rampage. Now I knew.

Ever since I'd been summoned, Saldrea hadn't stopped talking about some woman named Izzy and how much of a half-breed whore she was. I got the impression Saldrea's two previous guards, a dragon and a seraph, had helped this other woman and betrayed Saldrea. I couldn't help my vicious joy at that, even if I couldn't show it.

I hated Saldrea. I wanted nothing more than to test my skills and power as a titan against hers. Every fiber of my being called for me to destroy her... and her insane mother. But I couldn't, not as long as Saldrea held my sister captive. I had no love for my parents; they'd betrayed titan ideals a hundred years ago when they'd sided with Valnea and helped her overthrow the elven monarchy. Yet my sister was innocent, still young, and had nothing to do with this conflict. But that hadn't stopped my parents from handing her over to Valnea and Saldrea as a way to control me.

My parents' weakness, their willingness to yield to Valnea, only showed how far we titans had fallen. We'd once been a proud race, strong in our convictions, having shaped our bodies over generations to become the giants we were, no longer recognizable as the elves we'd once been. We and our minions had once outnumbered the elves five to one, but that didn't account for all the other races the elves had enslaved and brought under their sway. Had it just been us and the elves, we might have crushed those who'd once oppressed us, suppressed us. But all our strength hadn't been enough against the full might of Seial, and Urval, and Elysial, which the elves had summoned to fight in the last war. Titans now were a hollow shell of what we'd once been, and my parents had only further demonstrated how far we'd fallen. I alone was the last of the true, proud titans, and yet here I was, forced to serve this petty elven princess.

"And you'd better make sure no one gets close, I don't get so much as a scratch," Saldrea ranted. "Or I'll torture your sister to death then revive her and do it all over again."

How my parents could have allied with this woman and her mother — both raving lunatics — I didn't know. Saldrea's threats weren't idle. She sent me videos on my phone every few days of her tormenting my sister... just for fun, to remind me to do my part and play the role she and her mother had designed for me.

Up till today, I'd been tasked with making friends and showing all the races here at the academy that titans were harmless and wished for peace. The goal of the deception was simple: ease the fears of all races so they'd welcome more titans into society. Then, once we were established, we'd attack from within and kill most of the elves and their allies.

That's how insane Valnea was. She hated titans, but she hated and feared her own kind even more. From what I'd gathered, during my few encounters with the queen regent, she assumed everyone was out to destroy her. This belief most likely came from the notion that all other elves were like her: willing to betray everyone and crush their enemies. Her plan was simple, if completely mad: cull the elves. Her kind had flourished over the millenniums since the elves had defeated the titans and driven my kind into the barren lands. The elves had all the allies, all the fertile lands, all the assets and advantages, so they'd lived well and prospered. But to Valnea, that meant enemies everywhere. She desired nothing more than to exterminate her own kind, reduce them to a level she could control.

And what would the titans get for all of this? Valnea promised new lands and a place of power in the new government. My parents believed her, blind to the truth. Valnea would never share power. She'd betray us and we'd be culled as well, easy targets, our numbers greatly reduced after a war with the elves.

But there was nothing I could do, so long as my sister remained Saldrea's prisoner, held in some secret location, far from prying eyes. I had feelers out. The few titans here on campus were all loyal to me. When they weren't playing the role of friendly visitors, they were using their earth magic to seek through the ground and buildings for any hidden places where my sister might be. I'd find her eventually, free her, then kill Saldrea, even if I died in the attempt. I honestly didn't know if my earth magic was as strong as hers.

Saldrea slapped me. It turned my head but did little harm. We titans were as strong and tough as elves.

"Were you listening to me!" Saldrea shrieked.

I hadn't been, no. She'd been ranting for so long I'd tuned it out.

"Apologies," I said, voice tight. "I am now."

"Lower your physical defenses so I can hurt you," she demanded.

"No."

She blinked, taken aback. I wondered how long it had been since anyone had said no to her.

"If I can't hurt you, I'll hurt your sister," Saldrea hissed.

I ground my teeth.

"Do you really think it wise to threaten the man you've tasked with protecting you? Did you do that to your dragon and seraph? Did it work? Did they stay with you?" That hit home. She flinched, fury in her gaze. "I'm guessing not. So here's some advice, you keeping me in line with threats to my sister when I was your lackey was one thing, but now... what if I let an attack slip through, a fatal one? Then you'd be dead and my sister and I would be free. So perhaps, treat me with a modicum of respect and see if that gets you further than threats and violence."

Saldrea was practically frothing at the mouth, but some of what I'd said seemed to get through her thick elven skull.

"I said, follow me," she hissed at me, barely able to form words.

I nodded and when she turned, I followed.

Since even Saldrea's little crew of groupies couldn't know of her mother's plans, she always spoke to me and the other titans in private. Now we joined Saldrea's cronies, who were happily plotting ways to crush Saldrea's enemies.

"We've got the perfect plan!" Hana, the sylph, said as Saldrea arrived. I'd studied up on all of Saldrea's friends and allies: their powers and how dangerous each was. Hana was one to keep an eye on, because of her mental attacks, and her ability to take what she wished from your mind.

"Please enlighten me, I could use some good news!" Saldrea growled at her supposed friend.

"Dominion!" Hana breathed. "We challenge Izzy to a game of dominion."

Saldrea blinked. "How does that get rid of her?" she shot back so viciously Hana recoiled.

Neyalim provided more of an explanation. "It's a way to draw her out," the undine said, voice measured, clearly wary of Saldrea's temper. "We put it out that Izzy is a half-blood and must be exiled and give some insane reward for anyone who finds her and brings her to us, dead or alive."

Saldrea grinned at that.

"But... we also say that if Izzy comes to us willingly, she can stay... unmolested and safe... but only if she wins a game of dominion against us. It will be in her best interest to accept and not become a hunted fugitive. And when she does accept... well, it wouldn't be the first time someone died during a game of dominion. It's not like she could field a team strong enough to challenge us. She'll have dregs and outcasts and we'll crush them... literally. We can kill her and it'll all be legal and above board."

Saldrea's manic grin was in no way a good thing. "I love it!"

Well, whoever this Izzy was, she was screwed. From the little bits I'd heard around campus, especially after this Izzy woman had insulted Saldrea, she was a nymph who'd quickly earned Saldrea's ire and attention. Though it seemed she was a half-blood elf as well? That was curious. Anyone else who spoke of her, talked of a woman who stood up for herself and others, who seemed to care about people. That didn't sound like an elf to me.

Not that I trusted the rumors, or even Saldrea's perspective on the woman. I didn't trust anyone on campus, except the other titans, and even them I only entrusted with so much. Life was easier if you trusted no one. I'd learned the hard way that those closest to you could betray you in an instant. The only beings I trusted were my abominations. That's what all the other races called the wonderful creatures we titans created.

The elves were so damned focused on the purity of things, they couldn't see any beauty in the strange and fascinating mix of creatures we titans spent years perfecting. My Pegasus — Skycleaver — was a proud and noble steed, strong and agile, especially in the skies. To me there was no more beautiful being on the planet, but the elves called him an abomination because no horse should have wings.

I found it hypocritical for them to call themselves beautiful — their souls filled with filth — while calling my magnificent mount, whose heart was pure, an abomination. True... some of the chimeric beings we titans created were pretty messed up, but I'd never focused on creating beings of raw power or war, like others of my kind. I sought to create living works of art, truly beautiful beings, wonders of nature.

And I wished more than anything I could be among my creations now, instead of here with these women, all of whom had souls so filled with hatred and ichor it made me sick.

Elves and their minions were clearly the foulest things

on this planet, and I'd do whatever it took to save my people and my creations from the black hearts of these villains.

MYELAS

THE SICKENING ACHE IN MY GUT MADE IT HARD TO concentrate, Izzy was too far away. Safir had been so very wrong about the bond. And despite knowing Izzy was strong and capable, thinking of her in the capital, surrounded by elves, made my mind spin with scenarios of doom. If they found out who she was...

I understood now why she'd begged me to be careful not that long ago. She'd feared what would happen to her if I died. Now I feared the same.

I'd accepted my role in Izzy's life. I would serve her for as long as I could, protecting her and comforting her... till she decided she no longer needed me and was powerful enough to break the bond we shared. It seemed inevitable. She'd be a queen someday — if all our plans worked out — and when she was, she wouldn't want some insignificant shifter by her side. She wouldn't need my comfort. She'd have a whole harem of men to pleasure her and tend to her every whim. Stronger men than I. So, I'd take what I could get for as long as possible, but that wouldn't be long if she died before all our plans came to fruition.

Hence, I was more than a little distracted during the morning's sparring session. And in my job, any distraction during training could be fatal.

It was a good thing I wasn't fighting Artol. The wolf shifter was vicious and had it out for me. When we were young, he'd beaten me all the time, but as I'd slowly grown into my power and gained my shadow abilities, I'd started to win against him every now and then. That had only made him more vicious and vindictive. Of all of my cohort, he was the one I feared the most. He often said he'd gladly kill me, to be rid of the weak link in our team.

Today, I fought Saia, an eagle shifter. She didn't have it out for me, like Artol did, but of all my cohort, she was the one who beat me most often. I relied on agility and stealth to win, hiding and striking from shadows, whittling my opponents down. But Saia was equally as agile *and* the most perceptive of our group, meaning she often saw through my faints and ruses.

Since it was still midmorning, the shadow of the high wall around the practice yard stretched long enough for me to find it and quickly shadow-step away to avoid hits or get into position. But my distraction this morning meant every time I did, Saia was ready.

I emerged from shadows once more to attack her from behind, but she spun and raked me with her talons, tearing my practice armor to shreds and scoring three shallow bloody lines across my chest.

She pressed her attack. Since we both had wings in our hybrid forms, we flew over the yard. She forced me higher, out of the shadows and as soon as she had, I was done for. She wouldn't kill me, like Artol might, but I'd not be coming away from this practice session with just the wounds I had. She'd make sure I was truly defeated.

There was no calling surrender in these fights. The fight only ended when our cohort leader said it did. And my leader was a particularly vicious snake shifter named Essyma. She let Saia tear into me, while I sought to dodge and flee. It was only once I was at my limit, exhausted and shredded, that Essyma ended the fight. Saia and I landed, but I couldn't even stand, falling on my ass as soon as I did.

Artol laughed.

Svek, the last member of my cohort, a giant bear shifter, came to me and helped me up. "You're getting better, stronger," the big man tried to reassure me. "But you're still relying too much on shadows to win. You need to find other ways to fight or—"

"Or you're going to get yourself and your teammates killed when we're in a real fight," Essyma hissed. "What if we are attacked in broad daylight? What then? At night you *may* have the upper hand—" she didn't even sound convinced of that, "—but during the day, you're weak as shit." She shook her head, disgusted. "I should kill you now and put you out of my misery."

"I'll happily do it, chief," Artol said with a grin, showing off his long, sharp teeth.

"And you're a little *too* aggressive and bloodthirsty," she chided Artol. At least I wasn't the only one getting yelled at. "You could learn a bit of Myel's wariness. One of these days you're going to charge into a fight you can't win."

Essyma looked at all of us. "You're all shit. Saia's the only one of you with any real potential. Svek's afraid of his own strength, Artol charges in no matter the situation, and Myel is only a moderately viable warrior at night. Fuck me, I'm doomed."

As far as motivational speeches went, that one sucked.

It was Essyma's job to be hard on us, turn us into hardened warriors, but still...

"It's nearly noon. Grab some grub, then head to your afternoon patrols. I'd better see improvement tomorrow or I might report the whole lot of you to the commander."

None of us wanted that. Being reported to the commander meant only one thing: you weren't capable, and if you weren't capable you weren't needed. And since a shifter's only purpose in this world was to serve as front line troops and cannon fodder, if you weren't needed for that, you were simply executed so you weren't dead weight.

Admittedly, it was a threat Essyma made to us nearly every day, but today, I took it to heart. I hadn't done well in that fight and couldn't afford another bad day. I had to live, for Izzy.

I trudged away, aching and bleeding, to the infirmary, where I'd be stitched up and bandaged, but not magically healed. And while I was there, hissing through the process, since painkillers weren't wasted on shifters, I couldn't stop thinking about Izzy.

Perhaps if I sorted through my thoughts now, today, I could function tomorrow. I didn't think it likely my mind would let go so easily, but it was worth a try.

My feelings for Izzy hadn't changed, I loved her. The trouble was, no matter how she felt about me, she didn't *need* me. I wanted to protect her, but she had a dragon for that now. And the bond would ensure I remained her lover, but she had an incubus and a seraph to tend to those needs as well. The mate bond was the only thing keeping us together. And for now, I'd take it.

But the thought — the worry — I couldn't seem to get rid of was: *what will happen once she's fully trained, once she's come into her power and position?*

She knew who she was now. It was only a matter of time before she had the power to break our bond. Only a matter of time before she'd need to present herself as a royal, and having a shifter lover would only harm her image. I'd vowed to serve her for as long as she'd have me... but that had been back when she'd not been aware of her heritage. Now that she was, I couldn't help but wonder how limited my time would be.

And if I couldn't serve her, was of no use to her, not needed... perhaps I'd let Artol end me. Before Izzy had come into my life, I'd been nothing. Without her, I'd be nothing again. Life wouldn't be worth living.

While I wallowed in self-doubt, the three bells of a campus-wide announcement sounded. To ensure everyone heard these important updates and couldn't ignore them, announcements were sent directly into the minds of all those on campus by a powerful sylph.

"Attention all Veilblood Academy staff and students. It has come to our attention that Sa Brown Izzy is a half-blood elf. As such, she is to be exiled immediately. A reward of a thousand gold is offered to anyone who brings her to campus authorities."

Fuck me, a thousand gold? That's a fortune. Everyone on campus would be hunting Izzy!

"However," the announcement continued, "our generous and gracious princess Saldrea has offered an alternative option for this mixed blood wretch. If Sa Brown Izzy turns herself in to the main administration building by or before seventeen o'clock then she'll be granted leniency. Princess Saldrea offers trial by combat, in the form of a dominion match. Sa Brown Izzy will be allowed to form a team and take on the princess and her team. If Sa Brown Izzy wins, she will be granted a stay of exile and allowed to continue her education at Veilblood Academy. She will, however, be confined to campus and escorted to the human realm upon completion of her time here. Thank you all for your attention."

I couldn't make sense of this. Why would Saldrea offer such a thing? Then it hit me. Saldrea was hoping for one of two outcomes, both of which would get rid of Izzy, while leaving Saldrea blameless. Either Izzy didn't turn herself in and was exiled... or Izzy took the offer, and Saldrea "accidentally" killed her during the dominion match.

Fuck me, this was bad.

I needed to prepare myself. If Izzy was going to be exiled or flee back to the human realm, I'd have to go with her. That would be the safest option, not that Izzy would take the safe option, given what I knew of her.

I couldn't see Izzy winning a dominion match against Saldrea and her goons, all of whom were experts in their respective elements. Izzy was still too new, too fresh. Her chances of winning would be slim, especially with Saldrea out for blood.

First, I needed to let Izzy and Safir know about the announcement, since it wouldn't have reached them in the capital. I took out my phone and quickly sent a text.

I prayed Izzy would take the easy out, but that was selfish. It would mean we could be together... forever. She wouldn't need to learn her nymph or elven powers, just live as a human, with me by her side.

But I had a feeling Izzy would choose to fight. It was in her nature, who she was. And if she did, I would support her, even if victory wasn't a sure thing. But I had to believe she'd win... because if she didn't... if she died... I'd go mad or follow her to the grave.

AMARHUK (ROOK)

I GROUND MY TEETH AS THE ANNOUNCEMENT FADED.

Fuck.

This was bad.

As much as I'd hoped to distance myself from Izzy… I didn't want her to die! In fact, the thought of losing her was physically painful, a knife to my heart. Which illustrated to me all the more why I needed to keep away from her. My heart shouldn't be involved at all.

She was elven royalty for fuck's sake!

Never in my wildest dreams would I have imagined myself in *any* relationship, let alone with an elf, and certainly not with a royal! And Izzy being of mixed-blood made the whole thing even more complicated. I couldn't imagine many elves would want her on the throne, and yet — given the plans the people around her were making — that's where she was headed. I couldn't see that happening without violence, probably war. I'd fought wars in Urval and knew how brutal they could be. I didn't want to get mixed up in another life-or-death conflict.

Even if I already was.

I'd found Elnori, the dryad who provided my master — the dwarf Svokol — with much of his intelligence on the goings on around campus and in Seial. She'd been surprised that Safir had sent me. She admitted she'd been working with the old tiger shifter — who'd been pulling strings behind the scenes — for nearly ten years. They were part of a cabal of "lesser" races searching for a true royal to put on the throne and depose the tyrant Valnea.

We'd been on our way to talk to Svokol and convince him to join that cause when we'd heard the announcement.

I'd been wondering what Saldrea would do after finding out Izzy was a half-blood elf. This situation had two likely outcomes: Izzy's banishment or her death. The chances of her winning a dominion match against Saldrea were slim. Even if I had a sinking feeling that's exactly what Izzy would attempt to do.

And she'd probably pull me into it.

I sent a quick text to Izzy to let her know, in case Myel was tied up, then had to focus on the task ahead of me as Elnori and I entered my master's office.

Svokol looked up, saw the two of us together and raised his dark brows.

Elnori closed and locked the door. She closed her eyes, murmuring something, then looked up. "The wood will not hear us," she whispered.

Svokol did something similar, some spell, before replying with, "The stone has been silenced"

This must be some ritual between the two of them, some little spell they both cast to ensure no one would overhear what they said. Dryads were experts with wood and dwarves with stone and metal, so between the two of them — if they had the right abilities — they could ensure no one outside might listen in.

A common saying in Seial was: *the trees have ears*. Long ago the dryads had been the ultimate spies and gossips, since they could use trees to listen in on conversations miles away. The elves had not liked that power and had killed most the dryads who possessed such abilities, but it was rumored some still existed, serving the elves as spies. And Elnori might be one, though what she'd done just now had been to block such listening... so I honestly had no clue if she could do the opposite and listen in on others. Yet given the information she often provided to my master, I assumed she could.

"Why is he here?" Svokol said immediately, indicating me with a nod. "What's happened?"

Elnori turned to me. "That is his story to tell."

I grimaced at them both. I didn't want to be mixed up in this.

Safir had said I needed to work with Elnori to find a way to tell Svokol about Izzy and sway him to her side. The hope being that if Svokol — an influential dwarf — joined Izzy, other dwarves might follow.

Yet despite concubi being a very persuasive race in nearly any circumstance, I had no clue what to say. Luckily, my master was a blunt man and liked things straight. So, I told him everything. He already knew I'd slept with Izzy and roomed next to her. I didn't go into sordid details of our times together, but I explained Izzy's hopes to change this world and the truth of who she was: a half-blood elven princess of the true royal line.

"Fuck me," Svokol muttered, not looking happy. He put his elbows on his desk and his head in his hands, sighing. "If she'd been anyone else, anyone who'd been quietly flying under the radar, she might have had a chance... but..." He looked up at us. "You heard the announcement, Izzy's doomed. I don't know if there's anything we can do to save her." He sat back. "I certainly can't get involved, that would jeopardize all the work I've done to get in good with the elves and elevate my position."

Dwarves had once been elves, long ago, but they'd been considered "low" elves with no power over life and creation. They'd split off from the elves to live secluded lives underground. To elves they were considered lesser, like pretty much every other race, but still "acceptable company," having elven blood in their veins.

He sighed. "What is it you hope to gain by coming to me?"

I didn't really know.

Elnori piped up. "Nothing yet. But... if *you* support Izzy... in secret and slowly get the word out to other dwarves that if she becomes queen, they might once again be equal to elves... it would help our cause immensely."

The dwarf grumbled, "I still can't believe you were with *them* the whole time." It seemed he wasn't a fan of Elnori's extracurricular activities.

He shook his head. "I can't help her win this dominion match, I certainly can't participate, but if she manages to field a team and — by some miracle — win... I'll start spreading the word about her."

As far as I was concerned, that was the best possible outcome.

Elnori nodded. "I have others I need to inform." Then she excused herself.

"And you," Svokol asked me after the dryad had left, "you're taken with the woman? That's not like you."

It wasn't.

I didn't really want to go into the complexities of my feelings. The feelings I *shouldn't* have for Izzy.

"She's a good fuck," I said with a shrug. It was a lie. She was far more than that. And my master was shrewd enough to see right through me.

"No... she's more. What is she to you?" A faint smile caught his lips, a rare occurrence. "And why do I get the feeling she means more to you than I do?" His tone was light, but those words hit home hard.

Svokol had been good to me, taken me from a life of pain in the Urval military, elevating me to a position of relative privilege as one of his aids. He'd seen potential in me, as a warrior, as a spy, as a strong and capable man. And over the years I'd become something of his confidante. I could never repay him for the kindness and generosity he'd shown me. For him to think anyone in this world meant more to me than him... stung my soul.

Even if he was right.

Izzy meant so very much to me, even if I'd only known her a few days. I couldn't explain it. I didn't *want* to explain it, to admit how quickly she'd grown close, a friend and lover and... more.

"She's..." Fuck! How could I say this. I didn't want to admit anything. "She's intriguing in a way I've never encountered before," I said, and that was honest at least. "She's... powerful. And powerful people draw others to them."

Svokol grunted. "I've noticed that about her too."

Oh? Good.

"So, yeah... that's all. I'm still loyal to you."

"And what if I turned against her, which side would you choose?"

I didn't want to choose sides, didn't want to be part of the battle I sensed was coming.

"Yours," I said, but my words were a little too quick, too

forced and we both noticed it. Yet I couldn't afford to get any closer to Izzy. As much as I wanted her, my body and soul crying out for her... if I remained near her, she'd overwhelm me.

It had been torture last night, sitting in the same room while she'd fucked Myel. That angel's screen of light had done nothing to dampen the sexual musk which had filled the room and made my entire body sing. I'd wanted to be with her and Myel so damned much it had twisted my soul

No woman had ever affected me like that.

No woman *should* affect me like that. Incubi weren't meant to be with only one woman.

I shouldn't want to help her, hold her, be there for her. But I did. And now... if she died in this desperate gamble to put her on the throne?

No... I needed to step back, get away from her, distance myself.

If I gave in to these feelings, then I'd be banking on her somehow living through all the trials ahead of her. She'd have to beat Saldrea, then beat Valnea, then convince the elves a half-blood was worthy on the throne. The odds of her doing all of that and becoming queen were astronomical. But only then, once she was safe, could I let my feelings be known. Yet even as queen, she'd never truly be safe.

Hence, neither would my heart.

That was why I needed to get away from her, stop thinking about her.

But I couldn't. I couldn't forget the feel of her in my arms, how she tasted, the sounds of her soft sighs and pleading moans. I couldn't get over how much I simply wished to hold her close and feel her warmth, to protect her and help her, and be her friend, which was so very wrong for an incubus.

Caring only led to heartache and pain.

Love was dangerous. Period.

I wouldn't let what happened to my mother happen to me.

Svokol grumbled something, words I couldn't quite make out, a bad habit of his. Then he raised his voice and said, "Just... keep your head screwed on." His tone held a warning. "I get the feeling times are about to get... interesting, and that won't be good for any of us.

The dwarven ability for understatement was astounding.

"I'll do what I can," I said.

Svokol told me I could stay in his residence on campus, then dismissed me. I headed straight for the nobles' residence, since it wouldn't be safe to return to my room to retrieve my things. For now, I'd stick close to my master... and try not to think about the doomed woman who'd somehow stolen my heart.

IZZY

"WE KNEW SHE WAS GOING TO DO SOMETHING, BUT THIS..." Safir shook his head as he paced the large living area in Olinara's house.

He and I had received multiple texts. He from Myel and various other sources on campus and me from Myel and Rook. Myel's text seemed concerned. Rook's had been clinical, just the facts.

Lhorine had only just begun going over the fundamentals of earth magic when the messages had come in. That would have to wait now.

Olinara — I still had trouble calling her grandma or grandmother, it was easier to think of her as a friend or distant cousin — sat in thought, mulling over our options. At least today, she wore more than a flimsy robe, if not much more. Her white blouse strained against her chest, far too many buttons undone. Between the sheer fabric and how much skin was showing, it was clear she wasn't wearing a bra. Her skirt, if it could be called that, was a tiny scrap of fabric which barely covered her necessities. I couldn't take her seriously when she dressed like this. Yet she seemed to be taking my predicament very seriously.

Lhorine sighed. "It's the perfect strategy for Saldrea. Either you leave or she gets a state sanctioned way to kill you without making a fuss."

"You're assuming I won't win," I said, though I wasn't confident I could either.

Everyone looked at me.

"What!" I said, throwing up my arms. "You expect me to just... leave? Go home, forget about everything here?"

"You could go into hiding, much safer," Safir said. He'd calmed from earlier. Before I'd started working with Lhorine I'd had a quick word with him. I'd told him I appreciated all the work he'd done on my behalf and would seek his guidance, but that he couldn't be doing things on his own anymore. He had to run things by me first and learn to accept that others would be involved in the process.

He, in turn, had conceded that he'd been a bit of an ass lately. He'd been on his own for so long that giving up control hadn't been easy. I expected there'd be more clashes between the two of us... or him and others... but for now at least, he seemed to be trying to help me, not run my life.

"I'd still be hunted, so not *that* safe," I countered.

He conceded that point with a grimace and a bobble of his head.

Koar, leaning against a nearby wall, grunted. "Yeah, a thousand gold is too good for anyone to pass up. We'd not be able to trust anyone."

"I'm still not sure we can trust *you*!" Safir grumbled, mostly under his breath, but he quieted when I threw him a warning look. Even after our talk, he wasn't fond of Koar. The dragon *had* punched him earlier, so he may have good reason not to like the big man.

"I have to fight." I didn't want to, but it was my only option. "If we want people to follow me, I can't be some hidden princess who does nothing. I need to be fighting for this nation, for these people, and they need to *see* me doing it."

"Hidden princesses are much safer," Oli mused, then sighed. "But active ones would rouse the people far more. She's right."

Thank you, Grandma.

"And I'm well aware of my shortcomings," I said. "So what we need is a plan, how can I fight and win. Perhaps the others on my team...?" I glanced over at Koar, I wouldn't mind him backing me up.

He shook his head. "Dragons are forbidden from participating. We possess too many elements." He grinned. "We're hard to control."

Damn.

"You need a team of four," Lhorine said softly, almost as if talking to herself. "Do you know anyone with strong elements who'd fight for you?"

"Vyns!" I said immediately. However, I recalled something he'd said about himself and dominion. "But... he has light magic, and I remember him saying that wouldn't be useful."

"Not for the main purpose of the game, no," Lhorine said. "Light can't push people off the field... but he could still be useful, blinding your opponents, so they can't see you, can't attack properly."

"Oh... and he has a wall of light, like a shield-thing, he can do."

"More useful than he thinks," Lhorine agreed. "Anyone else?"

I sighed. I didn't know if I was still friends with Rook.

Safir brought him up. "What about that incubus? He's also half salmaeri, isn't he? That's fire magic."

Olinara grumbled. "As much as salmaeri have an affinity for fire magic, most of them are not incredibly strong. Saldrea's sylph friend would probably blow out his flames without a second thought."

"I have a nymph friend, Tala," I offered.

"Is she strong?" Oli asked, then put on a wide, cat-like grin. "Like me?"

"Ah... no." By her own admission, Tala wasn't strong in water magic.

"I could put on a new face and be some new nymph friend," Grandma offered.

"If we were fighting a bunch of guys, you'd be my first choice. You'd be one hell of a distraction, but I don't want to put you in danger."

"And if Saldrea figures out who you are, she might make the connection to who Izzy is. Though that's assuming she hasn't already," Safir added.

That was the big unknown: did Saldrea know I was a royal? In many ways it didn't matter. This was a trap either way.

"I have to believe she doesn't," Lhorine said. "I know the princess and her mother well. If she thought you were a royal, a true threat, she'd hunt you down and end you. But instead... she's trying to draw you out. She's toying with you. That's what she does to enemies she believes aren't a real threat to her status and power."

That made sense.

"It's still a risk though, revealing yourself," Grandma warned.

"But we all agree it's what I have to do?"

There were resigned grumbles all around. What a resounding affirmation.

Safir was probably right, as much as I hated to admit it. I probably should run, stay safe. But it wasn't in my nature to run from a fight. Though, I'd never been faced with a true, life-or-death fight before. I'd not be able to put together a team as strong as Saldrea's, that was a given. I had to hope we could fight smarter... or something like that.

I didn't want to fight that insane princess, not yet. I'd hoped to have a lot more training, in both water and earth magic, before I faced her again. But I had no choice. If I didn't do this, nearly everyone in this world would be hunting me. I had to show people it was possible to stand up to bullies like Saldrea.

But the truth was... I had no clue how to do that and win. I didn't have a lot of options for my team. As much as Grandma Oli was a very powerful nymph, I couldn't bring her onto the field. Although..."

I smiled.

"Grandma, you can be anyone you want, right?"

She blinked and nodded with a smile. "Of course. But I can't replicate the powers of other races."

"But if you were another nymph, everyone would think you're them, not you. You can change yourself that well, right?"

"Oh yes."

In which case, Grandma could pretend to be Tala. It would keep my friend safe, Olinara wouldn't be revealing herself, and I'd have a strong water magic user. The problem would be... Tala would probably be targeted by Saldrea and her minions afterward and wouldn't have Grandma's power to protect herself. I'd have to talk to her, make sure she was good with this.

I had to hope she'd say yes. If not...

And Lhorine's idea about using Vyns' light magic in alternate ways did seem intriguing. I was willing to bet none of Saldrea's crew had ever fought a seraph before or faced light magic like that.

Which left...

"Could Myel fight?" I didn't want to include him, but he was an option.

"Shifters aren't allowed to participate, we don't have elemental magic," Safir said.

Ah... so...

The only other person I knew was Rook, and I didn't know if I'd be able to convince him to fight.

"How common is fire magic among the races?" I asked. "How likely is it Saldrea or others would have faced someone with fire?"

"Unlikely," Lhorine replied. "Golana is the only one who might have, but from what I've heard, she's never actually been to Urval, despite her family's vast holdings there."

I turned to Koar. "You have fire, did you ever... spar with them?"

He scoffed. "Like they'd lower themselves to fight me."

Then it seemed likely none of them had fought anyone with fire. Even if Rook wasn't strong, he might be enough of a wild card to help win this. Which meant I had to convince him to fight for me, despite the stick he'd had up his ass lately.

"Okay, I'm doing this, and I know who my team will be. I'll head back to campus with Olinara posing as my friend Tala, and Safir. Lhorine, can you make your way there separately? I don't know if I'll have any time to train, but any time they might give me I'll use. Koar, find Vyns and get him back here."

Grandma smiled, proud. "That's my little royal, already bossing everyone around."

I had a plan, but whether or not it would work... remained to be seen.

VYNSIEL

"Izzy is a true royal, the last of her line, the real queen, and I love her with every fiber of my being," I said to my family, finishing the long tale about why I'd abandoned Saldrea. "She may not be a seraph, but we share a spirit link, a true and abiding connection. That's how much of a miracle she is."

I could see my impassioned speech had not swayed anyone. My father's face was hard, a mask of rigid disappointment. My older brother leaned against a wall nearby, a smirk on his face. He'd never much liked me, especially after my martial exploits had earned me a place at Saldrea's side. I'd outshone him and he'd been envious ever since. But now he was all snide smiles. He'd finally be the "good" son, not the disgrace. And my mother... she seethed with barely restrained rage.

I hadn't expected much from my family, but I'd hoped I might be able to convince them of Izzy's brilliance and sway them to her cause.

I'd failed at that.

"You left a position of privilege for a half-blood strumpet?" My mother shouted, the dam keeping her fury in check finally breaking. "You betrayed the empire and ruined us for a pretty face, is that what I'm hearing?"

Nope, not at all what I'd said, but there was no use arguing.

I sighed. If they wouldn't listen, there was no reason to stay here and have them yell at me. I had but one more thing to say. "Saldrea may seek you out in retribution for what I've done. For that I'm sorry. You should probably leave here and lay low for a while." Then, done with my obligations, I turned and headed for the door.

One might think I would miss this house, having grown up here. They'd be wrong.

I had a few pleasant memories of times within these walls, but they'd been a *long* time ago, as a small child. Most of my memories were of my mother's general displeasure, or abuse at the hands of my father and brother, which they'd called training for my eventual military service. There was nothing here for me.

Not anymore.

I'd returned to say my piece, tell my family the truth about Saldrea and Izzy and see their reaction, which had been everything I'd feared. They hadn't changed. They probably never would. Which meant I could release myself from the burden they'd placed on me and live my life without them, free and unhindered.

I felt… lighter than I had in a long time.

"Don't you dare turn your back on your mother while she's talking to you!" my father roared.

I laughed as I continued to the door.

I knew what would come next, my father and brother would resort to violence. Both my father and brother had served in Elysial's armed forces, fighting the nephilim, but they'd been away from the front lines for some time. Once I'd been elevated and my mother had obtained a position of power, she'd ensured her husband and son were safe, working desk jobs. I, on the other hand, had been Saldrea's bully for the past six years and endured her constant punishment. So, when my father and brother came at me — cowards attacking from behind — I was ready. I sensed their spirits moving and before they reached me, I spun and lashed out.

I cracked my father across his face with a back-handed fist and kicked my brother to one side. I was a lot stronger now than when they'd "trained" me as a boy, my spirit enhancing me, my body toughened by the rigors of Saldrea's service.

Before either could get up — too slow, by far — I delivered another hard blow to keep them down.

"I am *not* the boy you beat up all those years ago!" I hissed at them. Then I turned to my mother who gaped. "And if you will not accept me and the truth which I speak, then I am no son of this house any longer!"

"How dare you!" my mother sputtered.

I shook my head in disgust. The woman before me had never loved me. I'd only ever been a pawn to her. She saw no wrong in what she'd done. Just like she couldn't see the truth now.

"You were never my mother," I said, voice deathly calm. "You never deserved me as a son, and now you've lost me. I can only hope one day you realize what you've done."

I walked out.

The day blazed with light, a pale blue sky above me, and I smiled up at it, feeling true joy in my soul. I had Izzy, the light of my life, a beacon to my spirit. She was my family now.

I'd create a new life with Izzy and Myel and those around her. People who saw me and appreciated me for who I was, not how I could benefit them.

I spread my wings and soared through the skies. Elysial was a wondrous realm. There was no ground here, simply open air. Long ago, the first angels — led by Anchiel himself — had imbued the very clouds with a solid permanence, weaving them into floating islands on which the angels had settled and built their cities. Every building was made of cloud-stuff, infused with light and magic to make it a structure which would last the ages. The sky was filled with fields of white and cities of shining silver.

The denizens of this realm needed no farms, nor livestock. Sylphim fed on air itself and seraphim on light. We enjoyed the food of other realms but did not require it. Thus, our realm remained a pristine place, one which would always hold a special place in my heart… even if I'd probably not return for some time.

A giant shape flew over me, its shadow enveloping me.

Vyns, I have returned. Izzy needs your help, Koar's voice spoke into my mind as I glanced up at the massive form of his dragon above me.

Izzy should have been training with her grandmother. Why would she need me so soon?

I landed on a cloud nearby and Koar descended to me.

"What happened?" I asked as he transformed, then quickly dressed. He carried a special pack with him, which slipped around one of his "wrists" in dragon form, but would loop around his torso as a man. He'd been carrying clothes in that.

"Saldrea," Koar said, as he slipped on pants. "She's challenged Izzy to a game of dominion. It's clearly a trap, a means to kill Izzy in a semi-legal fashion, but Izzy intends to face her and needs a team."

I blinked.

"I'm no good at dominion."

Koar grinned as he slipped on a shirt. "They have a plan for that."

"They?"

"Her grandmother, Izzy, and the elf we found to train her, Lhorine." He reached out and put a hand on my shoulder. "They're creating a team of misfits, *wildcards* they call them, and you're in." He shrugged. "Who knows, it's a crazy enough idea, it just might work.

Then the world of light and sky spun into inky, oily darkness as Koar shifted between realms.

Me? On a dominion team?

I'd always been curious to play but never thought I'd be any good.

Apparently, Izzy had other ideas. I shouldn't be surprised. She was brilliant. And if I could serve her in some way — especially to humiliate Saldrea — then I was all for it.

Time to find out what my partner in spirit had planned.

IZZY

I DISGUISED MYSELF AS AN ELF, ONE OF THE MANY ILLICIT forms my grandmother had acquired over the years. This elf was exquisitely crafted to have all the elven traits, without standing out in any way. Non-elves would see an elf and let them pass, while elves would likely dismiss their rather "mundane" cousin.

That got me to the sigil point in El'Anderyn, and back to campus, travelling with Lhorine and my grandmother, with Safir as our attendant. We'd decided we could all go together since I wasn't myself and nobody was looking for two elves, a nymph, and a shifter.

Once back on campus, I quickly found Tala in the lesser residence, showed her my true form, and explained to her the plan to have my grandmother look like her for the dominion match.

"It will still be dangerous for you," I said, "simply by associating yourself with me, and by going against Saldrea in an active way."

Tala knew this, I could see it in her worried features.

"We can hide you, get you off campus for a while, till things die down," Grandma Oli offered.

"I will be creating a safe place where you could stay," Lhorine added.

Tala sat heavily, slumped in her desk chair. I had no idea what she might be thinking. Then her jaw went tight as she drew in a deep breath. She'd reached a decision.

"Many of us have known for ages that Saldrea and her mother are bad for this realm. If there is something I can do to stop them, I will." She looked at my grandmother. "I'm not strong, but if you could train me... maybe I'll find some way I can help... eventually. For now, yes, I'll allow this."

Then my new friend, whom I barely knew, but who had more of a backbone than I'd thought, turned to me. "And I want to stay. If you have some place you'll be hiding on campus, I'll join you. We can train together." She smiled.

I returned her smile. "Thank you." I went to her as she rose, hugging her tightly. "I have so few friends in this world, it's good to know you're one."

"After this, you'll probably be my only friend, so... here's hoping this all works out," she whispered. I realized then how much she was giving up: her life, her freedom, going into hiding... all for me.

I embraced her all the tighter.

Olinara took a picture of Tala on her phone, which she'd use to turn herself into my friend later. Lhorine assured the nymph that she would construct a hidden place off campus for all of us to hide and train. Though... if we lost the dominion match, Lhorine would take Tala with her when she left campus.

Next, we went looking for Rook.

Once again, I ventured out hidden as an innocuous elf,

Safir led us to Svokol's office. Lhorine knew the dwarf, if only in passing, so she led our little group in to see him.

"We're looking for a man in your service, the incubus Rook," she said, voice silken and soft.

Svokol eyed her. "Why?"

Lhorine smiled. Safir had assured us Svokol was no friend of the crown, but this was still a risk. "We'd like to recruit him for the dominion team fighting against Saldrea."

Svokol's brows shot up. Instantly his gaze searched the four of us, landing on Olinara and lingering there before he nodded, then looked at me.

"Izzy?"

A keen man indeed.

"Yes," I said, and let my form return to my nymph self.

"You've gotten good at that in a very short time." His gaze slid to my grandmother. "But I suspect you had a good teacher." He rose and bowed to Olinara. "Inamora Eofine," he said with reverence.

"Always nice to meet a fan," she said, brushing off the formal greeting. My grandmother's reputation preceded her, it seemed.

Svokol righted himself. "Rook has been laying low in my residence. I'll escort you."

The dwarf led us from his office to a moderately sized house in the nobles' residence area. I once again hid myself. And while we walked, I marveled at how things had progressed in less than a week. This man had been the one who'd taken me from the human realm. It said a lot that I didn't think of it as "earth" anymore. I'd been terrified of Svokol then, furious at being kidnapped and taken from my life. I'd been even angrier — certain Svokol had something against me — when he hadn't stepped in to stop Saldrea from assaulting me in the middle of his class.

But now… I knew the lay of the land. Svokol hadn't been able to speak out against Saldrea, no one could, not without repercussions. And from everything Rook had said about the man, he seemed like a decent and fair master, if not one who tolerated fools.

And here he was helping me now.

I shook my head at the strange contradictions of this world.

Svokol's house looked small, but only a small portion of it was above ground. Dwarves lived below the earth, and the main floor of his house was a large and well-lit sitting room for receiving guests, but the rest was underground. We descended into halls exactingly cut from stone, clean and spacious.

We found Rook in a large workout and training room. He was stripped to the waist, sweating, throwing himself at fire-proof practice dummies, striking with fists and fire in equal measure. I'd never seen the man fight, and he seemed to be going all out, working out some deep aggression. When I'd first met him, he'd been steamy and tempting. I'd learned since then that he could be soft and warm and friendly. But this was a new side to him: dangerous and deadly… and damned hot!

As an incubus he probably sensed my momentary spike in arousal. He stopped suddenly and turned toward us with a surprised twitch before we announced ourselves.

"Izzy!" he breathed, and his entire aura shifted from sexy, sweating warrior to sexy, sweating playboy.

I'd reverted to myself once we were safely inside, and his gaze landed squarely on me when he'd turned. A shiver thrilled over his skin, making all the little hairs on his body stand on end… But then he blinked and growled, mumbling something to himself, before shaking his head and looking away. When he looked up again, he made a point of *not* looking at me.

"Master?" he said, addressing Svokol. "What is this?"

I sensed his unasked question: *what is* she *doing here?*

"Izzy needs a team for dominion. I know you've never played, but she wished for you to join her."

Rook's jaw dropped, eyes wide: a deer in the headlights.

When he finally blinked himself back to reality, he looked at me again. "You want...?" He tore his gaze off me, back to Svokol. "Won't that expose you? I can't go directly against Saldrea. I... we'll... it's a death sentence."

Thanks for the vote of confidence.

"I can talk my way out of it," Svokol said. "Tell everyone Izzy seduced you." He eyed Rook and me. "Something tells me that's not far from the truth. I'll have to distance myself from you, but only in public."

Rook seemed heart-stricken to hear that. He really did appreciate his master, it seemed.

"No... I can't leave you... you've been so good... You've done so much for me."

Svokol's voice and demeanor turned hard, a default for the dwarf. "I have been good to you, and now *I'm* asking you to do this. Will you deny *me*?"

Rook was completely taken aback.

I was surprised myself. I had no clue why this dwarf was putting himself out there for me. Though, from what Safir had told me about the man, he had a good heart. He wanted freedom for the dwarves and other races.

"No... master," Rook said, defeated. "I'll do it."

Wow, what a resounding acceptance.

My anger rose. What was it with Rook? Why was he suddenly so distant? Had I done something? Why did I get the feeling he didn't want anything to do with me? Had my explosive outburst the other night truly pushed him away? Maybe that was it.

I sighed, frustrated but resigned.

Vyns would help me, which meant I had my team of four. That was all I needed to face Saldrea.

As for whether we could win...?

Rook didn't seem to think so.

IZZY

Vyns and Koar found us as we marched across campus to the main administration building. Vyns fell into step beside me, a brilliant grin on his face, his spirit warm as it brushed mine. Koar dressed quickly then kept pace behind me, my stalwart guard.

Lhorine hadn't come with us, neither had Safir, nor Svokol. They'd thought it best not to reveal their presence. Lhorine would find somewhere near campus and use her earth magic to create a place for us to live and train in secret... assuming I won this match. Grandma Oli had already taken Tala's form, so I had my full team with me, plus Koar.

Saldrea was there, in the atrium of the building, when we arrived. She blinked, seeming surprised I'd shown up. When she saw Vyns and Koar, she twitched, her beautiful façade faltering to show her fury — for only an instant — before a cat-like grin spread on her face. I may have stolen her guards, but the odds were in her favor.

Behind her was a massive man, even bigger than Koar, taller by a head, well over seven feet and built like a brick wall. His skin was well tanned, bronzed, and he was bald, with dark eyes under a heavy brow. In contradiction to his massiveness, his face was a bit... soft and smooth, with round cheeks, a baby-faced giant of a man.

Was this a titan? I had to believe it was. Tala had said they were the only beings larger than dragons.

"I'm here to turn myself in and accept the princess's challenge to a dominion match." I looked Saldrea straight in the eye, defiant. It infuriated her.

"When do we play?" I asked.

"I'm not without mercy," Saldrea said, acting benevolent for the group who'd gathered to witness this event. "We will have the match tomorrow at sixteen o'clock. That gives you some time to train with your team. Aren't I gracious?" She preened and presented a pleasant smile. Many of those assembled clapped and cheered her generosity.

"Then I'll see you after lunch tomorrow," I said and turned to go. I'd wondered if maybe she'd try to stop me from leaving, keep me detained somewhere.

"I will, of course, be sending a couple guards to keep an eye on you," Saldrea said, voice light. "Just to ensure you don't try to flee overnight. You *are* a fugitive after all."

And there it was.

I turned back and nodded, accepting this, though I had no clue how we'd evade our minders to train. We could train in public, but not if I wanted any lessons from Lhorine before the match, which I did.

Saldrea motioned and two more massive figures stepped out to escort us. Both titans, or so I guessed, one man, one woman. The two flanked my group as we left and quietly walked with us as I made my way...

...where?

I couldn't go to the shifter residence, which was where

I'd been hoping to meet up with Myel and Safir and find out where Lhorine's secret hideout was.

My room was still a blasted-out hole.

Vyns didn't have a room.

Koar... I had no clue if he had any place to stay.

Which meant: Rook's room it was. Not that he seemed happy about it.

The five of us returned to the lesser residence and crowded into the room. Luckily, our minders remained outside, one next to the main door in the hall, the other guarding the door from the adjoining bathroom into my old room. We were trapped in here, no other way out...

Or so it would have been, if Myel hadn't showed up in a puff of shadow smoke, finger to lips to indicate silence.

Grandma was surprised, then seemed to understand who this newcomer was when he and I instantly embraced passionately in front of everyone, our bond stretched thin. With my legs wrapped around him and our bodies clutched desperately close, I got a teensy little orgasm as I ground my core against the bulge in his pants. We were both fully clothed, but the bond didn't much care.

I released him, a bit breathless, and righted myself.

Grandma, ever quick on the uptake, whispered to us. "Let me touch each of you." She did, memorizing our features through touch and having us all talk a little to collect our voices. She would remain behind and impersonate each of us, talking quietly to herself, to assure the guards we were all in the room.

The rest of us were then shadow-stepped out by Myel, before sneaking across campus. Safir met us outside the shifter residence and from there we crept through the trees at the edge of campus to the well concealed entrance of Lhorine's new training compound.

It was amazing what a powerful elf could do in a few hours. The hidden entrance was under a bush. Safir knew where it was, but otherwise none of us would have found it. When the bottom branches of the bush were pulled up, a rectangle of earth lifted away. Otherwise, it looked like normal ground.

Stairs, perfectly carved from stone, led down to a spare, open space. Lhorine couldn't make furniture, other than stone benches along the walls, so there was nothing in the large room, but it would be a great place to train in secret. Two of the walls had open archways, leading to side halls. From one came the sound of running water. I went to look. Off the main room was a long hall which ran parallel to the room. There were three open archways off this hall, the farthest to the right led to a small room where Lhorine must have found an underground stream. It gushed out from the wall and fell into the room, the floor of which was sunken, making this room into a shower and bath. Any overflow of the bath then flowed out through a hole in the wall into the next room. The next two rooms had a stream running along a trough in the floor on the far side of the room. These must be washrooms. We could do our business in the stream and it would get washed away by the running water.

The other hall off the main area held six small rooms. I assumed these were individual sleeping areas, but since they had no furniture, just four bare walls and a floor, I couldn't quite tell.

This place was all function and no luxury, but it would do.

I found Tala in one of the bedrooms.

"I guess I'll be living here for a while," she said. I could tell the grin she gave me was forced, trying to make the best of this and failing.

"Thanks for putting up with this," I said and hugged her again.

"Just... beat Saldrea, okay? Don't get yourself killed."

"That's the goal," I said, but if I wanted to do that, then it was time to start training.

I went back to the large main area and met up with the others.

First, we talked strategy.

Our opponents would have two strong earth magic wielders, as well as a strong water practitioner, and a strong air magic user. All those elements were good for pushing people around, which was the main focus of dominion.

Our team would have one strong water magic user, but my grandmother would have to temper her abilities a bit so it wouldn't seem too odd that Tala had suddenly gotten so much stronger. I had no illusions about my abilities. I was still a beginner in water magic, and I'd only know as much earth magic as Lhorine could teach me in a day. But... we also had a moderately strong fire wielder, and a decent light wielder. They'd be our wild cards. Fire could push, but mostly as a byproduct. People didn't want to get burned and moved out of the way, which might move them back.

We decided to have Rook focus his fire on Neyalim, the undine. Her water could protect her, but if Rook managed to blast her with enough fire all at once, he might be able to force her back, potentially off the pitch entirely.

We decided Grandma, as Tala, would focus on Hana. Water would be the best element to force her back, since she could fly to avoid earth and spin wind to snuff our fire.

Vyns would use his light to blind them. There was also no rule in the game prohibiting violent uses of magic, which was wild, but which worked in our favor. Both Vyns and

Rook could blast away at the others with their elements and harm them, perhaps forcing them back.

That left me to take on Saldrea and Golana, both strong earth magic users.

Yikes!

Once we knew our parts, we separated. Rook and Vyns went to opposite corners — still not fond of each other — to work on their fighting styles. I stayed with Lhorine to learn earth magic. I didn't have Grandma here to teach me water magic, which was a loss, but I did know some of that already, so I focused on earth magic for now. Lhorine suggested we all head back to Rook's room a bit early, so Olinara could instruct me a little on water magic before the bout.

Luckily, dominion didn't require much finesse with one's element, just big, forceful effects or defensive magic. And since — according to Lhorine — I had a lot of potential and raw strength in earth magic, simple effects should be easy enough to learn.

Still, I was starting from scratch, so most of that afternoon and evening I spent learning the basics. Even before attempting earth magic, Lhorine walked me through anima control. It seemed like such a basic thing, knowing how much anima to use, but I had no clue. Once I had a better handle on that, we moved on to beginner earth magic exercises.

Lhorine got me to stand on the stone floor barefoot.

"Eventually, you can do this through your footwear, but don't worry about that for now... feel down into the earth with your feet. Don't try to feel anything other than the coldness, the hardness, the basic sensations. Focus on them."

I did, it was easy, my feet were freezing in this underground dungeon of a training room. The cold stone was seemingly all I could feel.

After a while she whispered, "Now, imagine the stone beneath your feet softening enough that your foot sinks, till the entirety of your sole, even your arch is contoured by the stone. As you do... release your anima, just a little, a sliver of a stream."

I released the power within me. To help control it, Lhorine had suggested I imagine a funnel, limiting the flow of this magical essence to a narrow stream.

The stone beneath my foot softened and shifted. It was the oddest sensation as I sank, not even an inch, so that the stone floor cradled my foot.

I lifted one foot and saw the perfect footprint in solid stone.

It was such a little thing, but I couldn't help marveling at it. You shouldn't be able to leave a footprint in stone.

"Good," Lhorine praised. "Now return your foot and concentrate. We have a long way to go."

By the time we broke for a meal, I'd learned the absolute basics of earth magic, namely, how to feel down into the earth and sense the soil and stone around me. I could only sense to the edges of this room, perhaps fifty feet in all directions. I thought that was pretty good, until Lhorine told me she could feel for miles. Yeah... I had a lot to learn.

Safir and Myel — with Zora helping them from time to time — had been working while the rest of us had trained. They'd brought down some basic furniture. I had no idea where they'd gotten it from, but three of the small bedrooms now had mattresses and the rest at least had thick blankets. They'd also brought down a small table with four chairs as well as food and water.

Rook didn't say a word as we ate.

Vyns and I chatted a little. He seemed... different from before he'd gone home. When I asked him about it, he smiled.

"My family wouldn't listen to what I had to say. I honestly didn't think they would, but I had to try, had to tell them the truth. They wouldn't hear it, and it only affirmed to me that they aren't worthy of my time and attention. I walked out on them and won't look back." He reached over and laid his hand on mine. "You're my family now. I... hope that's not too forward."

Hell yeah, it was! Still, I smiled.

I didn't have any family. Well, that had been true a week ago. Now I suddenly had a grandmother, though she didn't act like one. Still, I'd always wanted that feeling of belonging somewhere. Now I had a place: with Vyns.

A week ago, that would have freaked me out. I'd not wanted any sort of attachment or long-lasting relationship, but right now, with everything else going on, it felt good. Perhaps it was only because I might not live past tomorrow and I really needed someone to lean on, but still... Vyns' devotion gave me a soft, safe place to land.

After dinner we all went back to work and trained late into the night.

Progress was so very slow, though Lhorine kept telling me I was moving far faster than most young elves.

Since I wouldn't need to use earth-sense for any great distance tomorrow, we left off with that and focused on actual manipulation and movement of earth after dinner. I learned how to push up stone to create a basic wall to defend myself from attacks. We worked on that for a bit, making it sturdier, stronger, thicker. Then came a simple attack, using earth like a wave, rolling beneath people to topple them and push them back.

Lhorine could make a tall wave, which leaned forward, literally sweeping people away. I only managed a low roll of earth, but that was still apparently very good for my very first day working with earth magic.

Lastly, Lhorine taught me how to soften earth and sink down into it. This served several purposes. First, I wouldn't have to make my earth shield as tall. Second, it would help me stay in place and resist most attempts to push me back. Third, if someone tried to trap me in earth, I could soften it and get out.

After that... I was exhausted. It was well past midnight, and I hadn't slept much that morning.

I wanted nothing more than to collapse on a mattress and sleep... my bond with Myel, however, demanded attention.

IZZY

MYEL AND I SHOULD HAVE BEEN GOOD FOR ANOTHER DAY OR so, since we'd been together last night. God, it felt like an eternity since then. But perhaps because we'd been so far apart, or because we both knew things might go badly tomorrow, the bond had grown tight and desperate.

Myel went to reserve one of the rooms with an actual mattress, while I sought out Rook. The incubus had been cold to me all day, still I asked him if he wished to join us. He'd told me that being with Myel and me was like a drug, that he *needed* it.

Even so, the incubus shook his head wordlessly and left the training compound entirely, heading up the stairs and out.

Wow...

He couldn't even speak to me now?

What was up with him?

I let out a pained and frustrated sigh, then headed to the hall with the bedrooms. Vyns stopped me.

"I... am not ready to be with you and someone else at the same time," he whispered with an offhand glance to the stairs, where Rook had just fled. "But, if you need anything from me tonight... let me know.

"I... might?" I didn't really know. I might also fall asleep in Myel's arms, given how exhausted I was. "Thank you for the offer."

He smiled and let me go.

Myel waited for me, already naked. Yet despite the rather swollen and desperate look of his erection, he didn't rush things. Instead, he came to me more like a servant. He helped me undress, whispering soft pleasantries and compliments. And once I was naked, he urged me to lie down, massaging my back and feet.

Hot Damn! That felt good.

I let him know exactly which spots needed more attention with soft moans and breathy yesses.

"You can win," he whispered behind me, digging his hands into my back. Sometimes I forgot how strong my Goth hero was, despite his lanky appearance. He said no more on the matter after that, and I was thankful. I didn't want to think about Saldrea, or tomorrow. I wanted to let his presence soothe me and relax, after we both got our rocks off because... *the bond.*

Our connection strained, burning within me, making it impossible to completely unwind and enjoy this massage.

Eventually, I squirmed and when Myel shifted off me, I rolled over.

"Time for the front," I breathed, feeling my breasts swell of their own accord. Apparently, I didn't have complete control of my body yet. "Once the bond is satisfied, you can go back to that wonderful massage."

His eyes dilated in the dim light of the small lantern which lit the room. I opened my legs as he slipped between them, leaning down, hands to either side of my head.

"I am the luckiest man in all of existence," he breathed reverently. "I'll treasure you forever, no matter what."

I wasn't sure what that last bit meant. Did he think he'd lose me tomorrow? It broke the mood for all of a nanosecond before his heavy cock brushed my drenched and aching folds and I lost all coherent thought.

He thrusted in.

I cried out, back arching.

He pulled me up into his arms as our hips crashed together. The semi-sitting position was awkward, but neither of us cared, lost to our joining. His lips pressed to mine before desperately kissing all over my face and neck and chest as our ecstasy quickly escalated. There was something divine about knowing I did this to a man, feeling him lose control, his thrusts growing ragged, grunting desperately.

His raking teeth found my neck and he bit deep, drinking from me as a heady mutual orgasm swept through us. We clung to each other through that stunning release, time stretching, drawing out this bliss.

Eventually, Myel laid me down, kissing softly over my face and hair. He held me close, but something about his strong embrace made me feel like he thought I might slip away in the night.

And only then did his previous words return to me.

I'll treasure you forever, no matter what.

No matter what?

What did that mean?

Did he not think I'd win tomorrow?

It seemed the only logical explanation for this sudden clingy behavior. And that vote of non-confidence filled my gut with cold dread, despite how much Myel's presence soothed me.

"Shall I massage you again?" he whispered.

"No, we're both tired, just sleep," I replied.

But long after he'd fallen asleep, I lay awake, unsettled.

I didn't know what hour of the night it was when I finally slipped out of Myel's embrace. I put on a robe which someone — probably Zora — had left for me. I'd seen the hobgoblin woman coming and going, bringing so many of these small niceties into this otherwise cold and sterile compound.

The stone floor chilled my bare feet as I made my way out to peek into the other rooms. Vyns wasn't in any of them, but I caught flashes of light from the main room. When I looked, the angel was still practicing.

Much like earlier, when I'd seen Rook training on his own, Vyns was stripped to the waist, bathed in sweat. And even more so than Rook, he was a bronzed god of a man, heavy chest and thick shoulders and arms, with a narrow, chiseled waist. One hundred percent *yum*.

And despite my frenetic coupling with Myel earlier, I needed... more. I needed a man who revered me, trusted me, thought I was powerful.

And Vyns was that man.

I went to him, padding softly across the stone floor. It said something about how hard I'd worked on my earth-sense, that even without really trying, I felt his movements through the ground. If I closed my eyes, I could feel exactly where he was.

"Vyns," I called softly, interrupting his training.

He spun, surprised, then smiled wide as his gaze traced down over me.

"I..." I didn't know what to say. He'd offered *something* earlier and I needed whatever that was. I rushed to him, throwing my arms around him and clinging to him almost as desperately as Myel had to me. "I need you," I whispered.

And without even asking, he seemed to know what I meant, what I needed.

Strong arms enfolded me with a delicate yet passionate embrace. "We'll beat her," he whispered and the surety and confidence in his voice allowed me to breathe out the tension I'd been holding inside since Myel had fallen asleep. Yet, when that stress left me, my exhaustion returned and I went limp in his arms. He cradled me close, my body molded to his.

He gave a soft chuckle. "I'm a dripping mess," he whispered.

Yeah, so am I, my dirty little mind replied, thinking of something entirely different.

"I should have a shower."

"That sounds heavenly," I breathed.

A soft and gentle shower with Vyns seemed like just what the doctor ordered. Some calming shower sex before finally resting.

He lifted me easily and carried me to the other hall and the shower room. Someone had placed a small curtain of fire in front of the pouring water. The water poured through, heated, while steam filled the small room, making it nice and humid.

Vyns stripped and I removed my robe before we stepped down into the knee-deep bath and let the warm water flow over us.

"I have to hand it to the incubus, this is genius," Vyns said, indicating the fire. "*Maybe* having a demon on our side could be useful... *occasionally*."

Rook had done this? It made sense, he was the only one with fire magic.

"And... he can keep it up all the time?" I asked amazed.

"Well, he *is* an incubus," Vyns replied.

I didn't understand how that impacted the durability of his fire magic... till I got the dirty joke Vyns was making and slapped him playfully.

"Are you actually giving the man a compliment?"

Vyns sighed. "With you in my arms, I feel... generous."

Right answer.

My desire for this man spiked. I couldn't help myself, Vyns was... perfect! He was starting to accept Rook, and he was otherwise so giving and so damned certain of my strength and power. I climbed his amazing body, wrapping my legs around his waist and toying with his rigid hardness trapped between us, rocking my pubic bone over it softly.

"I need you," I whispered, and he got my meaning clearly this time as well. But to make it clear what I wanted, I added, "Make me feel powerful, like a queen, a goddess!"

Turning us in the warm spray, he pinned me to the wall. Steam had warmed the stone and given it a slippery sheen.

His kiss was intense, passionate, but also... giving, letting me take control as my hands slipped up behind his head to comb through his wet hair.

When he pulled back, he breathed, "Then I shouldn't need to do much at all, because you *are* a queen, quite literally, and I don't know about anyone else, but you're certainly a goddess to me."

Yup, all the right words. "More," I breathed. I needed more of everything he gave me.

"You're a goddess of love, of lust, of power and earth and water. You're a sexy vixen at night, and a true and benevolent ruler during the day. You have my heart and my spirit, my everything. I am yours, now and always."

Yes, yes, yes, yes, YES!

"Make me feel it," I gasped as his words brought tears to my eyes, wetness hidden by the water coursing over us.

"Kiss my neck, here," he breathed, touching a spot as he tilted his head.

I didn't ask why, just did it.

"Feel what you do to me, feel the pounding of my heart," he said as my lips pressed to his neck, and I felt his hammering pulse. "And feel the tempest of my spirit."

I did. A sweltering humidity, a billowing wet heat that matched the shower coursing over us. And it matched a wet heat *deep* inside me. His spirit had whipped up a torrential summer's storm and it raged with devotion as it linked with mine.

"Yes!" I breathed, voice trembling.

"*You* do that to me," he breathed.

I did something else to him too; his cock was practically vibrating between us.

I shimmied up over him, freeing that trapped hardness and feeling it brush my folds. When I settled back down, his tip slid effortlessly inside me.

He chuckled again, even if it was with a strain in his voice. "And you take control when you want it, when you need it."

I had, hadn't I?

Fucking yes, I loved how this man made me feel.

I sank fully down onto his thickness, grinding my clit against him. Pleasure and power filled me.

"Yes," Vyns gasped, clearly already on the edge. "Use me, take your pleasure from me, my goddess!"

I did.

I pushed his face to mine once more, devouring him as I rocked myself hard over him, riding that deliciously filling cock with sudden vigor. I'd been exhausted a moment ago, but now I felt renewed, vibrant and potent.

There was no imperative between Vyns and me, like there was with Myel, no bond demanding sex. I could take my time enjoying how epically good Vyns felt crushed against me, deep inside me, my lips on his, his hands worshiping me as they stroked my flesh.

And when I came, it was with a full body shudder of complete and utter release, all my worries and fears gone, replaced only with a sense of serene strength.

Vyns slowly shifted us, sitting down in the bath, warm waters all around us. Yet...

"You... did you...?"

His cock was still throbbing and rigid inside me.

He smiled. "Despite your heavenly beauty, I have withheld myself. Great feats of willpower and control are possible with a spirit as strong as mine," he boasted. "Even so, it took everything I had to resist your allure, your forceful vigor."

My look must have asked why...

"My goddess hasn't commanded my release yet."

Oh fucking hell!

"And if I command it now?" I whispered, breathless at the thought of another round.

"Then I'd ensure my goddess came again before I did, it seems only right."

Worked for me.

"Then, by all means," I breathed.

I yelped in surprise as he lifted me off his divine erection and placed me at the entrance to the shower, sitting on the steps.

He urged me to lay back as he kissed his way down my body. I opened my legs and let him feast on my folds. I'd thought myself spent, but Vyns' insistent tongue quickly whipped me back into a frenzy. I combed my hands through his hair as my hips bucked, body writhing. And when he sucked on my aching clit, sliding two fingers inside me to massage my G-spot, my pleasure rocketed toward a second peak. My back arched so high only the back of my head touched the ground.

That's when Vyns rose, yanked my hips to him and filled me with his throbbing cock once more. That's all it took. That one thrust hit some miracle place deep inside me and I shattered, crying out and squirming, fists slamming into stone as a raging orgasm swept through me.

"Thank you, goddess!" Vyns hissed.

He must have been pretty damned desperate for a release, because as soon as I came undone his cock pulsed hard inside me. His spirit exploded in bliss: a wave of sweltering heat washing through me, stealing my breath and elevating my pleasure to a mind-bending, body-breaking rapture.

I writhed and bucked so hard, I pushed Vyns out. The pleasure so intense, I rolled onto my side, curling up, shuddering and holding myself as I laugh-cry-gasped through the residual waves of that blessed orgasm.

Vyns laughed and swore and laughed some more before he regained himself enough to ask,

"Hey, you okay?"

I nodded, unable to speak. Then inanely, I lifted a hand and gave him a thumbs up. That made him laugh again.

He settled next to me, behind me, kissing my shoulder. "The goddess approves?"

I let out a *long*, whining moan, which I hoped said: *hell yes!*

"Oh... Wow... As if I needed more evidence of my

goddess's power..." Vyns' breathed in awe. When I looked at him, he was glancing at the stone floor. I followed his gaze to where... oh...

The stone was shattered in places, small craters, where I'd pounded the floor with my fists during that epic orgasm.

I'd done that.

And I hadn't even felt it.

Wow.

And wishing to feel my own power, prove what I could do, I smoothed my hand over the marred stone, using a hint of anima to level it out once more.

I couldn't have done that yesterday.

Maybe I was as powerful as Vyns thought me to be. I sighed and smiled, confident in myself in a way I'd never been before.

Vyns brought me back into the bath to wash me — and himself — off, his touch so soft and soothing.

I fell asleep in his comforting arms, in that warm water, and sometime later, woke to find myself in a bed. Oddly, I wasn't with Vyns. The angel had put me back with Myel and the soothing comfort I got from the shifter allowed me to fall asleep again for a while. And all I could think was: *The man gives me one of the most stunning orgasms of my life, then puts me in the arms of another man.*

What an angel.

Lhorine woke me early, but I felt oddly refreshed, considering I'd been up most of the night. Hooray for empowering orgasms!

Then we got back to work. We had only a few scant hours before our match with Saldrea and I still had a lot to learn.

IZZY

I WAS NOWHERE NEAR READY BY THE TIME WE ALL SECRETLY returned to Rook's room. I was far more prepared than I'd been a day ago, but still way out of my depth.

Seeing my agitation, Grandma Oli took me aside, into the bathroom.

"Get yourself together," she said, stern. "Half of any fight is your mindset, and I can see in your eyes, you already think you've lost."

She wasn't wrong. I leaned on a wall, tired. As much as I'd woken up refreshed, Lhorine's rigorous training that morning had been more than my sleep-deprived body could handle.

"So… what? What can I do?"

"First you need some energy, one sec." Olinara popped back into Rook's room, returning with Koar. "Take your shirt off," she commanded the dragon.

He raised a brow in question but obeyed.

"What are you doing?" I asked.

Olinara lowered her voice, we all knew there was a titan guard on the other side of that bathroom door.

"It's a rare healing technique. I shouldn't even know it, because it's meant for two earth practitioners, but Queen Leastrine once taught me, in confidence. I can do it, but I'm more of a conduit. Once you know, you'll be able to do it without me."

I hadn't really known Koar was an earth wielder, but some stray lesson from my scant class experience returned to me about how dragons were beings of earth, air, and fire. I assumed they were mostly fire, but... apparently not.

"Do I need to take off my shirt too?" I asked, starting to unbutton the blouse I was wearing.

"No, I just wanted to see Koar's magnificent chest," Grandma said with a grin.

Koar grunted, rolling his eyes.

"Give me your hand," Grandma Oli instructed, and I did. Koar went to give her his large hand as well, but she shook her head. "No, I'm going to feel up your chest, now get over here, big boy."

My turn to roll my eyes. My grandmother might be a wise and experienced woman, but sometimes she acted like a flirty girl. It was easy to forget she was over two-hundred-years-old.

Koar stepped in grudgingly, and she put a hand on his chest.

"Oh, yes, thank you," Olinara said with a sigh and a silly grin. Then she blinked herself back to reality and walked me through the ritual.

Healing was closely related to both earth and water magic, so theoretically, this should be quite easy for me. Though, in this case, it wasn't so much repairing an injury — which anyone could do — as it was restoring vital energy. And since that energy was a physical thing, not mental or spiritual, or emotional, it required two earth magic users. In this instance, Olinara acted as a conduit as Koar released his raw physical energy, and I received it. She told me to visualize taking part of Koar's physical essence, suggesting I imagine taking his kidney, since that was something he could give away and not die. Koar envisioned the same thing, giving up the organ and letting me take it, a willing donor.

"Repeat after me," Oli whispered to Koar. "My body to yours, my essence I give freely. Take what you need of me."

He repeated the words while she instructed me to say: "Your body to mine, your essence I receive. I thank you for your gift of life."

I repeated the phrase, imagining taking Koar's kidney as Olinara concentrated between us.

It came slowly, sluggishly. I didn't know whether this was how it was meant to be, or because there was a third party involved who possessed no earth magic. Still, it was like nothing I'd ever felt before: something akin to the best caffeine kick mixed with a massive sugar rush, but *so* much more. Muscles throughout my body tingled as my fatigue drained away.

Grandma grunted as she released us both. Then she swayed, and I had to catch her. Apparently, this took a lot out of her too.

Koar shrugged. "Doesn't feel that bad to me."

"You've got a lot of energy to give, this body doesn't do you justice, you are a dragon after all," Olinara said from my arms. Then she looked at me. "Better?"

"Lots, thanks."

She nodded, then dismissed Koar. "Now... to teach you some water magic."

"Are you in any condition to do that?" I asked, worried.

She laughed. "Oh, I'm just going to explain it. You'll do all the work. Now... fill up the tub."

Since we didn't have a lot of time, Grandma taught me one thing, an attack. There'd be small fountains on the dominion pitch from which we could take water, and she walked me through how to take as much as I could handle and simply push it, like a wave, at someone. I was surprised how much I could handle. When I'd taken my water magic class earlier in the week, I hadn't been able to do much. But now, gathering a ton of water seemed easy.

"It's because your binding is gone," Grandma explained. "It wasn't just suppressing your looks, but your power as well. You'll be far more capable now than you were then."

And it was a good thing too. I'd need every advantage I could get going into this dominion match.

I trained in that one technique over and over, surprised at how much energy I had after that infusion from Koar. I felt like a million bucks, even after training for more than an hour.

We all ate a small, energy packed lunch Zora had prepared for us, then, as time drew near, the titans guarding our door knocked and told us to come out.

We were escorted to the dominion pitch, where Saldrea and her minions waited for us. Also, it seemed the entire school had turned out to see the match. The bleachers were full and some elf must have used earth magic to make more tiered seating. Those who couldn't get a seat stood, crowding around the sides of the massive pitch.

Rook, Vyns, Grandma-as-Tala, and I marched onto the sandy surface, ready as we'd ever be.

Time to see if we could win this fight.

KOARTHANDRIS

IZZY WAS A BEAST!

I'd marveled at her training last night and this morning, how quickly and easily she'd picked things up. She didn't think so, but that's because she had no point of reference. Elves and dragons both had earth magic and were fairly strong in it, but the rest of us had mastered it over decades of practice, our long lives giving us plenty of time to learn how to harness our power. Yet in the span of a few hours, Izzy had mastered powers which some elves took years to learn.

If I'd needed any more proof that she was a royal, that had been it. The Anadendyra family had always been the best, the strongest, the quickest, the fastest at all things.

It's why I'd devoted myself to them, why I'd... loved them.

No... I couldn't allow myself to feel anything for Izzy. It had been my feelings for Mynrial, Talmarion's daughter, which had distracted me when I'd needed to be at my most vigilant. I'd failed that family, failed in my duty to the royals, and now I had a chance to make it right, and I wouldn't fail again. I'd never allow Izzy's perfection to distract me.

And Skies Above, she was perfect.

Strong and kind, gracious and resolute, resilient and bold while also being intelligent and damn-fucking beautiful. As an elf, she'd be able to take anything I could throw her way, but as someone who hadn't grown up in the filth and indoctrination of this world, she wasn't a stuck-up, nasty brat, like some princesses.

Perfect.

But off limits.

Even if every fiber of my being strained to touch her, hold her, give her what Myel and Vyns had given her last night. My dragon's senses had made me quite aware of both events, especially since I'd been on high alert for any danger pertaining to Izzy. She hadn't been in danger, and I was glad someone was giving her what she needed, but damn if I didn't want that someone to be me.

Yet, I couldn't.

I'd never allow myself to get close, not like that. I couldn't risk the distraction. I had to protect her with my life, had to make sure she lived.

And yet... I couldn't protect her now.

I watched her walk onto that dominion pitch, knowing Saldrea's power and spite, but unable to do a damned thing to help Izzy. My muscles twitched and my skin itched with the strain of holding myself back. It went against everything I stood for. Yet, I couldn't interfere. I was forced to watch over Izzy from the sidelines. And if Saldrea did manage to — Skies Forbid — kill Izzy, I'd make it my life's work to return that favor on Saldrea herself.

But I had to hope that the miracle that was Izzy could

pull this off. She'd amazed me time and again, ever resourceful and resilient and strong. She could win this.

She *could*...

But so could Saldrea.

I touched the still festering wound on my cheek. I knew how powerful the false princess was, how driven to destroy her enemies, how much she reveled in hurting others. Everyone watching today knew this was a state-sanctioned death-sentence. Saldrea would do her best to kill Izzy... because things like that happened in dominion; it was a brutal game.

Saldrea's team was stronger, there was no denying it. Elves, dwarves, undines, and sylphim were all at the top of their respective food-chains. Well, technically elves were above dwarves, but the underground dwellers weren't far behind. And against a barely trained elf, a nymph, a seraph, and an incubus... it *should* be no contest.

But Izzy's plan was solid. It just might work. And Saldrea had no clue Izzy had been practicing with an elven instructor, working on her earth magic, in addition to honing her water magic. As far as anyone knew, Izzy was a barely capable water magic wielder and that was it. Izzy had surprise and cunning on her side, versus Saldrea's brute force and raw power.

Skies Above, I hoped Izzy could pull it off.

She had to...

So I could... continue to protect her. That was it. All I would allow myself. I tried to tell myself it would be enough, service and duty. It had been enough for the past hundred years. But that had been before I'd met this stunning woman and realized that she, unlike every other woman I'd ever known, was ideal for me in every way.

I ground my teeth, though whether it was my fear for

Izzy or restraint of my deepest desires, I didn't know. Probably both.

I was so damn messed up it hurt.

If Izzy didn't live past today... a part of me would die, just like a part of me had died that day when the rest of her family had perished because of my failure. Living without Izzy would be hell, but... living *with* her would be perpetual torture of a different sort, denying myself the perfection which was right in front of me.

Yet I prayed Izzy would win, would live. Better her alive and me in pain, then her dead and the world denied its rightful ruler.

Izzy had to live.

She had to.

MYELAS

It killed me that Izzy was about to fight for her life while I was stuck here in training with my cohort. My bond demanded that I protect Izzy, and I couldn't. Not being with her was pure, unadulterated torture.

I'd tried to sound casual, make it an offhand comment, when I'd asked my cohort leader if we could skip today's training and watch the dominion match.

She shut that down instantly, saying our place was here.

"But half the shifter barracks have gone!" I pleaded, failing miserably at trying not to sound desperate.

"And perhaps this cohort could have gone as well, *if* you'd been half decent at anything," Essyma snapped. "But you're not. You're all crap, the worst of the worst, which means you have no right to leisure time until I say you do. So you'll stay here and you'll train. End of discussion."

Though even as she said this, her expression changed, considering.

"How many of you want to see this match?" she asked, curious.

I raised my hand slowly. Everyone but Artol, the wolf shifter, did as well. Huh... I wasn't the only one.

Essyma smiled. "Then I have the perfect solution. Saia and Svek, you two spar, whoever wins can watch the match." She turned to me and Artol and I already knew what she'd say. "Myel, if you can defeat Artol, you can go as well."

Yup.

I hated fighting the wolf shifter, mostly because he reveled in fighting me. He was stronger, faster, tougher and very perceptive. I rarely won against him and he thoroughly enjoyed ripping me to shreds whenever we faced off.

"Maybe, with the right motivation, this troop can actually get their act together and look like some semblance of a fighting force!" Essyma seemed proud of her decision.

I couldn't fault her.

I'd certainly be fighting harder than I ever had. Though that wouldn't guarantee victory, especially since my bond was being a dick and distracting as hell.

"Oh... and just for some added fun," Essyma grinned her viper's smile, "Myel, no shadows for you, fight in the sun. Let's see you win by sheer strength and prowess, no tricks."

And... I was fucked.

"Yes, leader," I said as my stomach bottomed out.

Artol laughed, an evil thing. "This should be fun."

The two of us walked to a sparring ring in the middle of the large training yard, in full sun.

"I hope you're ready to see your own bowels," Artol whispered as he shifted into his hybrid form. Wolves were the most common shifters, and though not the strongest, still apex predators. Long claws extended from large hands, his fangs grew as his snout elongated. He got about a foot taller, heavy with muscle which twitched, ready to launch him into this fight.

My shift was far less dramatic. I grew a few inches, but bats weren't large animals to begin with. My muscles stretched, a little stronger in this form, but not by much. My wings came out and my ears elongated. Bats had talons, but on their feet only. I could use them when flying, but my hands remained mostly human.

I had two slight advantages over Artol: my flight, and my hearing. But seeing as how I'd have to get within range of his claws to hit him, flight didn't do much for me, and despite that I could hear the pounding of his heart, my exceptional hearing didn't help much either. His hearing wasn't as good, but it was still superhuman and he'd hear me coming.

I took to the skies as Essyma called for the fights to start.

"Come down here and face me like a man," Artol taunted me.

"Why? I have wings, why shouldn't I use them to my best advantage?"

Artol growled.

Without my ability to shadow-step or hide, there was no way I could surprise him, which was usually my best approach.

Still, I had to win this fight... somehow.

As I tried to figure out some strategy to win, Artol called out to me again. "Why you want to see the match anyway? Just two elf bitches fighting."

My anger leaped to life at him calling Izzy such a name.

Artol must have seen me twitch and laughed. "What... you got a thing for one of them? Like to dream about sticking your dick in an elf slut?"

The bond responded viscerally to Artol's words. I swooped down. It was reckless, but even as my mind reeled at his insults, I managed to put together a vague plan of attack. I was slightly faster than Artol, but the margin was so small it usually didn't mean much. Still... perhaps I could use that tiny advantage.

Artol crouched, then leaped up to meet me. If the wolf-shifter had a flaw, it was his aggressiveness, an over-eagerness to fight. He threw himself into battle a little too readily and this time, it would hurt him.

He'd not be as nimble in the air as on the ground. I flared my wings and swiveled, just above him. His claws missed me. I then raked my clawed feet over his shoulders from behind, scoring a rare hit on the wolf. He howled as he fell, spinning in the air to try to swipe at me, but missing.

Still, he hit the ground in a crouch and waited for my next move. It didn't seem like he even registered his injuries.

Perhaps I could goad him into making another mistake.

"First strike to me," I quipped, throwing all the arrogance and spite I could into the words. "You're not so tough after all." And while I said this, I let myself sink a little, lowering myself to a height where he could reach me if he leaped.

"Never seen you get so worked up about an elf before," he snarled. Damn that perceptive nature of his. "Come to think of it, I've smelled something new on you these last few days. I thought you were fucking some shifter whore, but..." He made a face of disbelief. "Noooo... you can't be seeing this new elf in secret, can you?" He might be joking, talking out of his ass. He knew it was illegal. Still, I couldn't tell if he was serious, and I didn't like where this was going. He was far too close to the truth.

"You going to fight me or what?" I taunted.

He grinned and took the bait, launching himself at me.

I lifted myself, swiveling quickly as he got within range once more, but I should have known the same trick wouldn't work on him twice. His reflexes were lightning fast, and even as I tried to get behind him once more, he turned in the air. One of my claws raked over one of his arms, a minor hit, but his other hand wrapped around my ankle.

Fuck.

He pulled me down with him as he fell and with a twist, smashed me to the earth. He released my leg and pounced on top of me before I'd recovered enough to move. His claws raked my chest, sinking deep, bouncing over my ribs as he tore through flesh. His free hand secured my one arm, while he knelt on my torso pinning me.

Fuck!

He had me now.

But Artol's other weakness was his arrogance. He snarled down at me, savoring his victory. He sniffed, then whispered, "Is that what elf pussy smells like? Maybe I should find this new elf and show her what a real man can do."

He should have finished me off instead of talking. I took advantage of his lapse in judgment, my free hand snapping up to wrap around his neck. Perhaps he expected me to try to strangle him... or push him away. He seemed surprised when I pulled him down, allowing me to bring him closer. He went for my neck, but I was faster... biting into *his* throat.

Warm blood spilled over my tongue as I drank from him.

It wasn't Izzy's blood so it tasted like shit, but any blood would strengthen me. And I'd caught Artol off guard. That gave me another second to act before he regained himself. I brought a leg up and sank my talons into his side, using my currently heightened strength to push him off me and roll on top of him.

He lashed out, and nearly took my leg off, as I launched

myself high into the air… bringing him with me. My clawed foot still grasped his torso, and though I wasn't the strongest shifter I had more than enough strength to lift his bulky form.

Shock filled his eyes as he realized what I planned to do.

I pulled us higher, as fast as I could.

Artol attacked my leg. I used my other leg to fend him off, but still, my left ankle would be a mess after this. It didn't matter, my bond insisted any sacrifice was worth it to get back to Izzy.

"You sure you want to do that?" I hissed through the pain as I drove us higher. "Tear my leg off and you fall."

Artol stopped for an instant to see how far up we were, which was what I'd hoped he'd do. It gave me another second to pull us higher still.

"Go ahead," I gasped, just because I could lift the heavy wolf-shifter, didn't mean it was easy. "Rip my leg off and let's see how well you land."

My healing would restore a limb… eventually. For an ankle and a foot, it would take up to ten days and the whole process would be excruciating, but the bond didn't care.

"Fuck you, you little shit! Put me down!"

I shrugged as I dragged us higher and higher. From this height. I could easily see the dominion pitch. Though I couldn't make out people or what might be happening.

"Sure," I said… and let him go.

His eyes went wide as he fell…

…and fell…

…and fell…

I dove, driving myself down with my wings. I was injured and nearly at my limit, the high I'd received from taking his blood almost gone, but I wouldn't stop. I didn't know how much damage the fall might do to Artol, so I vowed to be there to finish him off when he landed.

He hit the ground with his feet, sacrificing his legs to absorb the impact. Bones crunched.

Good. The asshole deserved as much.

I hit him hard, driving him to the ground, even as he tried to claw my already torn up legs. His head cracked against the earth and his eyes rolled back. He went limp, but I didn't stop. I followed up with punches, driving my fists into his face and didn't let up until Essyma called the fight.

"Spirits!" Essyma said to me, wide-eyed. "Now that's the sort of thing I want to see from you every fucking day!"

"Getting my legs shredded so I can't even walk?" I hissed in pain as I flopped to the ground beside Artol. "How's that useful?"

"You won, didn't you?" she said simply. "We'll work on not getting torn up later, for now, it's that level of spirit I want to see in you every time you fight."

"Got it, boss," I said, panting.

"You've earned the right to see that dominion match. I'll even chip in for a healer to get you on your feet again, but only just. You need a reminder of how far you have to go."

That was unusually kind of her. Shifters rarely got magical healing.

A healer was summoned, for myself and Artol, since I'd nearly killed the wolf.

Artol wouldn't forget this. He'd be out for blood even more the next time we faced off.

Let him come. I had to survive, for Izzy. That bond-driven imperative had made the difference today. Perhaps I could use it every day.

And I had to hope he'd been talking trash during that

fight. Between that damned nose of his, and my own reactions to his words, he'd guessed at something which was far too close to the truth. I had to hope he'd forget about it...

...because if he didn't, and he told the wrong person...

...I'd be in deep shit.

AMARHUK (ROOK)

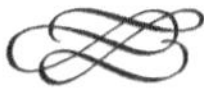

This was the last place in the entire world I wanted to be. I still couldn't believe my master had forced me to help Izzy. I'd been trying to stay away from her, for my own health and sanity, but here I was, by her side, facing down a psychopath. Not that I wouldn't have ended up here eventually. As much as I wished to avoid her, I still couldn't let anything happen to Izzy. I wanted her away from me, not dead. Just because I couldn't let myself fall for her, didn't mean I wouldn't help her if she needed it.

Still...

Now my life was on the line and my relationship with her out in the open. Well, not exactly how I felt, but that I'd sided with her. I'd have a huge fucking target on my back after this.

Assuming I survived.

And that was far from a given.

Our plan was sound, but what was that human realm saying? Something about no plan surviving contact with the enemy? Exactly.

Saldrea was powerful, as were each of her companions. I

knew exactly how powerful Hana was specifically. I'd had a fling with her a couple years back. Well, *I'd* thought it was a fling, but she'd gotten attached and kept dragging me back to her, dominating my mind to make me love her. She was a truly sick little woman, and I didn't like the way she was grinning at me now. Luckily — if I could say anything good had come from our horrid time together— I could resist her mental domination now.

Concubi fed off lust and sex. We drained it from our partners, not enough to harm them, but enough to feed ourselves. What most people didn't know was that if a concubi fed off the same partner for a prolonged period, they'd start to take more than just their lust, they'd learn their partner's powers.

From Hana, I'd eventually gleaned how to protect my mind, and I'd acquired a limited telepathy. That was how I'd been able to speak into Izzy's mind. It was limited in that I could only connect with one person at a time, and oddly, ever since I'd connected with Izzy… I hadn't been able to let go.

I still got stray thoughts from her from time to time… especially when they were screaming loud… like last night… twice. I hadn't needed to know how good of an orgasm that damned seraph could give her.

I pushed those thoughts aside. They wouldn't help me now. I needed to focus on the fight to come. It would take everything I had to win this.

"We can do this," Izzy whispered to each of us. "Keep to the plan."

A dominion match started with the ringing of a massive bell to one side of the field. The ringing of that same bell would also signal the end of the match; it was something loud enough that everyone should hear it.

Everyone on the pitch looked over at the troll standing by the bell with a massive hammer.

He swung.

We tensed.

The bell rang.

And dazzling light blasted to life on the far side of the field.

As much as I hated to admit it, Vyns really was our secret weapon. No one thought a light wielder would be any good in a dominion match, but they forgot one crucial detail. Of all the elements, light was the easiest and fastest to summon, especially for a simple dazzling effect like this. Where our opponents would need a second or two to bring their elements to bear, Vyns didn't.

The ladies on the far side of the pitch screamed and cursed.

Time to do our thing.

I summoned fire.

Yet even before I could get my shot off, Saldrea acted. Apparently, she didn't need to see to throw massive stones in Izzy's direction. The attack wasn't perfect, since Izzy had been on the move. Still, one of the massive boulders caught Izzy a glancing blow and she gave a clipped cry as she was thrown back, hitting the ground hard, and rolling.

Fuck!

No!

But Izzy recovered and caught herself before going over the stone line marking the back half of our field.

"I'm good. Go!" she shouted. The pain in her voice belied her words, but still, the rest of us had a job to do.

I usually threw small balls of fire from my hands, but our plan hinged on me being able to do more. That's what I'd been practicing yesterday and this morning.

I blasted fire at Neyalim, a massive cone, meant to hit her, no matter where she might go. If she dodged to one side or the other, I'd still hit her. Her only "safe" path was through the flames. A short jaunt through pain and she'd come out the front, relatively unharmed. But we were all counting on that being a counterintuitive move.

And it was.

She screamed, the sound shrieking up through a couple octaves as she tried to get out of the way of the fire and couldn't, or so I assumed. I had no way to see her. I blasted that cone of flame for as long as I could, before collapsing from the effort of the attack, my fire flickering out.

Neyalim was off the pitch entirely, completely out of the game, badly burned. A healer ran to tend to her. I had little sympathy, knowing she'd happily have drowned any of us to win this match.

I retreated. I wouldn't be able to do that again. It had taken too much out of me, but I'd done it, I'd taken one of their team out of the fight, right at the start of the match. Miraculously we were up by one.

Izzy's grandmother had blasted water at Hana, hoping to do what I'd done to Neyalim, but the sylph, though she'd been pushed back, managed to fly up out of the tidal wave and stay in play.

Still... our plan was working!

Saldrea screamed in fury, and the sand at our feet whipped into a frenzy.

Fuck! I shielded my eyes.

Izzy shouted through the storm of sand, "Keep on the move, Saldrea knows where we are!"

I flung out my wings and launched myself into the air. Yesterday, Izzy had been practicing feeling through the ground. I guessed Saldrea could do the same thing. She didn't need her eyes to know where we were.

But Izzy and her grandmother didn't have wings, stuck on the ground.

Unable to see anything I heard shouts and cries all over the field.

"Fuck!" came a distinctly male voice. "I can't concentrate, light's down!" Vyns shouted. I wanted to blame him, but I couldn't. This sand was infuriating.

The sand abated, but it still took me a moment to blink my eyes open.

When I did, two things happened at once. Izzy's grandmother — hidden as the nymph Tala — blasted Hana again. And she would have knocked the sylph out of the game... if the other thing hadn't happened. Golana and Saldrea teamed up on the nymph. Two massive waves of earth converged on the woman, pushing and crushing her at the same time. She was shoved behind the line, but not off the pitch, and when the earth subsided, the woman was a crumpled, mangled mess.

Blazes!

And the worst part was, no healer would come to her aid. The healers could only tend to those who'd been pushed off the field entirely.

"No!" Izzy cried.

And with Hana no longer under assault, and Vyns still recovering from that sand — which, now that I could see better, seemed to have been focused on him — Hana finally got in the game, blasting air at us. And she was one of the most powerful sylphim on campus.

Her raging tempest howled around us. My wings caught the gale and nearly blew me away entirely. I flashed my wings away to minimize my exposure to the attack. But now

I was falling. Though Hana's wind meant I travelled more horizontally than vertically.

Vyns, however, had been completely unprepared for the assault, wings fully extended. He was blown back, tumbling over the rough ground, to the back of the pitch, behind the line. A wall of earth rose and stopped him before he was taken completely off the field.

Izzy.

I would have been taken out by the attack as well... if Izzy hadn't caught me. I don't know how she did it, how she knew where I was, or how she managed to grab my arm as I flew by, but she did.

Izzy had blocked the wind attack with a wall of stone, and she pulled me down into that stillness with her.

"Thanks," I muttered as we huddled close behind that wall.

Blazing Fires! She was too close. I caught her scent of cinnamon and apples and my body responded viscerally, instantly on high alert... for sex, not danger. I didn't know how she could affect me so damned easily. One sniff, and I was gone.

I gritted my teeth. Now *really* wasn't the time for thoughts of ravishing Izzy. Yet, with her so close it was hard not to think about it.

"You good?" she asked.

"Yeah," I mumbled. I needed to be anywhere but here, so near to her I couldn't think straight.

"Then get ready. There's still three of them out there and we're down to two. We can't stay here or Saldrea and Golana will crush us."

"Now!" Izzy hissed, and we both darted in different directions.

Vyns had recovered and, since he wasn't off the field

entirely, he could still fight. Blinding light covered the other side of the field once more.

Hana gasped, her winds dying down.

Izzy summoned water as I summoned fire.

We'd worked out last night that water was the only element which would be effective against Hana. Fire she could blow away and snuff out with her wind, big earth attacks wouldn't reach her if she was flying and she would blow away any small stones thrown at her. That meant blasting her with water was the only option. Izzy took up where her grandmother had left off and blasted Hana with a massive gout of water. Meanwhile, I threw fire at Saldrea and Golana.

Izzy's water attack, though not as forceful as her grandmother's, hit true, pushing Hana behind the line and knocking her out of the sky, gasping for air and sputtering out water.

My fire did little to Golana and Saldrea, who blocked with quickly erected shields of earth. Then they both attacked with earth as I took to the air again, safe in the skies now that Hana was taking a second to recover. Or at least, I thought I was safe...

A column of earth rose up and seized my foot.

Fuck.

The grasping earth flung me back to the ground, hard, stunning me.

Then two crushing waves of earth converged on me. They pushed me behind the line while crushing my body. Bones snapped, blood burst forth. I remained conscious only due to my power with spirit.

And as the earth receded and I lay broken on the ground, Izzy cried out, reaching for me, even as she dodged more earth attacks.

She was the only member of our team still counting on the field. Vyns and I could fight — if I could manage to even get up and do anything more than bleed — but if Izzy was knocked behind the line we'd lose. And she was facing two very strong earth wielders, one of whom wanted her dead.

And technically Hana was still in this fight and could blast wind again once she'd recovered. Luckily, she was blinded by Vyns' light... but the other two, Saldrea and Golana, could feel through the earth, so Vyns' distraction would have little effect on them, now that they were expecting it.

And as much as I wanted Izzy to win this fight, the longer she stayed in, the greater the chance I'd bleed out and die from my wounds. A selfish shame filled me as I wished for Izzy to lose quickly... so a healer could tend to me once the game was done.

That was my last thought before I blacked out.

IZZY

Fuck.

I was so screwed.

I needed some way to end this fight now, before Hana recovered and Golana and Saldrea got their act together. Right now, they were both doing their own things, trying to crush me with earth or throw boulders at me, and I was only just managing to evade or block their attacks. But if they coordinated again, like they'd done with Rook and Olinara, I'd be toast.

Rook...

And my grandmother...

I'd gotten those two into this mess, and they might have paid with their lives. Neither was moving and the amount of blood...

Wait... if they were off the field... they could be healed.

As careful as I could be — while dodging and evading attacks — I softly scooped them up with earth and pushed them off the field.

Now they could get medical attention and hopefully live, but that meant only Vyns and I could fight and Vyns' blinding attack wouldn't be doing much at this point. It might dazzle Hana once she'd recovered, but by now Golana and Saldrea would know not to use their eyes, but their earth-sense.

And the distraction of me saving my teammates was all those two had needed to get me.

I didn't know who did what, but suddenly the earth under my feet softened to quicksand and I slipped, hip-deep, into the ground. The earth then solidified around me, trapping me. At the same time, rocks pummeled me. I put my arms up in front of my face, blocking the attacks while I summoned an earth shield. The stone wall jutted up in front of me, but not before my arms were a bloody mess.

I only had a second or two before the two earth users simply crushed me, like they'd done with Grandma and Rook... only instead of pushing me back, they'd simply kill me.

I needed a second to recover, heal, think!

But I didn't get it. The earth shifted as two massive walls closed in on me.

Fuck, fuck, fuck, fuck, fuck!

I did the only thing I could think of, a last-ditch defensive move Lhorine had mentioned. I'd never tried it, but if I didn't do it now...

I hollowed out the earth around me, shifting it aside, making a hole, which I fell into, then I covered over the hole with more earth, so I was completely underground and hidden.

The walls of earth meant to crush me had only been above ground and when they crashed together, I was below them. Golana and Saldrea would figure out what I'd done soon enough, but I hoped this little ploy would fool them for a second or two.

I quickly healed myself. When I'd healed Vyns from near death, I'd realized I could sense his injuries. And now, after learning how to focus my anima, I could target only those areas, instead of using tons of anima and hoping.

With pain no longer lancing through me, I could think straight.

I couldn't use water, not down here, which meant, if I was going to do anything while hiding, it would have to be with earth...

...Against two of the strongest earth wielders on campus.

Fuck.

But it was all I had left, all I could do.

I summoned all the power I had, which people kept telling me was significant now that my mother's binding had been removed. Then I pushed earth as hard as I could against Saldrea and Golana. I knew where they were through my earth-sense. I couldn't sense far, but across the pitch was far enough.

All I'd been able to manage yesterday was a rolling wave, which wouldn't do much more than knock them off their feet... maybe. But this time, perhaps from sheer desperation or fear of death, I created a tidal wave of earth.

And it was just in time, as — for an instant — the walls of my little hole began to close in on me. The two had found me, but once I initiated my attack, they stopped theirs, to block and cancel mine.

Their power pushed on mine, countering my wave with one of their own, two against one. My wave stopped... then inched backward.

No!

I couldn't allow them to win, couldn't let them block me, as soon as they banished my wave, they'd go back to crushing me and I'd die down here, having dug my own grave. I couldn't let that happen, couldn't stop fighting, I had to overpower them... somehow!

I dug deep, using everything I had: the power Koar had lent me, my bond with Myel, my spirit-link with Vyns, my fear for Rook and Olinara. I couldn't fail or I'd be dead, and this world would lose all hope. Saldrea and her mother would win and rule as tyrants.

I took all the fight within me, all the rage against injustice and tyranny and screamed in my little hole as I threw all of myself into one final push with earth.

Nothing happened.

I screamed louder, pushed harder...

The resistance against me faltered.

Yes... maybe!

I roared, punching the earthen wall in front of me and poured all the anima I had into one final push.

In an instant my wave of earth overcame the others and swept over the field, pushing Saldrea and Golana behind the line.

I collapsed against the side of my hole, breathing hard, shaking with the strain of what I'd just done. Had I really done that? Had I... won?

The walls of my hole began to close in.

What?

But...

That little fucker. She'd lost and was still trying to kill me!

I shot myself up out of the earth so fast I launched myself into the air, flailing, and couldn't stick the landing, falling unceremoniously on my rump.

The crowd was deathly silent as the bell rang marking the end of the match. Even then, they remained silent for a beat, perhaps wondering how wise it would be to celebrate

Saldrea's loss. But once one person did — a faint cheer and clap coming from somewhere — the entire crowd broke and roared with applause so loud it deafened me.

And that was the power of one person. If one person cheered, they all could, safe in the knowledge Saldrea wouldn't be able to pinpoint anyone to lash out against.

I laid back on the sand, chest heaving, heart pounding, but smiling up at the sun.

I'd won.

Somehow... me and my team... we'd won!

Fucking hell! We'd WON!

It was a damned miracle.

I couldn't help the laugh which bubbled up out of me, manic and pure.

The crowd's cheers slowly died out to silence once again.

I knew why. I felt it through the earth: the stomping footsteps of — it could only be — Saldrea heading straight for me. It was curious that even after I'd spent so much strength, I could still use my earth-sense. I guessed Lhorine's training had ingrained it well.

"You!" Saldrea spat, stopping to loom over me. "How...? What...?" she sputtered, clearly at a loss. "You can't defeat me!" she screamed.

"Guess again," I panted, smiling. I couldn't help but goad her. She was insane and dangerous, but she wouldn't kill me here, out in the open... would she?

"How? You're orange rank? You're nothing! How?" She was near to frothing at the mouth.

"I got stronger," I said with a shrug.

"That's not possible! You can't... HOW?"

Enough of this. I'd recovered enough to get to my feet, and I faced her down, stare for stare.

"Doesn't matter. I won, and unless you're going back on

your word, I'm free to stay here on campus and live my life... aren't I?" I made sure to say this all loud enough so the whole crowd could hear me.

This was it. Would Saldrea keep her word or break it in front of all of these people?

Hatred seethed behind her perfect blue eyes as she considered her options. I was fairly certain one of the options she considered was killing me and breaking her word and showing everyone what would happen if you fought against her. God... she was crazy enough that she just might do that.

I backed off a step, suddenly afraid.

She smiled, a grim thing... but then, through her gritted teeth she smiled wider. Her shoulders unbunched a little. She turned to the crowd, not me.

"Let it be known that I am an elf of my word and this half-breed is safe here on campus until the end of her schooling. Then she shall be escorted back to the human realm as an exile!"

I hadn't missed how she'd emphasized *this half-breed is safe*... as if to say, all my friends and any who followed me... they were fair game.

Fuck.

I should have seen that coming.

And Saldrea confirmed it when she turned back to me and whispered words only I could hear,

"I can't touch you, but that doesn't mean your friends are safe. I'll crush everyone close to you, everyone who helps you. I'll make your life a living hell without ever touching you... just you wait and see."

I'd won this battle, but I'd started an all-out war and my friends would be the casualties.

BAYN

I WANTED TO ASK SALDREA WHO THIS IZZY PERSON WAS — other than some upstart half-elf — but I suspected the princess wouldn't answer me, she was too worked up, lost in her own world, probably plotting vengeance. One thing was certain, once we were away from prying eyes, she'd take her fury out on *me.*

For now, I could only guess who Izzy might be.

I was one of the strongest earth magic users among the titans. Hell, even among elves there were few who could match me. Saldrea and her mother were among those few... now there was one more.

I'd felt the final clash of the half-breed's magic against Saldrea's and Golana's. It should have been no contest, no way for her to win against them... but she had. The raw strength Izzy possessed was on a scale I hadn't seen since... Queen Leastrine.

Absolutely stunning!

Which meant...

If I recalled correctly, Leastrine had had an even more

powerful daughter who'd married a nymph and been exiled to the human realm. And this Izzy was half-elf and half-nymph... who'd come from the human realm. It seemed only logical to assume she was the child of that lost princess.

And Saldrea had no idea.

If she'd known, she'd not have gone through the pretense of a dominion match, she'd have killed Izzy outright and been done with it.

I had to smile. The Tyrianel family — Saldrea and her mother — seemed to have a blind spot when it came to royals, so certain they'd killed every last one of them. Saldrea couldn't see what was right in front of her.

I considered — for half a heartbeat — telling Saldrea who Izzy was in exchange for freeing my sister, but that wouldn't work. Once I'd told her, she'd kill Izzy and not free my sister. And saying I knew of some "secret royal" and would only tell her who it was after she freed my sister was a longshot. She had no reason to believe there were any secret royals and wouldn't free my sister without proof, which I didn't have without giving Izzy's identity away.

I decided then and there, I'd never tell Saldrea the truth about Izzy.

Which meant... there was an old human realm saying: *the enemy of my enemy is my friend*. But trusting an elf, even a half-breed who was clearly against Saldrea and her mother, was not something I was comfortable with. Hell, I didn't trust anyone, not fully. Trust only led to betrayal, as my parents and the woman I'd once loved had shown me.

But maybe I could forge some sort of alliance with this Izzy? One where I got everything I wanted. Anything less and it wouldn't be worth it.

We'd see.

Saldrea turned to me the instant we were safely inside her residence.

"Defenses down, titan scum."

I ground my teeth and obeyed... to a point. I'd never fully submit to this woman, but I could play the roll of her punching bag, make it seem like she was hurting me. If I didn't, my sister would take the beating instead and I couldn't allow that.

I nodded, then knelt, lowering my physical durability somewhat, so the princess would draw blood, elicit a few groans and cries from me, that's what she really wanted.

And she laid into me hard that afternoon, venting all her pent-up fury at Izzy in a prolonged beating. Saldrea had stamina for days when it came to hurting others.

I took it all, making all the right reactions and noises, till I truly was a bleeding mess, face and body swollen from bruises on top of bruises. I could heal myself quick enough, but I'd wait till Saldrea was finished and had moved on to other things.

And as I took that beating, my fury rose. How could my parents have allied with this madwoman and her mother? How could they have handed Wensuria — their own daughter — over to them? Saldrea was truly mad, insane. I needed to get myself and my sister away from her, but my friends still hadn't found Saldrea's secret dungeon. They'd searched everywhere on campus, using their earth-sense to feel through the ground for any hidden rooms, and found nothing. That told me Wensuria had to be off campus somewhere, but where?

Once I found her, I'd free her and escape this hellish place. If I got a chance to repay Saldrea's debt of pain, I would, but if I couldn't, I'd just flee, my sister's safety more important than my own vengeance.

Yet... where could we go?

I couldn't take Wensuria back to our family. They'd already betrayed her, betrayed us. And we wouldn't be safe anywhere in elf-controlled lands. There was the Deepwilds, but that wasn't safe for anyone, and building a new life there would be hard as hell. The human realm was a possibility, *if* I could get some rogue dragon to take us, but my sister and I would stand out. From everything I'd heard, our size — I was over seven and a half feet tall and Wensuria was just under seven feet — even in these miniaturized bodies, would make us giants in that world, towering over others. That didn't seem like the best place to hide... but that might be our best option.

It wasn't like this world was going to change and accept titans anytime soon. Especially not after Saldrea and her mother's plan to have us wreak havoc amongst the population after we'd been accepted into elven society as "friends."

"Ah... mistress?" The tiny voice of Fini, Saldrea's mouse-shifter servant, only just managed to reach us. Saldrea paused her beating.

"What?" Saldrea snapped and Fini flinched.

"There is a wolf shifter here to see you—"

"Not now!"

"—with information on the woman you fought today," Fini rushed to finish, voice just a squeak.

Saldrea's head snapped around. "Say that again?"

"He says he knows something about the woman you fought today, something... juicy?"

"Show him in!" Saldrea snapped. She spun to me, "Get up."

I healed myself and rose as her attention turned to the wolf shifter being shown into the room.

Long ago, therianthropes had been minions of the titans.

We'd created the beastfolk through years of experimentation with animals, mixing them with our own blood, to create a strong and adaptable front line fighting force. They'd served us well, till the day the titans had surrendered to the elves after The Great War. The elves had taken the beastfolk and made them their minions, but the lowest of the low. The elves brutally pitted the shifters against each other with little care for who lived, so that only the strong survived to "protect the realm." But we all knew it was a farce. The dragons were the true protectors of Seial. The shifters' entire existence was an object lesson for all to see. The message was clear: side against us and we won't just kill off your race, we'll have you kill yourselves.

And this idiot of a wolf-shifter didn't seem to understand he was nothing but a pawn. It had been so long since The Great War that the shifters, with their short lives, had forgotten what they represented. This one probably thought he was getting ahead by giving Saldrea something she wanted, and that might be true, but he wouldn't gain any real power and Saldrea would dispose of him eventually. She, like most elves, hated shifters.

Yet she put on a bright smile to greet this one.

"Yes, welcome," she purred. "Come in and sit. Tell us what you know of the half-breed whore."

The wolf didn't sit, he stood respectfully and gave his tale.

"I'm in a cohort with a bat shifter."

"Bats!" Hana hissed. "Disgusting!"

"Exactly," the wolf agreed. "And today I learned something interesting. He was desperate to go see your match. He seemed... worried. Now, meaning no disrespect, but I don't think he was worried for you. So... maybe he was worried for your opponent, the half-breed."

I could see the wolf was losing Saldrea. A shifter worried for Izzy wasn't all that interesting.

"Now that on its own isn't much..." the wolf said, perhaps sensing he was losing his audience. So, when he spoke next it was in a softer, conspiratorial tone. "But... I've *also* noticed this bat shifter has had a new smell on him recently. Ever since that half-breed arrived here."

Saldrea perked up at this.

The wolf smiled. "The bat is close to her somehow. I don't know exactly how, and I have yet to confirm the scent I've caught on him—"

"Hana, get that item we took from Izzy's room!" Saldrea ordered.

The sylph shot out of the room and was back in a flash holding a small cloth item... Was that underwear?

"I thought this might come in handy, if we ever needed to track that bitch," Saldrea gloated as Hana handed the item over to the wolf, who gave it a good sniff.

"Ah, yes! That's what I've smelled on the bat! He's definitely been close to her... perhaps... traitorously close?" The wolf winked.

Shifters mating with anyone outside of their type of beast was cause for their deaths.

Saldrea smiled that vicious cat-like grin of hers.

"Thank you, so much," Saldrea said with delight. "What is your name again?"

"Artol, mistress."

"Artol, you shall be greatly rewarded for this."

The wolf grinned and was shown out.

Saldrea laughed, a light and airy thing, which to anyone else might have sounded mirthful, but I knew it was filled with hatred and spite.

"Oh... Izzy. What *have* you done? You've given me the perfect toy to play with." She couldn't have been happier.

Then she and her minions began planning what they'd do to this bat-shifter. And knowing exactly how it felt to have Saldrea hurt someone you loved...

I pitied this Izzy... even if she was an elf.

IZZY

DESPITE OUR WIN, THERE WAS NO CELEBRATION. WE WERE A solemn crew on our way back to Rook's room. That was until Myel found us.

He rushed to me, but managed to stop himself before embracing me, since we were still out in public.

"I'm so glad you won!" he breathed. "I knew you would."

Oh, we'd all had our doubts, even him, but his exuberant words helped lift my spirits.

"Thank you for your kind words, strange man," I said a bit stilted. There were far too many others around, most of them looking my way.

Myel looked hurt for all of an instant as he searched my face and I made the universal sign for *people watching*: eyes wide, looking side to side with subtle head tilts.

He blinked. "Oh, yes, of course. I... wished to congratulate you on your win." Then he turned stiffly and walked away.

I had no doubt he'd be in Rook's room when we got back.

"My room is yours, as long as you want it, I'll be staying

with my master," Rook said. He'd been sullen since the match. I still couldn't figure him out. Was he mad at me for involving him? Maybe he was mad at himself for not having won the fight all on his own? That would be a typical male reaction.

Gah… men!

Even with so many of the opposite sex around me, I didn't understand them.

"I'm… glad we… *you* won," Rook said stiffly, then broke away from us to head to Svokol's residence.

I huffed a sigh.

"He's mad at himself," Grandma Oli — still looking like Tala — said.

Huh… so maybe it was just a stupid man thing.

I'd been impressed that Olinara had kept her disguise even after nearly dying. She'd said something about locking her form, which I hadn't really understood.

"He cares, a lot," she continued, but then her face screwed up, confused. "But… he's frustrated too? I'm not sure I get that."

"Can you read everyone that way?" I asked.

She gave a low laugh. "Live as long as I have, in the rats' nest that is the capital, with intrigue around every corner, and you learn a thing or two about reading people."

Sounds fun.

Not.

And I wanted to be queen?

Wait… *did* I want to be queen? I'd been told I was a royal, that I was the heir… but since then I hadn't had time to think about what that meant.

Power, yes… but also responsibility… and politics.

Ick.

But if I wanted to help people as I'd always hoped... then I'd have to learn to deal with all of that, wouldn't I?

Great.

We made it back to the residence, and a crowd of people followed us up to Rook's room. Well, it was my room now. It hadn't ever been a secret, but now it seemed like everyone knew where I lived.

Good thing we could slip out to the training compound if we needed to. Though... we'd need Myel for that.

My group slipped into Rook's room, finally alone. And as I'd predicted, Myel was there waiting for us. He'd hidden in the bathroom and waited till the door was closed before coming out, to ensure no one saw him. *Then* he threw himself around me in a tight embrace.

"I was so scared... but... I knew... I did..."

"It's okay," I whispered, holding him, comforted in his arms. "I was scared too, I honestly didn't know if we'd win."

"We?" Vyns said with a grin. "*You* won. I still can't quite believe it... but I saw it with my own eyes. All that earth you summoned, and Saldrea and Golana straining to stop it and failing. You did that." He shook his head in awe. "Told you you were a goddess."

I smiled.

"She is," Myel breathed, then captured my lips in a *deep* kiss. When he pulled back, he sighed. "I can't stay, I'm technically on patrol. I'll be back later." Yet he didn't let me go right away. If anything he held me tighter for a second.

Huh... I'd thought his clinginess last night had come from him not having faith in me. Perhaps I'd been wrong? He seemed as needy now.

I didn't want to ask him about it, not yet, so I let it go as he finally released me and stepped back. Only then did I notice how tattered his clothes were, shirt and pants ripped, healing wounds on his chest and legs.

"What hap—?" I started to ask, but he'd already vanished in a puff of shadow-smoke.

He hadn't seemed that injured, so I had to hope he was fine and looked worse than he actually was.

"What do you need?" Vyns asked, coming to me, tone soft and comforting.

Grandma Oli cut in. "I need to be somewhere else while you give her what she needs." She winked at me and slipped into the bathroom.

That made me laugh a little, but it was a nervous thing. Fuck, I was still on edge, nerves frayed.

"Hold me," I whispered to Vyns.

"Of course," he said.

Koar stayed by the door, back to us, as Vyns drew me to the bed and sat with me, arms wrapped around me, not too tight, perfectly comforting. I wished he could give me the drugged high Myel did. As soon as my perfect Goth shifter had left, my mood had slipped back to darkness.

"I won," I breathed. "So why do I feel like I lost?"

But I knew why.

"Is it whatever Saldrea said to you afterward?" Vyns whispered.

I nodded. "She told the world I was safe, but then she told me none of my friends and family would be. You're all in danger. She's coming for you to get to me."

A loud rumbling growl came from the door.

We both looked over at Koar.

"I won't let anyone get to you." He didn't turn. "And I'll protect everyone precious to you, if that's what you wish."

"You can't protect everyone," I said.

"I can try."

"Not if you're by my side while Rook isn't... and Myel is out patrolling."

A deeper, longer growl echoed from him. He knew it too.

"But I appreciate the sentiment," I said. "You've been nothing but loyal..." *for all of a day and a half.* It still baffled me how Koar had gone from a threatening enemy to an incredibly loyal protector in such a short time. I still didn't know how far I could trust him, but for some reason I believed him when he said he'd protect me. Vyns said he was loyal to the crown, but it was more than that. I couldn't put my finger on it yet, but I felt safe with him around and since that's what I needed right now, I didn't dig any deeper into it. Perhaps I was picking up some of my grandmother's skill at reading people? But then why couldn't I read Rook... or Myel.

The dragon gave another, deeper, pained growl. "I... I couldn't protect you during the match, and it tore me apart. I vow to protect you from now on, no matter what. No one will *ever* hurt you again."

It was hard to argue with heartfelt words like that.

I leaned on Vyns.

"Thanks... you two... for being here for me." I yawned. A wave of fatigue swept over me. I'd slept last night, but not nearly as much as I needed, and I'd been working hard training for most of two days.

"Stay with me while I sleep," I said to Vyns.

He nodded and together we laid down, him close, holding me. Tears leaked from my eyes as I tried to find peace.

This was all too much. I'd won my life, but my fight was far from over. Now, everyone around me was in danger, and I'd have to train even harder to protect them. And eventually, I'd have to wage a war to claim a throne I wasn't entirely sure I wanted. Because if I won, I'd be mired in a different type of conflict, playing the political game amongst a nest of vipers… or was it rats? Which was better? None of it sounded good.

It felt like I'd never be safe or secure or at peace ever again.

Needless to say… I didn't sleep well.

MYELAS

When I returned to the shifter barracks after completing my afternoon patrol, I quickly popped into my old room to make sure it was undisturbed before heading to Safir's room to report in. The room was as I'd left it, except... someone had slipped a letter under my door.

I picked up the red envelope with a sinking sense of despair. I'd heard of red envelopes before but never seen one myself. Tearing it open I took out the note inside and read it quickly.

"Fuck," I breathed. Then instantly shadow-stepped to Safir's room, where he was talking quietly with Zora.

I threw the letter and envelope down on his table, interrupting them.

"I've been summoned to a punitive deathmatch," I hissed and the other two instantly went silent. Given how they usually dismissed what I had to say, their silence spoke volumes.

Safir picked up the paper and quickly read it.

"Fuck, this has to be a trap, but... how would she know?"

Zora read over his shoulder. "It could be coincidence." She looked over at me. "There was a bit of a hubbub around the barracks when I arrived, about you nearly killing a wolf shifter? Maybe this is a reward?"

Punitive deathmatches were meant to be a reward for shifters, despite how it sounded. It wasn't the shifter who was being punished or put to death. These sick spectacles had been going on for ages, a tradition here at the academy. When a shifter distinguished themselves, they were sometimes given a chance to show "the world" their skill by killing a condemned criminal. The criminal usually wore a binding collar, which limited their magic and strength, so the fights were often one-sided, but that didn't mean they were safe. More than once, it had been the shifter who'd died... since the reward for the criminal was not only their life... but their freedom, so they had a lot to fight for.

And as much as this might be a reward for defeating Artol, I had a strong suspicion it wasn't. It didn't sit right with me. I hadn't done that much by defeating him, even if my cohort leader had praised me. No, I was still a nobody as far as most people were concerned, far from a standout.

"No, I don't think so," Safir countered Zora. "The timing is a little too conspicuous. Just after Izzy wins her freedom against Saldrea, Myel gets a summons? No... this is a trap, I feel it in my bones."

Though we hadn't seen eye to eye on much lately, I fully agreed with Safir.

"What do I do?" I asked. I'd been ready to run with Izzy for days now, yet we were both still here. "Run? Fight?"

"We don't even know who your opponent is," Zora said. "And if this is a trap, there's no guarantee their binding collar will be working properly or at all."

"So... run?" I asked.

Safir growled and began pacing. "No," he hissed. "I've learned the hard way that our princess can't be too far away from you, not yet anyway. And I've also learned she doesn't run. Which means you stay... unless we can get Lhorine to break your bond."

My heart broke.

Had it come to that already?

I remained stoic. If this was what I had to do, then I'd do it.

"I need to talk to Izzy," Safir mumbled, then growled again. He was slowly getting used to the fact that Izzy was in charge, but at times like this, I don't think he liked it much. He wanted to be able to make this call on his own, but he couldn't.

He came to me. "Go... get Izzy, bring everyone to the training compound, we'll talk there."

I nodded and shadow-stepped away.

When I got to Izzy's room, I found her asleep with the angel wrapped around her, the dragon guarding them both. Koar raised his brows in question.

"I need to wake her, there's news."

Koar grunted. "That didn't take long." He nodded.

I gently shook Izzy, and she groggily opened her eyes.

"Just five more minutes," she mumbled.

The angel woke quicker, however. "What's up?" he asked, gently stroking Izzy's side, soothing her. Izzy had others to comfort her now, she didn't need me. Maybe it would be better if Lhorine broke our bond... before I got too attached. Oh, who was I kidding, I was attached like a leech.

Olinara came out from the bathroom. "I heard voices..."

Good, she should hear this too.

"I've been summoned to partake in a punitive deathmatch this Sulnari. The timing's suspicious, we think it's a trap."

Vyns nodded. "It is. I don't know how Saldrea found out about you, but she vowed to go after Izzy's friends. This has to be her first move." He cocked his head. "But... she probably doesn't know you two are bonded, or she'd just kill you. So... she knows about you, but not much more. Curious."

Curious? This was my life!

"What's that?" Izzy mumbled waking a bit more. Her eyes blinked open again and this time focused on me. "Myel?" Her beautiful brow furrowed as she registered trouble. "What's up?"

"We need to talk, all of us, at the training compound," I said. "I'll explain everything once we're there."

She sat up and Vyns rose with her.

"Sure," she said, wiping her eyes. Then she gave a harsh little laugh. "I guess I'll sleep when I'm dead."

All three of us men in the room stiffened at that comment. Izzy didn't notice, still waking up. Death wasn't something to joke about in this world.

All the shadow-stepping I'd been doing recently had improved my range and proficiency with the ability. I could jump much farther than I used to and with more people. Something good had come of all this chaos. I got everyone to the training compound in record time.

Once we were all assembled — except for Rook — I explained the situation.

Everyone agreed Saldrea was behind this, but we couldn't agree what to do about it. The easiest option was for me to run and avoid it, but I'd be a fugitive... and Izzy and I couldn't be that far apart.

"Can you remove the bond between them?" Safir asked Lhorine.

Izzy glared at him, jaw tight, but didn't stop the line of questioning.

Lhorine blew out a long breath. "I'm decent with bindings, but I've never tried breaking a mating bond. I've heard of them being broken in the past, but I can't recall details. It certainly hasn't been done often. Can I... inspect the bond?"

Izzy and I stepped forward, and the elf put a hand on both of us. I went cold at how final this felt. If Lhorine could do this... my time with Izzy would end far sooner than I'd hoped. Still, I put on a brave face. I'd accept whatever happened.

Lhorine blew out a breath. "Your bond is deep, solid. There's no way anyone but the strongest elf could break it."

What?

Really?

"What if Izzy tried it?" Safir suggested. Izzy sent another furious look his way and he held up a hand. "We need to know all our options."

"She probably has the raw power, but bonds are not something a novice can work with easily," Lhorine said. "We'd need to train hard. We *might* be able to get Izzy to a level where she could do this before Sulnari, but it would be tight."

"Then let's focus on other options," Izzy said, giving me a reassuring smile.

My heart leaped with joy.

Did she not want to break the bond? Did she truly want to be with me?

I tempered my elation. Even if that's what she wanted now... once she was queen... she'd not want someone like me weighing her down. Still, I couldn't help but smile at her. And her smile in return warmed my heart.

"I'd fight off the world for you," I said to her. "You worked hard to win your fight. I can do the same now."

She nodded.

"Then it's set," she said. "Let's find out what we can and help Myel train..." A twinkle came to her eye. "And I have an idea that might help him win."

IZZY

I TOOK LHORINE ASIDE.

"Elves can enhance themselves, make themselves stronger and tougher, but... can they do it to others?"

She cocked her head, then nodded. "Yes, but not all elves. I can't, but you probably could."

That's what I'd hoped to hear. "Then that's what I want to train on tomorrow," I told her. If I could enhance Myel, he'd have a better chance of winning his fight.

She nodded.

I probably should start training this evening, but I was still exhausted and could use a night's sleep.

We ate a simple meal together at the compound, and once again, despite my win earlier today, the mood was somber. Grandma Oli said she'd not return with us to Rook's room. She was no longer playing the role of Tala and probably shouldn't be seen on campus.

After dinner, I spoke to Tala in private. She could go back to her life, if she wanted. Though she was warned Saldrea might be out to get her. With that in mind, I asked her if she wanted to stay at the training compound for a while.

"Would I be in the way?" she asked, voice small. "You've got so much going on, you're... so important now... and I... I'm..."

I hugged her tightly.

She was trying to distance herself from me, for *my* benefit, and I wouldn't let her. "I need you, please stay," I whispered. "You're the only friend I have."

"You have... so many people to help you." I caught the hitch in her voice, the hesitation. I must have been getting better at reading people because I could hear loud and clear what she hadn't said: *you have all those guys*.

"You're my only female friend... around my age." I added that last bit thinking of Olinara and Lhorine. Zora was older too, just not the *hundreds of years* that my grandmother or mentor were. "I don't want to lose you."

Tala relaxed in my arms. She didn't want to leave. She was scared, and I didn't blame her. Saldrea was a psychopath.

"Thank you," she whispered, hugging me back.

"We'll make a trip and get some of your things tomorrow... or soon. Just... stay put for now and train with me when I'm working with my grandmother."

She smiled. "I'd like that, thank you."

I, however, wouldn't be staying here. I had to keep up appearances at school or Saldrea would get suspicious of my absence and might come looking for me. And the last thing I wanted was for her to find this place.

Myel took Vyns, Koar, and me back to Rook's room for the evening. This time Vyns let Myel sleep with me. I thanked him, loving the soothing feeling of my Goth shifter so close. Despite my many fears and worries, there were no tears when I fell asleep that night.

Morning came all too soon. I'd slept more than eight hours, but I still felt tired the next day. I'd been pushing myself too hard... and it wasn't going to stop.

I debated whether I should go to Magic 101 that morning. I didn't want to. Saldrea would be there and I wanted to avoid her. But I needed to be seen by her and others on campus, even if all my other time would be taken up with training at the compound. So, I went.

Perhaps Saldrea would let something slip about Myel?

Myel returned to the shifter barracks, as much as I wanted him to hide away for a few days. He said he couldn't. One missed training session and he'd be in a lot of trouble. Vyns said he'd watch over the shifter, for which I thanked him profusely with a very deep and passionate kiss.

So, Myel left with Vyns, while Koar came with me to class, never far from my side. I took a seat at the back and waited, having gotten to the room early. When Saldrea arrived, she made a beeline straight for me, a giant grin on her face.

Yeah, this didn't bode well.

"I feel like we got off on the wrong foot," she said, all mock-apologetic. "As a peace offering, I'd love for you to come with me to the punitive deathmatch on Sulnari. It's one of this world's rare delights, you'll *love* watching the fight."

Oh yeah... she knew. She was behind Myel's summons no doubt.

"Although..." she drew out the word as if reconsidering, "I hear the shifter they've chosen for this one is rather weak. I sure hope he doesn't die. That would be such a shame, wouldn't it?" The beatific smile and pleasant turn of her head told me everything I needed to know. She was enjoying this. "Would you like to join me?"

"Oh... I'll be there," I said with my own false pleasantness. "And I have a sneaking suspicion that shifter, whoever they are, is going to be a lot stronger than you think."

If I could train up my ability to enhance others, I'd make sure Myel was strong enough to beat whoever he might be fighting. I didn't even want to consider the alternate option of trying to break the mate bond.

Hana gasped.

I blinked as the sylph whispered something desperately into Saldrea's ear.

Wait... no...

Had she just read my thoughts?

Fuck!

She had.

I could see it in Saldrea's expression of shock, then sheer bliss. She knew about me being bonded to Myel.

Fucking, fuckity, FUCK!

I had to warn Myel.

Saldrea turned to her ladies. "Have that bat shifter arrested and taken into custody this instant!"

Golana took off running.

Neyalim took out her phone and quickly dialed someone.

I took out my phone to text Vyns and warn him, assuming Myel would already be in training, but Saldrea saw me. I expected her to grab my phone, take it from me, so I was completely unprepared when stone spiked up from the marble desktop and skewered my phone, shattering the magical glass.

Saldrea grinned so wide, it didn't look natural, creepy as

fuck. Then she laughed as she turned away and found a seat.

Fuck!

I rose… but there was no way I'd get across campus any faster than a dwarf with enhanced speed.

"I could fly you," Koar offered.

Would that be quicker? It might work. I nodded and we ran. But a wall of stone erupted up to block the door. From somewhere behind me came Saldrea's voice.

"Oops, did I do that?" Then laughter.

I used my own earth magic to push the stone back down into the floor, but we lost precious seconds as I did. Once we were out of the room, in the open, Koar didn't take the time to disrobe, ripping through his clothes as he became a dragon.

Despite the burning urgency to help Myel, I stood there stunned for an instant, marveling at the massive dragon. A dragon I was about to ride. So many of my teen-girl fantasies were coming true in this strange world. I shook myself out of my stupor and climbed onto Koar's back. He bent his front leg and lowered that shoulder to make getting up easier. Then I held on desperately to the many spikes along his back, seated between two larger ones, as he took off and flew with all haste across campus.

I held on for dear life as wind whipped around me, threatening to tear me off Koar's back. The campus blurred below us.

But despite our speed and direct route… we were too late.

As we neared the shifter barracks, descending, I saw Golana leap inhumanly high, over the walls surrounding the training yard. She'd get to Myel first.

Vyns, perched on the same wall Golana had vaulted

over, was taken by surprise. By the time he realized what was happening and flew down into the yard, Golana already had a hold on Myel and other shifters were coming out of the barracks to take him into custody.

For a heartbeat, I considered fighting them all. I could take Golana, and with Koar and Vyns on my side, the shifters wouldn't be too much trouble. But even as I thought it, Koar's head swiveled and I followed his gaze. Three dragons swooped in.

Could Koar take on three dragons?

Could Vyns take all the shifters in the yard?

Fuck!

We'd been out maneuvered.

Still, I hopped off Koar's back as we landed and went to Myel, even if Golana and a crowd of shifters kept me from getting close.

"I'll find a way to help you!" I shouted as he was dragged away.

Golana laughed, then she punched Myel in the stomach so hard he doubled over and coughed out blood. I screamed, but that was exactly the reaction the sadistic dwarf had wanted, laughing even more.

I shouted my fury, and with no other outlet, turned to a wall and punched it. I expected pain, broken knuckles... what I got was a one-foot-wide hole in the five-foot-thick stone wall. And my fist wasn't even bloody.

Vyns and Koar joined me. Vyns had loaned Koar his shirt to help cover the dragon who'd returned to human form, naked.

"We'll figure this out," Vyns said, but panic filled his voice.

"Blazing Skies!" Koar swore. "I'll take them all on if you command it."

"No..." I said through clenched teeth. That wouldn't help, not now. "We've lost this fight. We need to talk to the others. I don't know if there is a way to get to Myel, but if there is, we need to help him. He's hurt and probably in for more of a beating. I need to get stronger, and we need to make sure he survives, that's our only priority now."

Just like that, everything had gone to shit.

Again.

IZZY

There was no use in returning to Magic 101, that ship had sailed. I called an emergency meeting of Team Izzy, and we met in the training compound.

I looked at Safir and Zora, they'd always been the connected ones, the most informed. "What do you know?"

"We're still trying to find out where they've taken Myel, but I have all my resources focused on that," Safir said. "We'll find him." And I silently thanked the tiger shifter for not bringing up the issue of my bond with Myel. We'd all known it would cause trouble eventually, for both of us, but pondering that now wouldn't help anything.

"I did manage to find out who Myel will be fighting for the punitive deathmatch," Zora added. "A troll, condemned for a killing spree in the east, nasty."

"Will they still go through with that? If they know Myel and I are bonded, won't they..." I couldn't say it.

"No," Vyns said, voice hard. "Saldrea loves to torture people. She'll draw it out, make it as painful as possible. If she knows anything about bonds, she'll know killing him will potentially kill you, and she *will* do it, but she'll do it at the deathmatch. She wants you to suffer for days, then die horribly."

Koar nodded slowly, face twitching from a jaw clenched too tight.

"Well, isn't that wonderful," I said sarcastically, but actually it was a relief. I let out a sliver of tension in a heavy sigh. "But that means we have two and a half days to figure out a way to save Myel. I'm open to ideas."

No one said anything right away and I couldn't stand the silence, so I kept talking. "My plan had been to work on my ability to enhance others so I could make Myel stronger, tougher, ready for the fight. But—" I looked at Lhorine, "—I can't do that from a distance, can I?"

She shook her head. "If you were well trained and among the strongest of elves, you could do it from a short distance away, maybe a dozen feet, but no farther."

I nodded.

"What if... we could get you in to see Myel... in disguise?" Olinara piped up. "I've never paid much attention to deathmatches, but I seem to recall hearing something about the shifter having some last hurrah the night before, a special meal and a *conjugal* visit?"

Of course she remembered the part about sex. That's my grandmother for you. I'd only known her a few days, but I already knew she put the nymph in *nymphomaniac*.

Still... if this was true, it wasn't a bad idea.

Safir nodded. "That is usually the case, yes. The question will be will they allow it in Myel's instance?"

A grim, mirthless smile spread on Vyns' face. "Oh... they will. Think about it. Saldrea knows Myel is bonded. The only woman he'd wish to be with is Izzy... so of course she's going to send some woman up there to taunt him. We need to find out who and stop her, send Izzy in her place."

"On it," Zora said. The hobgoblin stood. "Do you need anything else from me?"

I looked to Safir. I did need the man, even if I sometimes hated to admit it. He gave a nearly imperceptible smile as he realized the same thing.

"No," he said. "Go."

Zora left and the rest of us got down to planning, though our plan was fairly simple. It had a lot of holes, unknowns.

We needed to find out where they were keeping Myel. Then we needed to find out who they'd send to be with him the night before. In the meantime, I'd work my ass off to learn transmutation magic and elven enhancements so when I went in, I could make Myel into an unstoppable force.

"No, that won't work," Vyns grumbled.

We all looked at him.

"Why?" I asked.

"They'd have put a binding collar on him."

"Fuck!" Safir hissed. "He's right."

"Pretend I know nothing about this world," I said, frustrated. "What's a binding collar?"

Lhorine answered. "Think of it like a slave collar, which also blocks a person's magic."

"Let me guess," I grumbled. "An elven invention?"

Everyone nodded.

Of course.

"So, even if you get in to see Myel, the collar will keep any magic from working on him," Olinara finished.

"Unless," Lhorine inserted, and we all listened. "Elves can break the bindings on those collars too." She gave me a pointed look.

Fuck, so I had two days to learn not only how to enhance and transmute Myel, but also to learn about bindings.

Yeah, sure, I can do that, I thought sarcastically. *It's not like I've only been in this world for a little more than a week.*

Yet, I had to... for Myel... and because if he died, I'd soon follow.

Nothing like the fear of death to motivate you.

Time to get to work.

To hopefully lift my spirits and help me feel like I was making progress, we worked on something I was already good at for the rest of the morning. I'd have to be able to take the shape of the woman going to see Myel with little time to study her, so Olinara ran me through my paces with nymph transformations. We started with pictures from her vast library of forms. She'd flash them, and I'd mimic them as fast as I could. Once I got better at that, the others then called out minor adjustments, facial features or details, which I had to alter in an instant.

Finally, Grandma Oli taught me how to lock my form, like she had with Tala, so if anything happened, I wouldn't change back to myself. It was more a meditation and metaphysical process than anything else, an inward seeking of permanence. That took me longer to master, but I forced myself to keep at it, forgoing lunch till it was done. That meant I did eventually master it, but also that lunch wasn't until midafternoon.

I ate lunch quickly then was back at it, training with Lhorine. I didn't know which I dreaded more, transmutation or bindings. I'd had one class on transmutation and it had hurt my brain so much I'd ended up snapping at Rook and Myel that night. That felt like a month ago, but it was only a couple days.

Wow.

Lhorine decided that we should focus on bindings first, for two reasons: it should come more naturally to me as an elf, and because if I couldn't undo the binding on Myel's collar, then everything else wouldn't matter.

But I was distracted. There'd been a lot of talk — mostly from Safir — about breaking my mate bond with Myel and I couldn't help but think that after I'd mastered this, that option would always be on the table, a looming threat to our relationship.

Finally, as afternoon turned to evening, then the edge of night — not that we could see any of that down here in this underground compound — Lhorine stopped, frustrated, and asked, "What's wrong? You're resisting this."

So I told her.

She cocked her head and sighed. Leading me to a bench at the side of the room, we sat.

"Do love him, the shifter?" she asked.

I shrugged. "How would I know? The bond says I do, but without it..."

She nodded. "Better question: do you want to love him? Do you want this bond?"

I leaned forward, elbows on knees, head in hands and sighed as I considered that. No one had put it like that before. Up till now, I'd assumed the bond would always be there, so I'd accepted that. But if I had a choice...

A smile crept onto my lips slowly as I remembered all the times Myel and I had spent together. Yes, most of it had been steamy and sexually satisfying, but I'd also found a hell of a lot of comforting serenity in his arms. And even beyond that, he was a good man, strong and dedicated. Not just dedicated to me, but to his friends and his mission. It also helped that he was my vision of a beautiful Goth hero.

"I don't want to lose him," I whispered. "The bond is... infuriating at times, throwing us together when we may not always want it, but... I do want Myel in my life. I don't know if I *love* him, but I know I... I need him."

"Then what's the worry?" Lhorine asked. "Once you learn this, you'll have all the control. If you don't want to break the bond, you can keep it."

Yet I couldn't help but voice my doubts. "What if... I... get angry at Myel though... or the bond? What if I break it without thinking or something like that?"

Lhorine laughed. "If you do that, you'll be stronger than any elf I've ever heard of. Bindings aren't easy for anyone. Breaking one *without thinking* is pretty damned hard."

I grimaced. "You know what I mean. What if I... *want* to break the bond because I'm in a mood or something?"

Lhorine placed a hand on my back. "All couples have trouble from time to time." She sighed. "I'm certainly no expert, despite my many years. I've not had a relationship which lasted more than sixty years." She made that sound like a short time, and for an elf, I supposed it was. "But I've never been so angry with someone I considered putting a binding on them. Something tells me you're more level-headed than you think and wouldn't rush into something so damning."

Was I though?

I sighed.

I did have a temper and a rather overinflated sense of justice, but I'd never completely gone off on anyone, at least, not someone I cared about. Saldrea made me want to punch her in the face constantly, but even with her, I'd resisted that urge for a while now.

"Thanks," I said softly.

"Are you ready to do this now?" she asked.

I nodded and got up. "Let's do this!"

"I have an idea," Lhorine said. "Something which might help."

"Whatever it is, I'm game," I said.

"Good." Lhorine rose and turned to Koar. "Can you join us?"

The dragon nodded and came over.

Lhorine pointed out the nasty wound on Koar's cheek. "Saldrea's work?" she asked.

He nodded.

That made sense.

"It's not easy to see," Lhorine said, "but it looks faintly like her house crest. And she put a binding on it so it wouldn't heal?"

Another nod from Koar.

Wow... that was cruel and vicious and... exactly something Saldrea would do.

Lhorine turned to me. "How better to learn than something practical? You're going to remove the binding on this."

I nodded, though I had no clue if I could do it, at least not yet. But Lhorine truly was an amazing teacher. She had Koar kneel while the two of us stood over him, hands on his face near the nasty injury. She guided me through how to feel the binding, how the anima around it felt, the strength and solidity.

"Yet, as permanent as it feels, all bindings can be undone if you're powerful enough." She looked me in the eye. "And I know you're powerful enough. From what Olinara told me, you wore down your own mother's binding, and she was one of the strongest elves of the age."

"I didn't fully break it," I said, feeling like I needed to stipulate that.

"You would have, given time."

That... was probably true.

Lhorine focused back on Koar's cheek. "Saldrea is strong, and most elves, myself included, could not break one of her bindings… but you can."

As the night progressed, she helped me work through it. How to feel the boundaries of the binding, feel its shape and gauge its power. Then how to use my own anima to overwhelm it, break it down. She described the usual process of breaking someone else's binding — or even one you placed yourself — as wearing it down, like a river slowly carving a gorge, since most of the time you were working with bindings of roughly equal power to your own. Yet once I fully understood what to do and how to do it, my breaking of Saldrea's binding felt more like a tidal wave washing away what should have been a sturdy, unmovable building.

"Wow," Lhorine breathed as she stepped back.

I pumped a little extra anima — not that I had much left — into Koar to heal the wound, now that the binding was gone. Then I too stepped back, a little unsteady on my feet.

"That was… impressive," Lhorine whispered. Then she seemed to recover. "You used more power than you needed to, but… yes… that's how it's done."

Koar stood and helped steady me, perhaps seeing I was about to faint. Yeah… I'd used up way too much of my anima… but I'd done it.

I smiled weakly.

"You should rest now," Lhorine suggested.

"No," I said, shaking my head. We couldn't stop, couldn't rest. Too much was at stake. I'd broken a binding, but like she'd said, I'd used too much power. I needed to refine the process, master it. We needed to push on.

I looked up at Koar, who had me wrapped so gently in his massive arms. Huh… this felt… really nice. I could go with more of this. But that wasn't what I needed from the big man right now.

"Care to give me some energy?" I was fairly certain I could duplicate what my grandmother had done, transferring his essence to me, before the dominion match.

Something in those golden eyes of his softened.

"Of course. Take what you need from me," he breathed, gravelly voice rumbling in his chest, vibrating against my side. "I'm here for you. I'll give you anything you desire, whatever you need, *always*." The softness in his eyes became something else, something far more intent. His gaze cut through my weary mind and spoke to something deep inside me, the part of me which couldn't get enough of being in this massive man's arms. Suddenly I was too warm, a deep heat throbbing in my chest and lady lava bubbling in my core.

I'll give you anything you desire... he'd said. *Whatever you need.*

Did he mean what I thought he meant?

This unflinching look of his made me think so.

And... did I want him *like that*? A big, sexy dragon, who would literally rip the world apart to protect me... Hell yeah, I did.

But that would have to wait. I had work to do.

VYNSIEL

I could still recall the grueling boot camp I'd gone through when I'd joined the Elysial Defense Forces. I'd been prepared, my father and brother had beaten it into me, and it had still been a test of my limits. And in battle against the nephilim, myself and so many other seraphim had found ourselves pushed past our limits.

And it all paled in comparison to what Izzy did now. I'd never seen anyone push themselves so hard. She was... there were no words. Even the title of goddess didn't fit anymore, because for gods, things came easy. Izzy worked harder than any god ever had, learning and growing and exceeding her limits. And now, even though she could barely stand and needed rest, would she stop?

Oh, hell no.

She took energy from Koar to keep going. Time was short and she still had a lot to learn. She wouldn't let anything stop her.

It would have boggled my mind... if I hadn't already been impressed with this astonishing woman.

With a spirit like the sun itself, she'd been a beacon in

my life ever since I'd met her. And she'd shown the world how amazing she was when she'd defeated Saldrea and Golana on the dominion pitch. She was strong and fierce and dedicated and didn't give up, no matter what.

She inspired me to be better, stronger, *more*.

I'd been feeling down, defeated, after the dominion game. I'd done my part, but still, I felt like I'd failed Izzy and the others. Yet, as I watched Izzy that evening, I vowed to be worthy of her, keep going, keep fighting, never stop, never back down, do whatever it takes.

And right now, since I had no part in the plan to save Myel, my job was to take care of her, be there for her when she needed me. Which meant, late that night, when she finally mastered bindings — a monumental feat to have learned in one night, Lhorine said as much — I was there for her, a soft place for her to land when she collapsed.

Her clothes were soaked through with sweat from her exertion, so first I took her to the showers, standing there with her, supporting her and washing her as she swayed, barely able to stay awake.

Then I carried her to her barely furnished little bedroom and laid her down, gently massaging her body, tending to her, helping her relax.

She sighed, still half awake. "That feels soooo good."

"Sleep," I whispered.

"Trust me, I'm trying, but… I can't. I don't know why. I'm exhausted and ohhhh—" She squirmed as I found a knot in her back and massaged it out. "You're doing such a wonderful job of relaxing me."

She rolled over suddenly, and I found my hands hovering over her chest. She saw my hesitation and licked her lips. Then a mischievous little smile took her face as her breasts swelled and pressed up into my palms.

"Better," she whispered. "Maybe I need... a different sort of release?" she hinted, biting her lip, feigning innocence.

I massaged her chest, feeling her nipples harden, digging into my hands. She smiled and sighed and gave the sexiest little moans. Her legs edged open and I knew she wanted more.

Leaning down to suck one hard nipple into my mouth, I let the hand which had been there slide down to her folds.

"Yes," she breathed, legs opening wider.

One brush over her seam and she opened for me. A gentle caress of her clit and her hips moved against me. I slid my finger back down and found her already wet. Heavens, she *really* needed this.

She practically sucked my finger inside her and let out the most guttural moan when I brushed her G-spot. Her body shifted, still tired but gently moving as her pleasure mounted, her heat blossoming.

I raked my teeth over her nipple as I massaged her clit with the base of my palm, my finger inside her stroking the sensitive patch within.

Her body shook with a soft release as she bit her lip and gasped, "Yes!" over and over. I teased out the orgasm till she was panting and spent.

Yet when she opened her eyes, a desperate need lay in those sea-green depths.

"More?" I asked, ready to give her everything.

A tear leaked from her eye as her face tilted. "If only you could give me what I needed," she whispered.

I didn't know what that meant.

She grimaced. "Thank you, that was amazing, you're amazing, but... I've realized why I'm so wired. I need... Myel."

Ah.

"The bond?"

She nodded.

My link to her in spirit meant we could feel each other, a limited sense, but it couldn't replace her bond with Myel. I'd accepted that.

"Thank you," she whispered again. "Can you give me a moment alone? I'm going to try something... now that I know more about bonds."

I leaned down to kiss her lips lightly. "Whatever you need." I covered her with blankets and rose, dimming the lantern in the room before leaving.

Koar waited outside the arched, open doorway.

The big man shifted uncomfortably when he saw me.

Something occurred to me.

"Is it... okay... me being with Izzy?" I asked in a whisper so as not to disturb her.

"*That's* not the problem," Koar grumbled. "*You're* not the problem."

I didn't understand... until I noticed exactly how he was shifting, why he was uncomfortable. He was aroused.

Oh!

"Wait... do you want...?"

His tight-faced grimace was all the answer I needed. He did, but he was denying himself for some reason.

"Izzy is very accepting. If you told her how you felt, I don't think she'd mind," I said quietly.

Yet his grimace only constricted more. "That's... *part* of the problem," he whispered.

I didn't understand.

"You want to be with her, and she might let you and that's a problem?"

He nodded.

"I... can't. I can't fail in my duty to protect her. I can't distract myself from this." He pointed at the floor, and I took his meaning. He needed to be right where he was, protecting her. "I can't distract myself from what I'm meant to do."

Huh.

"Okay buddy. I understand." I didn't really. He could protect her and be with her. Though being with Izzy was *one hell* of a distraction, so I guess I understood that part.

Yet it pained me to see my friend tormented like this.

I patted his shoulder, gave him a reassuring nod, and moved away, but I couldn't get that interaction out of my mind. Why couldn't he protect her while he was with her?

It felt like the man was putting up barriers to his own happiness that didn't need to be there. Perhaps I'd talk to Izzy about it and confirm she'd be okay with Koar as yet another lover. I had a feeling she wouldn't mind.

That made me laugh as I found my own bed that night. It hadn't been that long ago that I'd been torn up about the thought of Izzy being with others, but something had changed.

It didn't take me long to realize what.

I'd left my family, left my old life and old ways behind. Izzy was my family now, and her joy and happiness was all that mattered. And I couldn't deny that Myel made her happy, and as much as it pained me to admit it, Rook did too. Though I didn't know why the incubus had pulled away from her. I had a feeling Izzy's large heart would accept Koar into the fold as well. And if the big man made her happy, then I'd be happy too.

I tried to let that thought lull me to sleep, but another kept nagging at me. Koar was putting up barriers to his own happiness... was I doing the same?

For a while now I'd been hesitant to fully give myself to

Izzy because of my past. I'd done horrible things in Saldrea's name and that stain on my soul felt... wrong next to Izzy's bold brightness. I'd hoped being close to Izzy would heal me, and in many ways she had, but I still kept a part of myself from her.

But... why?

Given what I'd seen and learned about Izzy, she'd probably accept me, all of me, even the dark parts... even if I still couldn't.

Which meant... I *was* putting up barriers.

And the question which lingered in my mind as I tried to find some rest was: what did I need to do to get out of my own way and give Izzy the love she deserved?

I didn't know yet, but I vowed to find out, for Izzy's sake... and my own.

IZZY

It had only been a day since I'd been with Myel, but once again the stress of our separation had amplified the bond's call. I needed him… and he was far away, probably in pain, suffering for my sake.

I needed to rest, so I could do everything in my power to help him, but I wouldn't be able to rest until I'd done something about the bond's call echoing deep within me.

And since I'd learned a hell of a lot about bindings in the last few hours, perhaps it was time I put that training to the test.

Most of what Lhorine had taught me had been about elvish binding, which was meant to limit another person in some way. The easiest way to think about it was like binding someone's hands with rope. Magical binding worked the same way, only instead of limiting movement, they limited a person's power in some way. We'd focused on that, and how the binding collars worked, and about breaking bindings, for most of the night. Yet, she'd also spent some time talking about the difference between a mating bond and elven binding.

A mate bond didn't limit a person, instead it expanded a person's awareness to include another person and bound them together. It did "limit" Myel and I a little, since we'd always have to sate the bond or we'd suffer... like I was now. But mostly a mate bond gave more than it took. It soothed the soul and elevated emotions. It warned of danger and connected the two individuals.

And it was that connection I sought now.

One of the distractions this past evening had been feeling his pain. I'd tried to ignore it, turn that part of the bond off so I could concentrate, but now I steeled myself and faced it, dove into it. I needed to connect with my bondmate and to do that, I needed to fully commit to this link between us.

Tears leaked from my clamped shut eyes and whimpers escaped my lips as I sank into the agony Myel had endured. I gave myself over to that pain... and it was indeed horrific.

He'd been savagely beaten.

In addition to Golana's punch, which had crushed his abdomen and destroyed organs, myriad other pains seared and throbbed and ached all over his body. And I felt it all as if it had happened to me.

I cried out, sobbing. I couldn't help it.

But I hadn't sought through our bond just to feel Myel's pain. I'd hoped to help him, reach him, even though we were physically apart.

I laid a hand on my stomach, feeling Myel's destroyed bowels, and let my healing flow. I sent it into myself, then through the bond to Myel. I expected it to be difficult... but it wasn't. Lhorine had said our bond ran deep, solid. I felt that true connection now.

Myel's pain eased as his innards mended.

And so I went, healing Myel's injuries through our bond.

I had no clue how he'd experience this, but it didn't matter, as long as I could help him.

Izzy? Is that you?

Myel's voice seemed distant, but I heard his tenuous call.

Yes, Myel, I'm here.

How? The hope and pain in his voice shredded my soul. This wasn't a physical pain anymore. This was the pain of speaking to his beloved but not being able to be with her. A pain I shared in equal part.

I spent the day learning about bonds. I... I used that to reach out to you, heal you.

Oh Spirits, Izzy, thank you, you are... you're a miracle!

I smiled softly, the tears I'd shed in pain not that long ago cold on my cheeks.

I... may be able to do more... but I was exhausted, even more so after healing Myel from a distance. I could barely move, every muscle ached with deep fatigue.

"Koar," I called softly.

"I'm here mistress, what's wrong?" The dragon's voice was closer than I'd expected. A large hand took one of mine, lifting it to enfold it in both of his. Koar was already next to me? He must have heard me crying and come to see why.

"I'm with Myel, through our bond, but... I need more. I can do more, but I need your help yet again. I'm so sorry to ask." I was still floating in a place beyond my body, connected to Myel, my eyes clamped shut. But I knew Koar would help.

"You need energy?"

"Yes, lots... and... I'm sorry, but... this may get... awkward, intimate. Will you... will you stay by me and help me through this?"

He gulped, then sighed. "Yes mistress, whatever you need, as I promised."

God! I'd never known anyone so willing to do anything and everything for me. Even Vyns had kept some distance between us at the start. But Koar had been one hundred percent devoted from the get-go.

"Thank you."

We quickly performed the ritual which siphoned his energy into me, for the third time in less than a day. The man was a deep well of energy, always willing to give. That was dragons for you. And when his life force filled me, rejuvenated me, I delved even deeper into my bond with Myel. I had the energy to seek the metaphysical barrier between us, the thinnest of veils in a realm of soul and spirit... then I crashed through it, into Myel's very essence.

My awareness expanded.

Koar's hand still enveloped mine, giving energy as I needed it, close and comforting. Yet all of that felt far away, my physical body a memory. It was spirit and raw life essence which dominated this place. Reality shifted, feelings became physical. Myel's love for me was a heated breath coasting over my skin. Except I didn't have skin, I was a soul made substantial.

And so was Myel

"Izzy?"

No longer did his voice sound like it came from a great distance. He was right here with me. His spirit shifted and formed into a glowing manifestation of his body, which was somehow even more real than his true physical form. He seemed... taller, back straighter, dark soulful eyes shining brighter. This was Myel as he was meant to be, without an entire life of oppression having ground him down. And God, he was even more gorgeous than usual. He usually kept his hair short, but here his dark locks were long, floating behind him, like some story-book faerie prince, dashing and proud and…

…did I mention clothes didn't seem to be a thing in this strange place of spirit, so he was stark naked.

And so was I, I realized, as I looked down to see my own spirit form.

Myel looked around with wonder.

"What is this place? How did we get here?" The joyous smile on his face warmed my heart. I couldn't wait any longer and rushed to him. And as I'd hoped, even though this place wasn't physical, his presence still soothed me. He wrapped strong arms around me, and his love flowed through me, peace easing the tension in my not-body.

"This is our bond," I breathed as I held him tight. "Lhorine told me tales of bondmates of old who shared a connection so profound they could meet in a realm of spirit or essence or whatever. So I sought that out and broke through the last of our barriers to find you."

"Izzy," Myel breathed my name like a prayer, clutching me even tighter. "My miracle."

And our not-bodies being crushed together in this place seemed to have the same effect as our physical bodies doing the same. Our arousal spiked.

I pushed back enough to find his lips and kissed him. And when my ethereal lips touched his, it was like some long-lost part of me had come home. It wasn't just a kiss, it was the last piece of a puzzle, the final joining of our souls in this bond.

And through that kiss all our emotions flowed, not only his abiding love, but his heady lust, his need for me. And deeper than all of that, his unflinching devotion… mingled with a terrified doubt.

And because of this deep connection, I understood that dread-dismay instantly: he feared I'd leave him someday.

I had to hope this ultimate joining of our spirit would show him how much he was wrong. He knew how I felt, even if it wasn't full-on love yet, it was nearly everything else. I needed him as much as he needed me. He was my partner... for life, and I appreciated everything this man had done for me.

As our emotions flowed, our metaphysical bodies began to merge in a way our physical bodies never could. He wasn't just deep inside one part of me, but everywhere within me. And I slid inside him as well. We became one. It was sexy and steamy and hot and wonderful, but so much better than messy physical sex. It was pure and utterly sublime, heavenly.

We touched each other in ways I'd never thought possible, sinking deeply into this heated connection, giving and receiving in waves of building bliss. Our bond demanded we come together, and in this place we did... over and over again.

We remained like that, joined in a perfect union of ecstasy and devotion, for a while before I felt a pull.

My body needed me back. It had taken far more energy to be here than coupling in person.

"I have to go," I whispered as we slowly separated, though still in each other's arms, just not mingling spirits completely anymore.

He nodded. "I feel my body growing weary as well."

"I'm coming for you," I breathed. "I'll find you and we have a plan to help you win the fight. Hang on, be brave my perfect hero." I pushed an ethereal hand through his long thick hair.

"I will, I'll never falter. I'll hold on. I'll wait for you, always."

We drew apart, the pull of our bodies too demanding.

And yet, as that place of wonder faded and my essence settled once more into the heavy and weary confines of my body, I had to smile.

Because the bond between Myel and I was even stronger now. It was complete. And having sated its desire, I finally, thankfully, rested.

MYELAS

I OPENED MY EYES IN THE DARKNESS AND SIGHED HEAVILY.

Izzy truly was a miracle.

Only she could have breached the metaphysical barrier between us and somehow come to me in spirit to sate our bond.

That had been... there were no words to describe our ultimate joining and the bliss which had flowed out of it. Pure emotion had somehow translated into raw sensation beyond anything I could ever imagine.

I shouldn't smile, but I couldn't help it. I rolled over to hide my joy from the guards outside my cell, in case they checked in on me through the small sliding grate in the door. I hated those men, there to make sure I didn't sleep, didn't rest, was always in pain. They'd soon come again, to beat on me, ensuring I didn't sleep. I'd try not to let on that I was healed and whole when they did. And until then, I held my miraculous moment with Izzy in my heart and reveled in this stillness and peace.

Yet the stink of this cell, the cold and damp and bare

stone beneath me, all slowly ate away at my joy, till doubts crept back in.

During our time together in spirit, I'd felt the full extent of Izzy's feelings for me... and though there had been so much passion and joy, she still didn't love me. I tried to tell myself she simply didn't love me *yet*, that it would come... but could she? Would she?

Because the other thing I couldn't get over was how powerful Izzy had become in such a short time. She'd changed so much. Yesterday, after only one day of training, she'd bested Saldrea and Golana with earth magic. And now she'd used her ability with bonds to join with me.

She was an elf. There was no denying it. She had proven her power.

And she was royalty.

Would she come to know her own kind and relate to them? Would she see her own power and realize how far beneath her I truly was? Because I'd never known an elf who was kind to a shifter.

What if, despite how much she cared for me, she didn't grow to love me? She was becoming more like an elf every day... what if her feelings for me changed completely?

Given what she'd done with our bond I had no doubt that she could also *break* that bond if she wished.

Would she?

Given what I'd felt from her... no.

But... if she changed even more...?

People knew of our bond now. I had no doubt others would tell her to be rid of me, that shifters weren't worth it, that I was dead weight pulling her down. She wouldn't listen to them... not at first. But since she'd changed so much so quickly, I had to wonder how much more she might change after a month... or a year.

And even if she didn't grow to despise me... if she remained loyal... I'd always be a target, a weak spot for her. I'd been taken hostage so easily. What if it happened again? What if, instead of drawing things out, they just killed me?

Perhaps it would be best if Izzy broke the bond. Then I wouldn't be a liability to her.

The longer I lay there, in the fetid stench of that cell, the more my thoughts twisted in on themselves, sinking me deeper into despair, until I desperately clung to my last shred of hope... Izzy had promised to save me, to help me, and I had no doubt that she'd do that. She hadn't changed yet. I wasn't dead yet. I had to have faith that she'd keep her word, that she'd live up to her promises, but it was so hard to hope in this horrid place.

Leather rustled; low voices mumbled outside.

A key in the lock.

I tensed as the door opened.

"Time to wake up, little bat. You need a few more bruises, I think." The head guard was an ogre, big and heavy of limb with fists like anvils. The other two were both hobgoblins, not nearly as strong, but just as fervent in their administration of injury.

I rolled away from the guards and tried as best I could to smear the grime and dirt and filth of this place over me, hiding the fact that my wounds had healed. Then I huddled against the wall, not needing to feign fear. If I hadn't been collared, I could have shadow-stepped away from this horrid place, the cell was certainly dark enough, but all my magic was restrained and I was helpless against these brutes.

They closed in, I couldn't see the grins on their faces in the dark, but I heard their chuckles. They enjoyed this nearly as much as I feared it.

Then the blows began to fall and all I could do was take it, steeling my will to survive, crying out in pain to give them what they wanted.

And when they left, I huddled in on myself and wept.

And I prayed.

Shifters had no gods, the elves were meant to be our gods, so I'd never prayed before.

But that night, I prayed to Izzy. I prayed she'd come for me, help me, heal me, save me. I prayed she'd stay with me, even if it was unlikely. I prayed she'd become the woman I knew she could be, and change this wretched world, even if she had to abandon me to do it. I'd sacrifice myself for the greater good, for all the shifters who came after me, that they might live in peace. If Izzy had to give up her bond with me to rule, to gain the respect of the elves and change thousands of years of tradition, then I'd gladly give up my love and my life for that cause.

That was my only solace that night.

KOARTHANDRIS

Izzy settled, her breath even, her body cooling and serene. She'd stopped pulling at my life force, so I assumed she was finished whatever she'd been doing and was resting. I laid her hand back on her stomach but lingered by her side.

She'd taken a lot from me, draining me. Fatigue was not a sensation I was familiar with. Dragons didn't tire or sleep the way others did. We went through cycles of centuries, sleeping for hundreds of years at a time, then active for even longer. I'd last slept once I'd become an adult — around my twentieth century — for a couple hundred years, waking roughly seven-hundred-and-fifty years ago.

Yet it wasn't my weariness which kept me here.

The scent of Izzy's arousal filled my nostrils and sang to every cell in my body. My dick was so damned hard I couldn't move. I was beyond overwhelmed. Whatever Izzy had done, it had been extremely erotic to watch, and I'd had a front row seat. She'd moaned with abandon, the sound filled with raw passion. She'd thrown off the covers over her,

her naked form writhing before me, flushed, aroused, exposed...

I tried to cover her, only to have her throw off the blanket again.

Having witnessed that, how could I not be stunned with extreme arousal.

Hearing Vyns pleasure her earlier had been bad enough. And it certainly didn't help knowing she was my ideal mate, strong and intelligent, witty and kind.

Dragons *never* came early. Our control of our wills and bodies was matched only by elves and dwarves. Yet it had taken every ounce of energy Izzy had left me with to resist losing control of myself.

Izzy was... perfect.

Yet... she didn't need me.

Vyns seemed to think she would accept me, be with me, but I couldn't allow that. So, I had to settle with knowing she had others who could give her stunning heights of pleasure and be her ideal mates. Myel may be a shifter, but a mate bond was a serious thing. I wouldn't get in the way of that. And Vyns loved her, of that I was certain. I was less certain about the incubus Rook, who I'd thought her friend at least, but he'd not been around at all for her, other than to help with the dominion match. Still, Myel and Vyns were probably enough for her. They could take care of her in every way she needed.

She didn't need me.

And that shouldn't have bothered me — since my one and only duty was to protect her — but it did.

I sank back, sitting next to Izzy, waiting for my body to settle, which might take a while. I took that time to remind myself of why I could never let my guard down, even once, to be with Izzy.

It had been roughly a hundred and twenty years ago. I'd been the guard captain — The Sentrea Prima — of the queen's brother's household. Talmarion had been a good master and I'd served him loyally for hundreds of years, working my way up through the ranks of his personal guard. I knew his family well, and they knew me.

His daughter, Mynrial, in particular, had come to know me *very* well. She'd pursued me romantically for over a hundred years, and I'd denied her. It wasn't uncommon for elves to have flings with dragons, but I had my duty to consider. Even during my off hours, I was loyal to Talmarion and wouldn't give in to his daughter's desires.

Then, one night, Talmarion himself had invited me to dine with him while I'd been off duty. I'd been honored to share his table, a reward for my many years of stalwart service. Mynrial and been seated next to me, fawning over me. I'd denied her... but then Talmarion himself had asked why I'd rebuffed his daughter's advances. I'd told him it would affect my duties, that I could not allow myself to be distracted, even by a most amazing woman such as she.

Mynrial had been nearly as perfect as Izzy. She too had been witty and strong, determined and fierce. She hadn't had the same sense of justice and kindness as Izzy, but she'd had a good heart. Despite being raised a royal, indoctrinated into the superiority of elves, she'd done charity work for the less fortunate. At the time, I'd thought her the epitome of womanhood.

Had I wished to be with her? Certainly, but my duty came first.

Yet Talmarion had shrugged off my objections and had told me, in no uncertain terms, I should enjoy myself every now and then, his meaning clear. I had his blessing to be with his daughter. He'd known it would be nothing more than a fling, we'd never be married. Elves could only mate with other elves, but they were allowed to dally with whom-so-ever they wished before that.

That night, I'd given in.

And it had been a mistake. For that was the same night assassins had attacked the royals. I'd been distracted until we'd heard a scream. Even then, I hadn't reacted instantly, lingering with Mynrial, believing other guards could handle whatever was afoot. It had only been once guards had sought me out and told me there were attackers all over the palace that I acted. I'd left Mynrial with other dragon guards and run to her parents' suite, but it had been too late. Talmarion and his wife Hyessa had been killed.

I'd raced back to Mynrial, only to find her, and the guards I'd left with her, dead. Perhaps, if I hadn't been with her, I'd have been able to save her parents. Or perhaps, if I hadn't left her, I could have saved her. I hadn't made any good choices that night.

And being with Mynrial would have been a mistake, even if the assassins hadn't come... because she'd been everything I'd wanted. It would never have been the case of "getting her out of my system" and going back to my duty, but quite the opposite. Once I'd been with her, she'd put her mark on my soul. I'd have wanted more, constantly distracted while on duty. I know it to be true.

That's why I could never be with Izzy. As much of a distraction as she was now... being with her would only compound the issue.

A guard should never have any sort of relationship with his charge, period. I'd been weak once, and I would never allow it to happen again.

Never.

No matter how much my soul cried out to be with Izzy.

No matter how much my body yearned to hold her, touch her, please her.

I had to be strong, for her sake, and for my own. Because I'd never forgive myself if I lost her, lost another of the family I'd sworn to protect.

Besides, I didn't even know if she wanted me in the same way. She had Myel and Vyns after all… and maybe Rook as well.

Although…

After she'd removed Saldrea's binding and healed my cheek, when I'd held her in my arms… there had been something in how she'd looked at me. I'd been filled with gratitude at first, then, realizing how close she was, my desire for her had nearly overwhelmed me. I'd wanted desperately to kiss her… and something in her eyes had made me think… she'd let me, that she wanted it.

Still, I'd never presume.

And asking her would only open a door I dared not even touch.

No, going down that road would only lead to failure of my duty and pain. I had to believe she didn't need me, didn't want me. I *could not* be with her.

I stayed with her that night, in her room, not outside. I watched her sleep, waiting for my body to cool, to calm. It didn't.

And I began to fear that maybe when she'd taken my life force… perhaps some of hers had fed back into me…

…infecting me…

…filling me with a need I could never fulfill.

IZZY

"I NEED MORE FROM YOU," I WHISPERED TO KOAR. "MORE OF your life, your essence."

Why were we naked?

Why was he so close?

How could any man — even a dragon — have a dick that damned huge?

"I'll give you everything, my all, my life, my essence," he breathed as he stepped closer and our bodies pressed together. His arms wrapped around me, that mega-dick pressed into my belly, so long it tickled the underside of my breasts. There was no way that would ever fit inside me, but I sure as hell wanted him to try.

"But if you need more from me, we'll need more than the touch of a hand," he breathed as he bent his head. I tilted mine back and our lips met. His were hard and pressing, ordering my mouth to open, and I did. His tongue swept into my mouth, dominating me, and his life-force flowed into me.

But it wasn't enough.

"More," I hissed, when we broke apart. "I need all of you!" I demanded.

"Yes, mistress," he breathed.

And yeah, I had to admit, it was damned sexy when he called me mistress. This big, hard, brute of a man deferring to me played into every domination fantasy I'd ever had. Not that I'd ever owned a pleather dominatrix outfit. But I may have perused the options online a few times and let my imagination run wild.

Koar lifted me easily. I wrapped my legs around his thick torso as he pinned me to the wall and...

Oh.

My.

God!

He penetrated me in a way no man ever had, so forceful and deep, so filling, I'd never be hungry again. He was so huge it broke my mind. I let out a very unladylike series of noises as he thrusted deep into my soul, breaking me, too big, tearing me apart, but also giving me all his essence, healing me, strengthening me, putting me back together.

Then he was a dragon, and I was pinned to the ground as he had his way with me, so damned huge over me I couldn't comprehend it...

...and *that's* what made me wake up.

I sat up, sweating, searing hot and more than a little turned on.

And across the room, sitting against the wall... Koar stared at me, with a bulge in his pants reminding me of my dream.

"I'm sorry," I blurted, still only half awake. In my head I was apologizing for leading him on, because clearly — according to my dream — he wanted me, yet I'd also been denying him here in reality, when it was clear — according to his pants — he wanted more.

Koar raised a brow in question.

That was when I realized none of what I'd been thinking made sense. I blushed furiously and stammered, trying to come up with a real reason for apologizing.

"For... taking so much energy from you yesterday." I couldn't even remember if or when I stopped drawing on his life-force last night. I'd sated myself with Myel in that strange realm of bond and spirit, then fallen right asleep. "Are you okay?"

His other brow rose to join the first and a slow smile broke the stony features of his hard face.

"I have a lot to give," he whispered.

I'll give you everything, my all, my life, my essence. His words from my dream echoed in my head, and I was blushing even hotter now.

He frowned. "No... I didn't mean like that," he stammered.

And my dirty little mind took control of my lips, overpowering my wake-up brain.

"And what if that's what I wanted?"

I blinked, surprised I'd gone there.

I had enough men in my life... didn't I? At one point I'd had three paramours, but now... Myel felt so far away, and if he died, the best-case scenario was that I'd go insane. And Rook had once been a friend, but he hadn't been around at all since the dominion match.

And here I was being all inviting to this dragon, whom I barely knew. Admittedly, he'd been doing a damned good job of being one hundred percent dedicated to me, a fierce protector. I believed him when he said he was on my side, but still...

Oh... who was I kidding? I'd wanted to climb that mountainous body of his since I'd first met him, and that had been back when he'd been protecting Saldrea.

Vyns probably wouldn't mind. He seemed to have accepted my other lovers.

Myel was okay with all that... I think. We hadn't really talked since our argument over me being with Vyns that first time.

And Rook... he didn't get a vote since he was being a dick.

So... yeah.

I didn't retract my words. I just smiled at Koar in a sexy little way.

I was pretty sure that bulge in his pants twitched before the dragon rose quickly.

"I can't give you that," he said sharply and left the room in haste.

Oh.

Huh.

Well, that only made me want him more.

So few men turned me down. And since it was clear I was his type and aroused him, that meant he had some good reason for not wanting to be with me. I respected the hell out of that.

As opposed to Rook, who seemed to have flipped a switch and wanted nothing to do with me anymore.

Grandma had said he was mad at himself? That he cared but was frustrated at something?

Out of anyone, I'd have thought the incubus wouldn't have had any reservations about being with me. Sex with him was stunning and he'd said it was the same for him, so... why had he disappeared? The more I thought about the fiery man, the more frustrated I got.

But Koar...? He hadn't given me a reason for his resistance, but then...I didn't expect one from him. Maybe the big man just had boundaries. And with Rook ghosting me, maybe I'd leave the door open for the big dragon... if he changed his mind.

I dressed and left my room. Koar dutifully followed me into the main area where Zora had laid out breakfast. The others were up already, but the mood was subdued. We ate in silence.

Afterward, Lhorine and I went to work, focusing on the elven ability to physically enhance themselves and others. And so began another long day, as time ran out for Myel...

And for me.

AMARHUK (ROOK)

My master was at his office and the servants had done their morning rounds of cleaning and tending to Svokol's sprawling underground residence. The place was quiet.

I'd just showered, after yet another grueling workout and training session, in the vain hope that physical activity would overpower my thoughts and feelings about...

Izzy.

Perhaps seeing her would help? Some part of me knew the *one last hit and I'm done* philosophy didn't work for addicts, but it didn't stop me.

I crept through the silent stone halls to a secret room, which only my master and a select few were aware of. The fact that I knew about it signaled Svokol's trust in me. And I was about to break that trust, since I shouldn't be in the room without him.

But I couldn't risk going outside. Saldrea might have someone watching the house, ready to drag me to her for some good ol' torture if I left. And even if that didn't happen, I couldn't risk getting too close to Izzy in person. Maybe I'd be drawn back to her side. She had that effect on me. And I couldn't risk getting close to her physically or emotionally.

So, I'd did something I shouldn't, to catch a glimpse of her from a distance.

In the lowest level of Svokol's residence was a meditation room. The stairs descended into an open area. There was no furniture, dwarves needed no cushions or chairs, they preferred hard stone. The walls were one giant stone carving of a scene from dwarven history: the conquering of Urval. The four surfaces were intricately detailed, showing the dwarves, and their armies of trolls and ogres, passing through a massive gate between realms. It showed the first meetings with the salmaeri and concubi and the pact which was forged between those races and the dwarves, then the combined might of that force pushing back the pyrkai giants to the Shadow Lands.

It was an epic tale, which all Urval residents knew by heart. The dwarves had saved us and allowed the salmaeri and concubi to flourish once more.

I found the hidden knob in the carving and pressed on it, making a section of the wall swing inward silently.

I entered and closed the stone door behind me.

This small room also had no furniture, except for a four-foot tall stone column at the center, on which sat a sphere of glasstone in its raw state.

As far as the other races were concerned, glasstone had two possible states and uses. The first was anima-saturated, where it became a silvery color. Such stones were used to test a person's magical power. The second was anima-desaturated, where all the innate anima was drained out and it lost all color, becoming completely clear. Then it could be used to create magical devices such as phones and computers, or windows, and so on.

But there was a third state, somewhere in between, which only the dwarves knew about. With no anima added nor taken away, the glasstone was a milky silver color, translucent and cloudy. In this raw state it had an extraordinary power, which the dwarves kept secret: it could scry on others, viewing people and places far away. Anyone with even a hint of anima could touch the stone and think of a person or place they knew well, then see the result in real time.

This stone was so much of a secret, that before Svokol had had it put in this room, he'd had a sylph enchant this area, such that any thoughts and memories from this room would be sealed away, unable to be taken from one's mind.

I laid both hands on the cool surface and didn't even have to consciously think of Izzy, the stone instantly flashed to a view of her. That's how much she dominated my mind.

She was at the training compound, working hard with that elf, Lhorine. I couldn't tell exactly what they were doing, there were no clear physical effects, but strain painted Izzy's features, sweat covering her body. She was pushing herself to her limits.

Myel had been taken into custody. It was all over campus. Even the servants in Svokol's house had been chatting about it. Rumors and speculation swirled about why this unheard of shifter had been brought in, but I knew exactly why.

And I had to imagine Izzy was working her sexy ass off to help him.

If this was how hard she worked when I wasn't around, perhaps it was a good thing I stayed away. Some part of my brain knew that didn't make any sense, but I held onto that thought.

I had to.

She's better off without me. That tenuous mantra was all that kept me from rushing to her side. I had to believe *she* wanted it this way, because I certainly didn't. I wanted nothing more than to be there with her, helping her, cheering her on, giving her quiet little orgasms to help relax her and refresh her and help her rest when she needed it. Okay, maybe not *quiet* orgasms.

Izzy was too... perfect. Beyond her obvious physical attributes, she had a soft soul. She wanted to help the people of this world. I'd never met an elf like that. And as a royal, she had the power to change things, if she could defeat Saldrea and Valnea to take it. She was everything this world needed... everything I needed.

As much as I didn't want to admit it.

I shouldn't *need* anyone. That was counter to everything concubi stood for. We gave to others and fed off others, but we never settled down, because we'd always be called to keep giving to anyone in need. We were for everyone, not just one person.

But I didn't want anyone else anymore and that frightened me. It scared me more than that terrifying dominion match, more than death.

Death was easy, simple, an ending. I wouldn't worry about anything after I was dead. I'd come to terms with death a long time ago. When I'd been in the Urval army, I'd accepted death as an end to pain and suffering. It was peace after a world and life where that was so damned rare. So yeah, death didn't scare me...

...but love? Caring for someone? Giving them my heart?

Yeah, that freaked me out more than anything else, because that was the source of the worst pain and suffering in all of life.

Heartbreak.

And I feared Izzy had already stolen my heart.

She'd certainly captivated my mind.

My telepathy had yet to release its hold on her. I still caught stray thoughts from her now and then, especially the stronger ones. That was how I'd found out Saldrea knew of Izzy's bond with Myel. I should be able to move my mental connection at will, but I couldn't. It was stuck on her.

And the longer I stayed here, watching Izzy the more I *needed* to be close to her.

This wasn't working.

I tore myself away from the glasstone orb and rushed out of the secret room.

Hurrying through the halls, I found a door and knocked quickly before letting myself in.

The woman inside was one of Svokol's household, sometimes a servant, sometimes a spy. Eshta was a full-blooded succubus who'd been saved, like me, from a life in Urval. This was her private time, away from her duties, so she was completely naked when I entered, preferring no clothes when they weren't needed.

She raised one brow but smiled as well.

"Please, Rook, come in," she purred. "Finally ready to take me up on my offer?"

As odd as it may sound, incubi and succubi did not often couple. The only reason for doing so was procreation, since we couldn't feed off our own kind. Well, that wasn't entirely true, incubi and succubi also coupled as youths, to teach and learn and grow in the art of sex.

Since Eshta and I were the only concubi in Svokol's household, she'd offered to have my children before.

"Not that," I said. "But I could use a good fuck to..." *forget about someone?* Yeah, I couldn't say that. "... just... 'cause."

"I can do just 'cause," she said with a grin and came to me.

Yet when she pressed her bountiful body against me, hand reaching up to bring my face to hers in a long, deep, passionate kiss... my body didn't respond at all.

No, it wasn't that it didn't respond, it did... but in the opposite way it should. Revulsion flooded through me, the complete antithesis of arousal.

I pushed her away, her taste sour in my mouth.

"Sorry... no... I can't."

Both of her brows went up. She searched my gaze.

"Oh... I see." She sighed and turned away. "Your loss."

But it wasn't. I didn't feel like I'd lost an opportunity, more like I'd avoided a catastrophe.

What was wrong with me?

I fled Eshta's room and returned to my own, throwing myself on my bed.

This was messed up. I couldn't even make out with a succubus?

As they always did, my thoughts returned to Izzy. I only wanted one woman. Sex only made sense with Izzy.

Blazes, this was bad.

I was going... monogamous!

Fuck me, I was so damned screwed.

IZZY

SOMETHING WAS WRONG.

I'd taken a break from my relentless training, learning elven enhancements, to have a drink and catch my breath. The work was mostly internal, whether I was enhancing myself or others, so there wasn't much to show for my efforts, but my skill in making myself stronger or faster or tougher was progressing. I still couldn't do it to others yet, but that would come.

And while I'd rested, I'd gotten a strange sense, a deep ache, like a migraine, but... in my very soul. I knew this feeling. I'd felt it once before... the day Vyns had nearly died, beaten by Saldrea.

Fuck.

Vyns had left a little while ago, escorting Tala, who'd hoped to sneak back to her room and collect some things.

"Vyns is in trouble," I said.

Koar perked up.

"Spirit link?" he asked.

I nodded.

We both rushed out of the training compound. I shouted

an apology to Lhorine, then we were out and away, racing across campus, my spirit guiding me, pulling me toward Vyns.

Thankfully, he wasn't on the brink of death when we found him. He didn't look good, but he looked better than Tala, whom he held in his arms. Whether from my spirit-link with him or my training in magic in general, I was able to sense him feeding spirit to Tala to help her hold on.

Both of them had been attacked, the assailants long gone, but I knew who'd sent them.

I reached Vyns and knelt next to Tala.

He looked up, tears in his eyes. "I'm sorry, Izzy, I tried to protect her, but..."

I saved my words for later, laying my hands on my friend to feel for her injuries. I'd heal the serious ones first, then save my strength. Vyns looked like he'd be able to walk and as long as both of them were safe and not going to die, I'd conserve my energy, I needed it to train, since I was far from where I needed to be.

Tala's wounds were nasty, but someone had been very careful in beating her, maximizing pain, while minimizing risk of death. They'd wanted her to live...

...because this was a message: *I can get to your friends.*

Saldrea must have had people watching Tala's room day and night, in case she returned. It reminded me of the stark difference in our resources. She had all the money and practically the entire world on her side. I had a few friends and my grandmother's wealth.

I healed the worst of Tala's wound, till she roused.

"And you?" I asked Vyns. "Can you walk?"

He nodded.

Koar carried Tala, while Vyns limped along and I kept an eye out for anyone still watching us. I didn't want Saldrea to find our secret base. There were many prying eyes, curious onlookers, as we made our way across campus, but no one stayed with us for long.

We got Tala back to the compound and made sure she was resting comfortably before I broke down.

Shakes took me, and I had to sit, losing my strength.

I couldn't live like this, my friends — my chosen family — always in danger, not able to go out for the simplest things.

Wait...

Rook.

I'd assumed I hadn't seen him since the match because he didn't want to be around me anymore... but what if something had happened to him?

My strength returned instantly, and I shot to my feet.

"I need to go out again," I said as Koar returned from getting Vyns settled.

"You need to train," Lhorine said, stern. "You still have so much to learn."

"I will, but I need to check on Rook, make sure he's okay."

Koar nodded and the two of us headed out once more.

We were admitted to Svokol's house and when I asked if Rook was here and healthy, the servant nodded.

I sighed, relieved.

But all the built-up tension thrumming through me wouldn't go away so easily. My anxiety turned to frustration and irritation.

"Where is he?" I asked the servant who'd greeted us.

"Training."

I hurried through the underground complex to find him. Like the last time, he was stripped to the waist, sweat covering his body as he attacked a wooden dummy over and over with a series of strange martial arts moves and fire.

"You!" I shouted at him and he stopped, turning.

I marched over to him, Koar waiting by the door.

"Avoid me all you want but at least tell me why!" I hissed at him, poking him in the chest. A hard-muscled, glistening, sexy chest.

No... stop that! I'm mad at him.

"You want to know, fine," he said, voice strained as those fiery eyes focused on mine.

I was suddenly very hot, but it definitely wasn't because of those eyes, or his sexiness, or anything like that. No... it was from the fast march over here and my fury... yes... that's why... nothing more...

"Suddenly you're a princess, an elf, and that changes everything," he said, worked up. "Before, I could be your friend, we could have some fun and it wouldn't hurt anything, but now... being seen with me... I'm a lower race. Right now, you need to be showing the world you can be an elf, a ruler, and having an incubus on your arm would only tarnish your reputation. I'm bad for you. It's that simple."

I hope she buys that. The thought was faint, but I heard it softly in my head.

Right... he could communicate with me telepathically, though I assumed he hadn't meant for me to hear that.

"And..." he went on, "that night when you found out you were a princess, before all of that, you'd yelled at me and I honestly wasn't sure where we stood, or if you wanted me back as a friend or anything more."

I blinked.

There was no thought to accompany that, he seemed honest enough.

I *had* yelled at him, but only because he'd been a dick

about me seeing an angel, Vyns. I had the feeling he didn't mind now, but since our communication was clearly off, I asked him,

"Are you okay with me having Vyns in my life?"

He blinked. "Ah... yeah... sure, I guess. If you don't need me, then—"

"That's not what I said!" I yelled, frustrated. "Are you okay with me as a friend and fuckbuddy if I'm also doing an angel!"

Wow... that hadn't come out quite liked I'd hoped.

Rook shrugged.

"Whatever, sure, but like I said. I shouldn't be seen with you."

"Yeah, tarnishing my ever-so-bright image, I heard you... and I don't believe a word of it."

He flinched back.

"I don't give a flying fuck about my reputation. I'm going to change this world. Once I'm queen, there won't be any restrictions on who people can be with. I'm going to change all of that. So why would I care about being seen with you?"

He grimaced. A guilty look. He'd known all of that.

"Which means you're not avoiding me for my sake, but for your own." Though as for why, I had no idea.

Does she know? I only barely caught the stray thought.

Did I know what?

"I... just can't... be with you," he stammered. Something flashed in his fiery eyes. Was that... fear?

Fear of me?

"What are you so damned afraid of!" I demanded.

He looked away, face tight.

Enough of this. "If you're not man enough to tell me what's up, then maybe you aren't the man I thought you were!"

I waited to see if he'd say anything.

"You're... an elf now..." he mumbled.

An elf?

He was afraid of me because I was an elf? Sure, elves in this world were generally asshats, but he knew me better than that, didn't he? I guessed not.

Fine. Whatever.

I shook my head, disgusted that this man had turned on me for something I couldn't control.

Spinning on my heel, I stalked out of the room, Koar falling in behind me. I'd come here to make sure Rook was okay. He was, but as for clarifying where we stood... I was even more upset and frustrated than before.

And sad.

Rook had been a friend when no one else had. He'd been there for me, even when I'd been upset at him for betraying me, even with no bond compelling him. He'd kept my secret about my bond with Myel, he'd helped me learn the ways of this world.

So, why was he pulling away now?

What had happened?

Was it really that I was an elf?

How shallow could a man get?

By the time I returned to the compound, it was noon, and the others were sitting down for lunch. Lhorine and Olinara had helped to heal Vyns and Tala, who both looked a little sheepish for having been caught like that.

I sat, clearly grumpy. Zora broke the tense silence to tell us Myel's conjugal visit was a succubus named Alistora. Safir took over from there, saying he'd found out who would be guarding Myel at that time. The three jailers were already being paid by Saldrea to beat Myel, so bribing them probably wouldn't work. Also, it wasn't out of the realm of possibility that they'd actually watch Myel's conjugal visit, if they were so inclined.

Great.

"We can put them to sleep," Lhorine said, looking at me. "It's like a binding, but lesser, an enchantment. Elves are usually quite adept at enchantments. It shouldn't be hard for you to learn."

Yet another thing for me to master before tomorrow night.

Yay!

There wasn't enough time. I couldn't learn it all by then. I'd fail.

I didn't say anything. I gave a tight-lipped nod, then faked a smile to reassure everyone.

But my mood only carried over into my afternoon training, which did not go as well as Lhorine hoped. By dinner I'd managed to learn how to enhance others, but I couldn't give them much. Still, it was something.

"You're off today," Lhorine said as we joined the others for a meal. "We won't train any more this evening. Get some rest, you're tired. We'll start bright and early tomorrow. Okay?"

I nodded, dreading our next lesson. Just learning to do what came naturally to an elf had been hard enough, but now I needed to add enchantments and transmutation. I'd had a class on transmutation earlier that week, which had only left me feeling overwhelmed and confused. Could I really learn it in a day?

I wasn't so sure.

IZZY

After dinner, I had a shower, then slumped into bed, exhausted, but unable to rest.

My bond with Myel had been sated last night, but I still felt his pain, physical and emotional. That, piled on top of my frustration over Rook, meant I couldn't settle.

Vyns came to me.

"Your spirit is in chaos," he whispered. "Allow me to help you relax."

I sighed thankfully and nodded.

But as he shed his clothes, he paused. "Unless... you'd like someone new?"

New?

Vyns sent a meaningful glance at the door. "Koar?" he whispered.

The dragon entered, lips tight.

"I told her I can't," he grumbled.

"Don't be another man turning her away, she's had enough of that today." I guessed Koar had told Vyns what had happened between me and Rook.

"If he doesn't want to..." I said, trailing off, leaving it open.

"What do *you* want?" Vyns asked me.

Did I want Koar?

My dream from the night before returned. It had been an exaggeration, a fantasy, but still I shivered with desire. It had been more than Koar's powerful physical presence and size which had moved me, but his dedication. Would he dedicate himself as much to my pleasure as he did to guarding me?

The dream suggested he would.

Koar's hard expression suggested he was not interested.

I was more than a little curious what being with a dragon would be like, but only if it was what he wanted.

"I... wouldn't mind... exploring a new partner... *if* that's what you want," I said this directly to Koar.

The big man seemed torn, like he had that morning. His jaw twitched and bunched as he stood there, fighting some inner war.

"I... can't, mistress," he said, somehow seeming both relieved and upset about this. "I do not feel I'd be able to perform my duty as your guard if I was... so close to you."

"We're safe down here," Vyns tried.

Koar shook his head. "I can't allow myself to think that way."

So the big man was on alert twenty-four-seven? I'd known he was dedicated, but... wow. I'd never had a man quite so devoted to my safety.

Yet even after he'd said he couldn't, he didn't leave. Something made him linger.

A thought popped into my head. "Do you want to watch?" I wasn't really into exhibitionism, but maybe that's what Koar needed to get over his issue, whatever it was. Because I agreed with Vyns that I was as safe as I was ever going to be here and now. Even if Saldrea figured out where we were, I had Vyns and Koar and Lhorine and my grandmother to help fight.

Koar returned to jaw-twitching stillness.

Maybe, if I just did it...?

I slid my legs apart and touched myself.

Koar grunted, that tell-tale bulge growing in his pants. He backed off, standing in the doorway, eyes glued to me. I grabbed my breast, hard, groping myself with one hand while working my slit with the other, till I was nice and wet.

Koar grunted and looked away.

I'd gone too far...

But no... he checked the hall, then his gaze slid back to me.

Okay... so we were doing this.

I looked at Vyns and nodded. He finished stripping and sat behind me, legs to either side of me. His hands replaced mine. Vyns knew exactly how to touch me. One hand high, one hand low, playing me like a cello, hitting *all* the right notes. I slid my hands up through my hair and gave a soft, heartfelt moan.

God, I'd needed this.

Forgetting about Koar, I closed my eyes, head lolling back on Vyns' shoulder, letting him work my body to a soft, shivering orgasm.

"Relaxed enough?" Vyns asked. "Need more?"

I did.

God, I missed Myel's soothing presence, that serene high, calm and content. Not only did I not have that, I had the exact opposite, feeling pain like jagged glass in my soul. I didn't just need to relax, I needed an orgasm so powerful it blew my mind and stilled my spirit, numbing the pain from Myel long enough for me to fall asleep.

"More," I begged. "An orgasm so strong I can't feel anything else." Wow... had I really demanded that?

Vyns' lips pressed to my shoulder. "Yes mistress."

A thrill sang through me at his use of that word. Usually, only Koar called me that. Was this his way of involving Koar as well. I didn't mind at all.

Vyns then whispered in my ear what he was thinking, and we quickly shifted into the new position. It was a reverse cowgirl, but with Vyns curled around behind me, able to use his hands. And once I was seated on him, his erection deliciously full and throbbing inside me, he opened his legs even more. My legs, already on the outside of his, were forced open as well, giving Koar a really good view of what was happening.

I glanced at the dragon once more. He leaned on the wall at the entrance to the room, his gaze darting from outside to in... to me. Both his fists were balled, everything about him tense and taut.

Then Vyns shifted, thrusting a little from below, hitting deep inside me so perfectly that my eyes crossed, vision blurring. Vyns' hands massaged my chest, my nipples so damn hard it hurt, breasts achingly sensitive. I moved on him as he moved below and the feel of him, of this position, of his hands in front and his hard chest behind, his kisses on my shoulder...

Tears leaked from my eyes at the contradiction of the pain in my soul and the pleasure of my body. Just as I'd asked for, the world melted away as I focused solely on Vyns.

Just a little more and I might tune out the pain.

"He's touching himself," Vyns whispered behind me.

I blinked, trying to focus my vision once again, and when I did... oh, God!

Koar had liberated the trapped erection from his pants, and he was every bit as big as I'd imagined. Well, not as impossibly big as my dream, but as far as real life dicks went...

So, they do make them in extra-large, I thought to myself as Vyns slid one hand down from my breasts to my clit and gently stroked me. And seeing the tightly-wound Koar stroking his dick as he watched me, combined with Vyns' perfect touch on my clit, his cock so damned deep inside me... was everything I needed.

The sound that issued from me was unlike anything I'd ever heard, a roar of primal lust and release. My body shuddered, my eyes crossed. I lost sight of Koar, though the image of him lingered in my mind. Vyns grunted, finding his peak and the feel of this dick pulsing hard inside me blasted the top off my pleasure. The orgasm swept through me in a torrent of heated bliss, followed by powerful aftershocks of ecstasy, which washed through my soul until I was a limp noodle of contentment.

Vyns lay back and I went with him, breathing hard, feeling only joy.

A part of me felt bad for denying Myel's pain, but I'd be no good for the man if I couldn't rest. And Vyns had made sure I was well and truly relaxed.

When I opened my eyes, Koar was gone.

But Vyns was close and warm, so I didn't feel unprotected.

Vyns and I slowly drew apart, but then cuddled close again, him behind me as he drew covers over us.

"Sleep well," he breathed.

I didn't have the words or energy to respond, half asleep

already. My last thought before falling into blessed darkness was:

I'm sorry, Myel.

For just as I'd felt his pain, he must have felt my pleasure and I honestly didn't know how that must feel, being in agony while his bonded was in bliss.

KOARTHANDRIS

I GRIPPED THE TIP OF MY COCK, WARM CUM OOZING BETWEEN my fingers, as I hurried across the compound to the bathroom. I didn't want to make a mess in Izzy's room. And I was going to make one hell of a mess.

I hadn't been with a woman in over a hundred years, since Mynrial, since that fated night, and that was a lot of pent-up arousal to deal with.

I found an empty bathroom, rushed in, and released myself... blasting the wall with cum. Heavy stream after heavy stream flowed out of me as I grunted, jerking my dick, the image of Izzy coming locked in my brain.

Blazing Skies, she'd been... divine, perfect, erotic and beautiful and powerful. The way her body arched back, chest thrust out, sweat glistening on her as she shook and shuddered... And that sound she'd let out. I'd never heard any woman make a noise like that, so full of release and relief, torn from her soul. Through that one intense utterance, I'd felt not only her pain, but also the therapeutic deliverance of her spirit from suffering. It had been pure and needful and raw, like a dragon's roar.

And that, more than anything else, had pushed me over the top.

I let my release spill out in waves, hard and pulsing at times, till I was spent. I leaned on the wall, one hand supporting myself, looking at the mess I'd made.

This was... unheard of.

No dragon had ever masturbated before. We had complete control of our bodies and minds and spirits. Self-pleasure wasn't forbidden, just... not needed. We kept ourselves for when we mated and we were fine with that. We didn't jerk off, because we didn't need to. But I'd needed to tonight.

The sight of other species copulating and mating shouldn't have affected me like this, but it had. Izzy had. She was... everything I desired, even if she wasn't a dragon... no, *because* she wasn't a dragon. My own kind were much like me, stalwart and hard. I'd mated with other dragons in the past, but our kind didn't see the act as one of love or desire, only procreation. It was a graceful and beautiful display, done high in the sky, in flight. But afterward, the female went her way to lay a clutch of fertilized eggs, ensuring they hatched safely, before giving them over to the elder females to raise as she went back to whatever she'd done before. Dragons... didn't care. But Izzy did.

She'd wanted me to join her tonight. She'd been good to me ever since I'd come to her side, rarely questioning my motives, accepting me. She was kind and generous and smart and beautiful. And she was also a beast, hard and tough and durable. She was what I wished the females of dragonkind were like. I'd spent too long around royalty. I expected more of my mate than a short time together, then parting ways. I expected them to be witty and compassionate, and most dragons weren't those things.

That's why Izzy was so perfect for me.

That's why I'd not been able to help myself tonight.

That's why I couldn't be with her, because, like tonight, I'd be distracted. I shouldn't have watched her and Vyns, but I'd not been able to stop myself, and look at me now. I'd abandoned my post. I needed to get back to her, but I also really needed to clean up in here.

What. A. Mess.

I washed up quickly, cleaning the room and myself before hurrying back to my post.

Yet nothing had happened. Izzy was safe, sleeping with Vyns.

There was even a guard outside her room: her grandmother.

Olinara raised a brow at me as I returned. She'd been in the main chamber of the compound when I'd run by, dick out.

"You're torturing yourself. You don't have to. Just be with her!" She sighed heavily. "Or be with me, I could look like her if that helps. Might help you get her off your mind if that's what you want?"

I growled.

She held up her hands. "Okay, that's not what you want... but Spirits, man, you can't keep going on like this. I've seen the way you look at her."

"It's nothing," I lied.

She saw right through me with a grimace and a look which said: *yeah right.*

"You can't keep beating yourself up for what happened over a hundred years ago!" she whispered intently.

She knew?

"How...?"

She rolled her eyes. "I hear things."

"Does everyone know of my failure?" I hissed, voice low.

"No. There are so very few who know the truth of what happened that night. I've pieced things together over time. Most don't want to look at it, don't want to see, don't want to aggravate Valnea. I don't really care. I'd wanted the truth, so I dug deeper than most. I know what happened."

"How I failed?"

"You made a mistake, a bad one, so what? You learn from it and move on, but you're not moving on. You're stuck in that night, in that place. And you're denying yourself and my granddaughter something you both want in the name of what? Duty?" She stuck out her tongue.

"Ever stop to think maybe you would have failed even if you'd been on duty?" she asked. No... no I hadn't. "Maybe it was an unwinnable event, they happen. We have to accept it, learn from it."

"I have learned. Learned not to forsake my duty."

"No..." She sighed heavily. "You haven't learned a damned thing. Or rather, you've learned the wrong damned thing."

"Oh, and what's that?"

She eyed me. "I'm so very tempted to tell you, and I would, if I thought you'd believe me or it would do any good. But you won't believe me, not yet, not now. You'll have to figure it out yourself for it to have any meaning."

I growled at her again.

She waved it off and left. "Back to your post, little guard dragon, since that's what you've made yourself. You could be so much more..."

And she was gone.

What had she meant?

What was the *wrong thing* I'd learned?

I shook it off. Olinara had always been an infuriating

woman. I'd keep doing what was right, protecting Izzy. That was my duty, no matter what my heart or my body might want.

No matter how much it hurt to see her with others.

No matter how good it had been to see her in bliss and know some tiny part of that was for me.

I sighed heavily, taking up my position outside her room once more.

I could never let Izzy down the way I had with Talmarion and Mynrial. I swore I'd never let that happen again.

Even as some part of me wondered what Olinara had been talking about. Maybe there was a way I could do my duty *and* be with Izzy?

No...

It was impossible.

Wasn't it?

IZZY

I ROSE FEELING REFRESHED AND A LITTLE MORE HOPEFUL THAT this final day of training might be enough to save Myel tonight.

I started the day with enchantments. This, thankfully, wasn't hard to learn. I didn't know why some magic felt far more natural to me than others, but simply putting someone to sleep, that didn't take long to master. Like Lhorine had said, it was like a binding, but far less invasive and intense. I had a good grasp on that after about an hour and a half, then moved on to transmutation.

This required a change of instructors since my grandmother was better with transmutation than Lhorine. I had to hope Olinara had some miracle way of describing transmutation that made it make sense, like she had with my nymph form.

"Now... I can't use earth magic," Olinara began. "But that doesn't mean I can't move earth." She focused on her hand and I watched as her fist turned from flesh to diamond.

It didn't look comfortable. Granma Oli winced and

grimaced as she finished. Then she dropped to one knee and punched the floor so hard stone bits went flying.

Holy crap-buckets!

Olinara rose and hissed as she returned her hand to normal.

"That didn't look like it felt good," I commented. "Also, damn, Grandma! That was amazing!"

She smiled. "You're right, it hurt like hell. Skin and bone and muscle weren't meant to be turned to diamond. I couldn't feel my hand anymore, and honestly, what hurt was the area where the rest of me connected with that bit, since it didn't know how to merge with such material. But yes, pretty neat, huh?"

I nodded.

"But let's start with something a bit easier." She gathered a bit of stone shard from the floor and clenched her fist around it. When she opened her hand, it had turned to a rough diamond.

"No wonder you're rich," I mumbled.

She laughed but shook her head. "No, as much as I can change this, it will revert to stone eventually. I've tried to lock its form, like I do with my own when shapeshifting, but I can't. You may be able to, with a binding."

I nodded. That was my hope. Though my goal wasn't to turn stone to diamond but turn Myel's flesh into something much more durable.

"So… is transmutation like shapeshifting?" I asked.

She bobbled her head. "Yes and no." Dropping the diamond, it clattered to the floor and slowly returned to stone. "When we shapeshift, we're only really changing our outsides, the rest of us, our inner organs and such, remains the same. We may stretch bones and make things a bit bigger or smaller, but that's not the same as turning all of that into something else entirely."

That made sense.

"And, like I said, it hurt when I turned my hand to diamond, the connection between flesh and diamond isn't natural and it resisted the change."

That didn't bode well for my plans with Myel.

"Would it be easier to change all of you to diamond, then?" I asked.

She gave me a stern look. "*Never* try that."

I raised a brow at that warning.

"Think about it, if your heart was a diamond, if your brain was a diamond, would you be a living thing anymore? No. Doing that essentially kills you, turns you into an unliving lump of material, a statue. You should technically return to normal eventually, but the damage is done, you'd be dead."

"Oh." Right... so I wouldn't be able to change all of Myel into diamond or stone or steel to make him tougher. But I didn't give up. There might be other things I could do. First, though, I'd have to learn more about transmutation.

"So... how do I think of it? What's the easy trick for me to understand this?" I hoped there was one.

Olinara sighed. "The trick — if there is one — is to believe it's easy. I can see it in your eyes, you're stupefied by me turning one thing into another. You have to believe it's as easy as snapping your fingers. And for someone who knows what they're doing, it is. I wanted that stone to become diamond, and I used my anima to make it so. Now... it should be said that the closer something is to the desired state, the easier the change. Flesh and bone to diamond is *a lot* harder than stone to diamond."

I nodded, lips tight. That certainly was a lot simpler of

an explanation than I'd been given in transmutation class, which had focused on the theory behind the changes, the molecular shifts and such. But as much as Olinara's description seemed simple, I wasn't so sure that would mean it was easy.

"Try it," Olinara said, picking up the same stone and handing it to me. "You won't learn until you've tried it... and failed... a few hundred times. So, let's get going on that." She gave a sweet smile. "Let's start with something easier than a diamond. That's a metamorphic rock... so try changing it to... marble."

And so began a morning of frustration. Grandma hadn't been wrong about the *failing a few hundred times* part.

Hours later, as noon drew close and I still hadn't made any progress. I threw the stone across the room and shouted in frustration, before collapsing to my knees in tears.

Transmutation wasn't a key part of my plan, I might be able to do without it, but I'd been worried that enhancing Myel wouldn't be enough, that I'd need to change him fundamentally for him to win. And I needed him to win. I couldn't let him die.

Then I'd die.

I had to do this... but I couldn't!

I was putting too much pressure on myself, but I couldn't not.

"Let's stop for now," Olinara said softly, kneeling next to me, a comforting hand on my back. "Believe it or not, you're doing well."

I huffed a snarky, sobbing laugh.

But then I wondered... "How would you even know that?"

That's when it hit me. "You... can sense what's happening with the stone?"

"And there it is," she whispered.

I wiped at my tears and swiveled my head to look at her. "Why didn't you tell me?"

"Yes… because me saying "feel the stone," would have helped you and not frustrated you more?"

I grimaced and bobbled my head accepting this.

"What… am I feeling for?"

Her turn to grimace. "That's the hard part. That's where all that theory you didn't like comes into play. If you know the essence of stone, you can see how to shift it to something else. Think of it like healing, searching within a body for the injured parts to fix, only they're not injured they're just… not the material you want them to be, and it's the whole thing, not just a part. All of which is easy to say, but there's still a lot of chemistry involved, and if you're like me, it took me a while to understand all of that."

I rolled my eyes, my frustration returning

"But… luckily… you're not like me," she added quickly.

I raised a brow.

"You're part elf… you know earth magic. Use that! Unfortunately, I can't help you with that bit."

I blinked.

Use earth magic?

Of course!

Still on my knees, I laid my hand on the stone floor and softened it, so I could scoop up a handful. Then I hardened it again. That I could do easily enough. So… could I just…

I tried changing the stone to marble with earth magic, not transmutation…

Nothing.

Oh…

So earth magic could *manipulate* earth but not change its nature.

I tried to *feel* into the stone. I closed my eyes and concentrated on the lump in my hand. I did feel something, but since I didn't know what stone was supposed to feel like it was all a mystery to me. Still, I used my connection to the stone — probing deep within it — then added some anima, to will it to change to marble.

The stone shifted… slightly.

"Oh! Hey… you did it… sort of…" Oli cheered. "I think that's quartzite!"

Opening my eyes, I looked at the stone in my hand. It had changed, just not to marble.

"Huh…"

That… hadn't been so hard.

I smiled at my grandmother, got up and went back to work. An hour later, I could transmute stone to marble. I was still a long way from changing flesh to something harder, and I still didn't know if it would work without Myel being in constant pain… but I'd taken the first step.

We kept going after lunch.

Since my goal was to be able to do this on another person, that meant we got Koar involved. He volunteered, ever eager to help. He had no clue what he was getting himself into, however. He spent the next few hours screaming in pain as I tried to change him into stone or steel and failed repeatedly.

As evening set in, I finally had some success. I changed Koar's hand to steel, which I'd found easier than stone. The only hitch was… I could only do it while holding his wrist and actively maintaining the barrier between his flesh and the steel, which took a lot out of me, and was far from my ideal result.

But I'd run out of time.

In a couple hours, I'd be infiltrating the arena prisons to see Myel.

I ate my dinner — a large one, since I was famished from all this grueling work — in silence. After dinner, Koar gave me more of his life essence to help revive me further. I wanted to practice a bit more after that, but both Lhorine and my grandmother said they had a better idea.

"You know the basics at this point," Lhorine said. "Everything you wanted to know, you know. You need time and practice and hopefully you'll have that tonight with your bonded. And perhaps the bond will help the process?" She didn't sound convinced of that.

"And since you need to conserve your energy," Olinara picked up the thread, "we thought we'd take this time to tell you more about your parents."

My parents?

Now?

"Do you think it will help?"

The two shared a look, then nodded.

"Yes," Olinara said softly. "You need to know the legacy you carry, the power and potential within you. Maybe, once you understand that, you'll see how powerful you really are."

IZZY

"Your mother, Ysania, was... different," Lhorine began with a wistful tone. "Everyone saw it. She wasn't like most elves, didn't see herself as superior. She was the most... down to earth elf I've ever met and also not afraid to call out the inconsistencies and prejudices of her own kind." The woman sighed. "Even I wasn't that brave."

"And she loved freely," Olinara added. "Not afraid to tell the world she loved my son and that there was absolutely nothing wrong with that. It... infuriated a lot of elves. Her mother, Queen Leastrine, tried to quiet such speeches, smooth things over with elven kind, but in the end Ysania was too vocal, too brazen. She was dedicated to changing this world and the real trouble was... some people were starting to listen. That made the traditional elves furious."

"That's why she was exiled." Lhorine picked up the telling. "The queen was wise enough to see that things were starting to change... but that Ysania was pushing things too far too fast. If Ysania had stayed, she'd probably have been assassinated. So, the queen sent her away and let things cool down, all the while subtly encouraging the changes her daughter had instigated."

"Twenty years later, and the views of nearly all the royals and many others had shifted, enough that..." Olinara pursed her lips.

"That Valnea killed my family," I finished.

The two women nodded.

"Your mother did more to change elven culture in twenty years than anyone had done over the many millenniums of elven rule."

I smiled, suddenly damn proud of my mom. Then a tear leaked from my eye, sad that I'd never gotten to know her.

"But it wasn't her ideals that changed things for the elves," Lhorine said with a note of awe in her voice. "It was her power."

I perked up.

"If she'd just been some third-rate earth wielder, I doubt many, perhaps even her own family, would have paid her much mind," Lhorine continued. "But she was one of the strongest earth wielders in generations, perhaps ever. When her older brother Jyrandion got married, she and a dryad friend built the happy couple a new castle outside of El'Anderyn. She single-handedly summoned marble from miles away, shifting it through the earth to become gleaming towers and sturdy walls. The legend was, she could snap her fingers and shatter mountains."

"And there was good reason for that belief," Grandma picked up the telling. "When she took the test of power, the glasstone shone with blinding white light, then cracked and crumbled. When sparring with her brothers and sisters, who were no slouches themselves, she regularly bested them without much effort."

"That's the legacy you have inherited," Lhorine said softly.

"But when I tested, I was only orange, which I'm guessing isn't great," I said.

Lhorine shook her head. "Olinara told me you were under your mother's binding at the time. She must have limited your strength and abilities. You are most definitely *not* orange rank anymore. I was here, off campus, when you fought Saldrea, yet I *felt* your last push of power. The earth itself shuddered. That was something I hadn't felt since your mother."

I blinked.

"Oh..."

I mean, yeah, I had overpowered Saldrea and Golana together and that had been a herculean feat, but... these two were saying I was some super-elf? Or at least the daughter of a super-elf.

"We're telling you this, so you can be confident in your abilities tonight," Olinara said, laying a hand on my shoulder. She smiled. "My son was a fairly powerful nymph as well, and if I had to guess, you got the best of both your parents."

A wave of self-consciousness swept over me.

"Really?"

I certainly did *not* feel that powerful most of the time.

The two nodded.

"You have your mother's power," Lhorine whispered. "You are her legacy. Let that guide you tonight."

This was a lot to take in, but I wasn't upset that these two had taken the time to tell me. I certainly felt more confident knowing what I was *potentially* capable of.

"Thank you," I said, bowing my head to these women,

my mentors. "Thank you for everything, all you've taught me, all you've told me. Thank you."

The two stepped closer and embraced me tightly.

Then Vyns gave me a long kiss for good luck and we headed out.

We had a narrow window in which to apprehend the succubus, who was to be Myel's conjugal visit, and take her place. We had to wait till after dark, so we wouldn't be seen out and about on campus, but that didn't give us long before she was likely to leave.

She lived in a small residence for non-students attached to the campus bar and lounge. Grandma Oli had spent all day yesterday staking out the place and learning the forms of others who lived in the dorm. She and I snuck in, disguised, found the room in question and walked right in. The succubus hadn't locked her door.

Olinara quickly enveloped the woman in a cocoon of water, ensuring it wouldn't get into her lungs. That suffocated the succubus to the point of passing out. At which point I healed her, to ensure she'd be okay, then we bound and gagged her. The others were let in through the window. They'd remain here, watching the succubus and hiding.

I studied the woman, ensuring I had her form down pat, then used Grandma's trick to lock in the form, so it wouldn't slip on my way to see Myel.

The succubus had been dressed and ready, so I put on her dress, in case it was known to anyone else. And by dress, I meant lingerie: a barely there baby-doll in black lace with nothing underneath. Why did it not surprise me that a succubus wouldn't mind showing off *everything* to the world?

Sigh.

At least it wasn't my body I'd be flaunting when I went out. Also, thankfully, the arena wasn't far away.

"Ready?" Vyns asked.

"As I'll ever be," I said and blew out a breath, trying to relax and act casual.

"I wish I could go with you," Koar said, frustration lacing his voice. He'd not be able to protect me during this covert mission. "I know your voice, your spirit. If you're in trouble shout as loud as you can, I'll hear you and come."

Good to know.

"Thanks," I said, laying a hand on his chest, feeling his sturdy form. I wasn't sure if the gesture was to reassure him or me, but it seemed to do both. I breathed a little easier and Koar let out a long sigh as well.

I headed out, trying to act like a nonchalant succubus in next to nothing. It was a level of body-confidence I wasn't used to. Being confident wearing something revealing was one thing but being brazen enough to wear next to nothing... this was new. I tried not to think too much about the few lingering looks I got as I strode to the arena. Oddly, I didn't get as many oglers as I would have thought.

How common was this? Did succubi walk around naked all the time? There were still so many things about this world I was getting used to.

A few people called out this succubi's name and waved as I passed, I waved back, keeping responses to a minimum.

Entering the arena was easy. Guards let me pass, knowing who I was. Koar and Vyns both knew the way to the dungeons and had given me instructions. I only got lost twice making my way into the dark depths of the massive structure.

The holding area wasn't pleasant, smelling of human waste and rotting flesh. I cringed at the conditions and tried not to gag or vomit. After all my training, I had rather strong control of my body now, so I sturdied myself and continued.

"Hey! Here she is boys!" one of the three guards called when I came into view. He was an ogre, heavy with muscle, but something in his eyes made me think he wasn't too smart. "Finally!" he cried out, then began undoing his pants.

Sorry? What now?

The other two men began doing the same.

It hit me. They never intended for me to see Myel. I'd be pleasuring them instead.

Yeah... no.

"You boys ready for a night you'll never remember?" I asked.

"Don't you mean, never forget?" one replied absently as he dropped his pants.

"No... I do not."

I put the three of them to sleep.

I found the keys and unlocked the door. There was no light within. I brought in a lantern from outside and hissed when I saw the limp, naked, beaten and filthy form on the floor.

"Myel?" I whispered, shocked. I shouldn't have been, I'd known what he was going through.

The form cringed and whimpered and tried to roll away.

I went to him.

"Myel, it's me!"

But he still flinched when I touched him.

It was only as I sent soothing healing through him that he blinked open what had been swollen-shut eyes and looked at me.

"Who?" he asked, confused.

Oh... right.

I shifted my form back to myself.

"Izzy?" he breathed in surprise. "You came?"

He'd doubted me. Though perhaps I'd doubt everything if I'd endured what he had. I didn't blame him.

"Yes, I'm here," I whispered. "I'll be right back." I rose and checked outside quickly. No one around but the three guards. I quickly positioned them so it looked like they'd fallen asleep naturally, one slumped in a chair, one sitting with his torso over the small table, the last leaning against the wall in a corner. Then I closed the door of Myel's cell — ensuring I still had the keys — to make sure no one saw what we were about to do. To make double sure, and to block out any noise, I also raised a stone wall in front of the door on the inside.

There. We were safe, blocked in, but safe.

I returned to Myel and finished healing him.

I didn't know if it was the intense magical training I'd done or the supposed power I possessed, but I wasn't winded at all after: putting the guards to sleep, healing Myel, and using earth magic to block the door.

Hopefully that meant I could do what I needed to do tonight.

"I'm so glad to see you," Myel whimpered, seeming like a shell of the man I'd known only a few days ago: so weak and uncertain.

"And me you," I said, as I stood back and summoned water to douse him. I did it several times, scrubbing off the filth in between showers to get him as clean as I could. His clothes were shredded, no longer even worth calling clothes, so he'd have to remain naked.

A drain in the floor collected the water I'd summoned, and a byproduct of having cleansed him was a semi-clean area of stone floor as well.

"I don't know how long this is going to take, so I should

get started," I said. "I'll explain as I go," I added at his confused look. "The gist of it is, I'm going to enhance you, make you stronger and tougher and faster... and if I'm able... I'm going to turn part of you into steel. Then I'm going to undo the binding on your collar so you can use all your powers tomorrow. Got it?"

He looked baffled. "How...?"

"I'm still working on the how, so bear with me." I tilted my head, sweeping hair off my neck. "And you should drink. You'll want to be strong for what is to come. We have a long night ahead of us."

MYELAS

As I drank from Izzy, the delirium in which I'd floated, a place of weariness and pain and confusion, slowly dissipated as my body regained strength, feeling whole again. I was still exhausted, not having slept more than an hour or so at a time — and probably not more than five or six hours total — over the last few days. And I'd only gotten that much sleep because of the laziness of my three captors. They'd taken a few too many breaks. A tiny blessing.

But now Izzy was here, looking like something from my fevered dreams in that lacy black "dress."

Once I'd had my fill, which was a lot — and Izzy was somehow still standing strong — I backed off and let her do what she'd come to do. We sat, and she got to work remaking me, enhancing me, making it so I could fight and win tomorrow.

"Why not... take me away, hide me from the world?" I asked now that my mind had cleared of the heavy fog which had bogged it down for so long. "Why remake me?"

"Huh...?" Izzy said, stopping the work she'd just started to give a confused little laugh. "I hadn't even thought of that." She seemed to consider the option. "Is that what you want? I'd figured you'd be free if you won this fight, and it's better to be free than hidden away."

She said it so matter-of-factly that I almost missed the significance of it.

She didn't want to hide me from the world. She wanted me free, to be out in the world, even with everyone knowing we were bonded. I shouldn't have been surprised, knowing Izzy, but I still was. I'd convinced myself, during my delirium, that Izzy had no more need of me, that I was useless, a burden.

And here she was, reminding me *yet again* that that wasn't the case.

Why did I always fall back on my fears so quickly, so easily?

It took Izzy time, and it was damned uncomfortable — sometimes downright painful — as she *changed* me. I hissed and grunted and she apologized a lot, apparently she hadn't fully mastered doing this yet and was learning as she went, but I didn't mind. I would endure any pain for her, especially to get stronger. And frankly it was nothing compared to what I'd been put through these last two days.

To distract me from the pain and my dark thoughts, Izzy and I talked. It was an awkward conversation, happening in fits and starts. She was often too busy concentrating on her work, and I slid easily back into my own thoughts, trying to understand why my fears always returned to haunt me.

"I'm so sorry you have to endure all of this," Izzy whispered. "This cell, those guards, the pain of this transformation... all for me."

"I'd do anything for you," I breathed, gasping as Izzy ran her hands over my wings, changing flesh and bone to strengthened steel.

Izzy sat back with a huff, perhaps needing a break. I flashed away my wings, since it hurt to have them partially transformed and exposed. When I vanished them, they didn't bother me at all. That had been Izzy's solution to the problem of joining steel to flesh. If she only transformed my wings, I'd be able to use them as shields or even weapons — since she was putting a razors edge on them — then put them away to avoid the pain. I'd also lose my ability to fly in my human or hybrid forms, but that wasn't a huge loss, since I had other ways to travel. Also, it seemed my wings returned to normal as a bat, so I could still fly that way if needed.

"Are you sure it's okay?" Izzy probed. "You've seemed so... distant lately."

She'd noticed.

I sighed heavily. Here and now, in this disgusting dungeon, with both of us tired and our future hanging in the balance, didn't seem like the best time to discuss this. But then, if I didn't survive tomorrow, this might be our last and only time to talk.

Time to be strong: be honest.

"I'm worried that you'll discard me, that you won't need me once you've come into your power, once you're queen."

"What?" She sounded completely taken aback and shifted around to kneel on the grimy floor in front of me. "Why would you think that?" She grimaced. "Is this because of Safir?"

My mentor had mentioned — more than a few times — how much better off Izzy would be if she broke our bond.

I shook my head. "I've... always worried." A faint, sad smile lifted my lips. "You've been such a blessing upon my life. But you have to understand, I've never had anything solid to hold on to. My life has always been a struggle. No one has ever given a shit about me. Well, that's not true, Safir cared... but only insofar as I was useful to him. To everyone else... I'm an expendable pawn. I've never had any hope for a bright future... until you came along."

She smiled softly, but I could see the sadness behind it. My words hit her hard. She hadn't known the depths of despair I'd suffered before I'd met her.

"You give me hope, but... you're an elf." I didn't mean to say the word with as much contempt as I did. "A royal." I hung my head. "I'm nothing. I know you keep saying you want me in your life and you'll keep me around, but... you've changed so much this past week. What if this world changes you *too much* and you don't see me the same anymore? You will always have the power to break our bond and there's nothing I can do about that."

She raised a hand to cup my cheek.

"I'm so sorry you've had to endure what you have," she whispered, then leaned in and kissed me softly. My lips tingled, the bond thrumming contentedly between us. When she drew back, she continued, her face close, her scent of apples and cinnamon filling my senses.

"But you know I want to change this world, break down the power structure the elves have built and make sure everyone can live free and love who they want. You... know that, right?"

I nodded, but my lips were tight. "I know that's what you want *now*... but what if you get a taste for power and..." I shrugged.

"Do you trust me that little? Do you really not know me?" She seemed hurt.

"I... want to trust you, want to believe you, but you have to understand the weight of this world and thousands of years of oppression."

She nodded and sighed heavily. "Yes, I'm sorry, I didn't mean to question your faith in me. I can't imagine how hard it must have been, living with the horrible traditions of this place." Her gaze locked onto mine. "Which is why I *need* you in my life, Myel."

I raised a brow.

"I need you to keep reminding me of your previous pain and my purpose. I..." She pursed her lips and blew out a breath through her nose. "I know I've changed, and frankly I have no clue what I'll do if I become queen. I want to change things, but I have no clue *how* to do that. Hopefully, with you by my side — with all my friends, my new family — helping me, and keeping me in line, then *we all* can change this world."

I wanted to believe her so damned much, but it was hard to have faith in this dark, dank cell. Even with Izzy here, helping me, altering me so I'd be able to win my freedom tomorrow, I still had doubts.

She must have seen it.

"Let's take it one day at a time, one horrible misadventure at a time, okay?" she said with a half-smile. "I care for you now... that's what matters. And once you've survived this... we can talk more, check in again, communicate as often as we need to. That's what people in relationships do, right?"

I nodded, giving my own wary smile.

She gave another breathy little laugh. "I thought so, but I haven't had a stable relationship in... ever. So, you're my first." It was meant to be a joke, but I couldn't appreciate it. "Just... keep letting me know what you're thinking, what you're worried about, and I'll keep being there for you, like you've been there for me," she finished.

I smiled truly at that. "As long as you'll have me, I'll be

there for whatever you need. I've made up my mind to serve you every way I can, for as long as I can, be that a few days or the rest of our lives."

She nodded. "Let's hope it's that second option."

By the spirits, I hoped so.

"Who knows," she said wistfully. "Maybe our love will change the world!"

Maybe.

I couldn't quite imagine what that looked like, but I loved that she believed it was possible.

"Now, are you ready to fight for your freedom?" she asked, sitting up on her knees a bit more. "I'm ready to get back to work."

I turned, giving her my back and flashing out my wings again. "I'm ready," I said, wincing and hissing at the pain. Even just having my partially transformed wings out hurt like hell. Once they were fully converted, I didn't know whether that would hurt more or less. Whichever it was, I'd get used to it. Because Izzy was doing all of this to help me, and I'd endure any hardship or pain to win my freedom and extend our lives together.

Izzy worked through the night, turning my wings to steel, filling me with strength and speed and fortitude as only an elf could, then binding it all in place. She also broke the binding on the collar that restrained my abilities.

A couple times during the night, she left the cell to ensure the guards remained asleep.

And when she was done transforming me, I felt like a whole new me. I'd thrash Artol if I fought him now.

"There's one last thing I'd like to do before I go," she breathed as we both stood. She doused us both in water, sluicing off the filth we'd acquired as she'd worked. That plastered her dress to her form. Spirits, she was stunning.

Even more so than her beauty, her entire aura and demeanor was sexy as hell, strong and determined and kind.

The bond tugged and... since I had no clothes to hide it — and Izzy had given me the strength and vitality to fuel it — I couldn't conceal my arousal.

She looked at my rising cock and smiled.

"Oh... I see you had the same thought." She slipped off that barely-there dress and came to me. Her sexy-as-sin body pressed against me, fulfilling all my dreams and desires, as her needful lips found mine.

Our bond wasn't demanding it, but with the pressure and expectation of the fight to come, we both needed this.

MYELAS

Izzy hopped up, legs wrapping around me. Even before she'd added to my strength, I could hold her with ease. Now, she was light as air.

Izzy lifted herself a little more, her lips pulling away from mine, my face in line with the bounty of her chest. I feasted on her perfect breasts, sucking a hardening nipple into my mouth as she spoke softly.

"You know," she breathed, gasping as I flicked her nipple with my tongue. "That spirit sex we had was *damned* hot and so *deep*, but I missed *this*... touching you.

As had I, and she had to be aware of how much I'd missed her, given the raging hot hardness of my cock trapped between us. She slowly shifted her pubic bone over it, rousing me even more.

But there was no way I'd give in to my desire just yet. There was a chance this might be our last time together, and if so, I wanted to leave a lasting impression.

I buried my face between her heavenly breasts, kissing over her heart. With her death-grip around my waist, I didn't really need to hold her, so I slid my hands between her thighs and my hips, cupping under her legs once more before lifting her suddenly.

Izzy yelped in surprise as I pulled her up, till my face was buried in another heavenly place. She put her legs on my shoulders, hands on my head to steady herself as my lips sought to please her.

She was already molten, so damned hot and wet. I licked my tongue over her, raking deep through her folds and flicking off her clit. She gasped above me, her legs tightening around my head, even as she angled her hips to give me better access.

Most people didn't know that bats had particularly long tongues. I shifted that one part of me and speared it into her.

"Holy fucking, what-the, YES!" she cried out, fingers raking over my scalp as she tensed. My tongue lapped at her G-spot as I created suction over her clit, sucking hard and savoring this amazing moment.

"Fuck! Oh, God! How...?" Izzy gasped, then her body tensed and convulsed, her core flooded with liquid desire. She tasted like the purest nectar on my elongated tongue. I kept my mouth over her, drinking down her release as she trembled and gave the sexiest little gasps over and over.

Finally, she laughed through her panting breaths. "Well, no man's ever gone down on me like *that* before."

I let her down, her mouth meeting mine with fierce desire, seeming to care little for her taste still on my lips. She devoured me as I — still holding her thighs and controlling her hips — played my rigid tip over her searing hot core.

She pulled her lips off mine, leaning forward to breathe steamy whispers in my ear.

"You need to put that thick fucking dick inside me and fill me with your hot cum."

I groaned at her heated words.

She pulled back, hands on my shoulders.

"Unless your goal is to destroy me with orgasms before you get yours?" she breathed. "Though that might make it hard for me to walk out of here." Her sea-green eyes flashed with excitement at that thought.

In that instant, I admired her control. Her eyes usually changed color when aroused, but they were as solid a sea-green as when she'd come in. She had changed, but not all of it was bad.

"If that's what you want," I said with a grin.

"I— Oh!" Whatever she'd been about to say was lost as I took her nipple in my mouth again. At the same time I dipped her body to let my tip play in her folds, then drew it out and ground it over her clit.

Our bond made every contact so much more sensitive, heated, and impactful. So, even sucking on one nipple, while alternating between penetrating her and rubbing my dick over her clit, eventually made her come.

"Fuck me!" she hissed as she trembled in my arms, soaking my cock with her release.

Then I forced her hips down while thrusting up to meet her, filling her perfectly before she had a chance to recover.

Her body arched, tense, hands clasping my shoulders as her hips crashed against me, rocking and bucking with abandon. Her head lolled back, mouth open but making no sound.

There was something utterly divine about Izzy mid-orgasm.

I savored this instant, drinking in my lover's perfect form, her heavenly ecstasy. I relished the feel of her scorching wetness clamped around my cock and luxuriated in the pounding need hammering through our bond. My own desire elevated to match hers, my dick throbbed, seeking release, but I restrained it. Instead, I thrusted harder, our hips crashing together, our passion run wild.

With her legs like a vice around my waist, I no longer needed my hands to support her and slid them up her sweat-slicked body to her breasts, grasping hard.

A primal scream echoed up from deep within her. Then, her head whipped forward. She couldn't speak but her lips formed the words: "Yes! Now!"

I let out a savage roar of my own as I gave into the demand of my body and filled her with my release. My cock pulsed so hard it hurt. Izzy's eyes crossed, her body convulsing in time with mine, her fingers digging into my shoulders as her body twisted and writhed.

Tears left my eyes at the perfect completeness of our merged desire, the utmost fulfillment of our bond.

I pulled Izzy close, hugging her tight as we trembled through that sublime moment.

And when, eventually we finished, she remained holding me tight, legs around my waist.

I didn't want to let her go either.

But then slowly, she pulled back.

"Vyns' spirit has shifted," she said. I didn't know what that meant, and she didn't seem entirely certain herself. "He's... worried? I think he's trying to tell me something, perhaps that it's nearly morning and I should go."

Still we lingered, kissing lightly, brushing lips and holding each other close.

Then, with a sigh, which seemed to blow through both of us, we separated. And yes, she wobbled as she tested her legs.

Mission accomplished.

She doused us both again, then put on her little dress and brought down her stone wall, heading for the door before blowing me a kiss.

"Your form," I reminded her.

"Oh… yes. Thank you." And she became a different woman, a succubus if I had to guess.

She locked me in, then shouted at the guards to wake up.

"Really? I was so uninteresting you fell asleep? I've been waiting for you to wake up and give me a good time all night! You three are fucking losers. I'm outta here."

I hid the sound of my laugh, then blew out a breath.

From here on out, I was on my own. Izzy had done her best to ensure my chances of winning, but now it was up to me to fight.

And fight I would.

I'd do anything to get back to Izzy, my heart, my home. She was the reason I fought. And maybe, if I fought hard enough for long enough, I might eventually feel worthy of that miraculous woman.

AMARHUK (ROOK)

I SHOULDN'T BE OUT.

I shouldn't be here.

But I also couldn't sit in the confines of Svokol's residence while Myel fought for his life. I barely knew that dark and sexy shifter, but he was important to Izzy, bonded to her, and I knew what would happen if that bond was broken. So, I'd sneaked out to the arena to watch the match, as macabre and vile as it might be.

It was easy to get lost in the crowd; everyone had turned out for this event. Cliffside Arena could hold the entirety of everyone on campus plus a couple thousand more people, and it was packed. I blended in and took a seat high in the top ring of the stands.

I'd been playing my encounter with Izzy two days ago over and over in my head and I'd hoped the hubbub of the throng around me might drown out my thoughts, but no... my churning mind tuned out the white noise of the assembled on-lookers.

What are you so damned afraid of, she'd asked me.

I'd told her it was her being an elf, and I'd seen the

pain that had caused. I shouldn't have said it. I shouldn't have said anything. I should have taken the coward's way out and stayed silent. Instead, I'd taken the jerk's way out and thrown it back on her, when it had nothing to do with her.

Well it did, but not because of who she was.

I was falling for her, and it was tearing me apart. Incubi were not meant to be monogamous. Even if we married, which wasn't common, our mates knew we'd still have other partners. It had to be an open marriage or no incubi would agree to it. But something was very wrong with me, because I didn't want anyone but Izzy. No other woman interested me, roused me, did anything for me.

It was so damned wrong!

And so damned right!

How could that be?

But I'd already screwed it up by telling her I was afraid of her as an elf.

I was such an idiot.

She hadn't wanted anything deep; I'd known that from the first time I'd met her in the human realm. So how could I tell her I was falling for her, that she was starting to mean something to me, far more than the friends and fuck-buddies we'd been?

Even if I *could* mend the tear in our relationship... it wasn't like I knew anything about being a dedicated lover and caregiver and *husband*. Ugh. That word made me want to gag.

I'd only make a mess of any sort of committed relationship.

And that wasn't fair to her.

It would also only break our hearts. She was about to fight one hell of a battle against everything this world stood for. What if she died? What if I died? That sort of heartbreak tore a person apart. I'd seen it happen to my mother.

As a succubus, she was supposed to have many partners and not love any of them. Lust was all that mattered. My father shouldn't have been anything more than another one of her lovers, but he had been. Yet, as a salmaeri, he'd been called to war and died. And it had shattered her. She'd made sure to tell me, over and over, that love only led to pain, and I believed her.

Blazing hell, Mother would be so ashamed of me for being this tied up over a woman. Though, oddly, I had a suspicion that Izzy and my mother would get along great. Even so, Mom would scold me for falling for anyone, even someone she liked, like Izzy.

And what made matters all the worse was my mental connection to Izzy. I literally couldn't get her out of my head. I'd caught a ton of stray thoughts last night. Her frustration, matched by her drive to help Myel. Her anxiety and worry for her bondmate. Then her rather stunning euphoria, which had invaded my dreams, then woken me in a sweat of desire. My dick had been so damned hard for so long. I'd had to get up and beat it down, fantasizing about — you guessed it — Izzy to get any sort of relief.

This was so messed up.

I was so messed up.

Izzy messed me up in ways I'd never imagined.

I banged my forehead with my fist, eyes clenched shut, somehow hoping the physical action would knock thoughts of Izzy out of my mind. It didn't.

The thing was, I couldn't really deny it any longer.

I had feelings for Izzy.

As strange and uncomfortable and abnormal as that

was. I wanted her and only her and if I didn't have her again soon, I might explode in frustration.

But first, I'd have to apologize for the whole *scary elf* thing.

That would be fun.

Not.

Still, avoiding her hadn't done anything. Like the old saying said, her absence had made my heart grow fonder. The part of the saying most people left out was how my blue-balls had gotten bluer.

I needed her. So. Damn. Bad.

I'd find her after this match and tell her as much. Even if I didn't know what I'd say.

As for what would happen after that? I had no clue. But what other options did I have? Avoid her and be in agony or be with her and enjoy it while it lasted... then be in agony when I lost her or know she'd be in agony if she lost me. There were no good choices.

I stopped banging my head. All that had given me was a headache.

A voice rang out, saying the match was about to start.

The crowd hushed.

I opened my eyes and leaned forward.

"Come on, Myel, shred this bastard," I whispered.

He needed to win, or I'd lose Izzy even before I'd had a chance to really be with her. Now I was even *more* upset about that potential outcome.

Fuck me.

Just...

Fuck me.

MYELAS

I WASN'T SURE IF IZZY HAD DONE SOMETHING TO THE GUARDS on my cell — perhaps some lingering effect putting them to sleep — but they didn't come in and beat me up before my match. I had to smile when this fact got them chewed out by Golana when she came to get me. I made sure to hide that smile when she entered the cell.

Golana saw me standing there, unbruised and clean as a whistle, and raised a brow.

"Were the guards not supposed to send for a healer and douse me with water this morning?" I asked... getting those three jailors in even more trouble. It wasn't like they could deny what was right in front of them.

Golana said nothing, but I could tell she was suspicious as hell.

"Saves me the trouble of bathing you before sending you to your death," she muttered, then jerked her head for me to follow her. I did, my three captors falling in behind us as we wound through the dungeons, then up to the level of the arena floor, where I was outfitted.

I was given a simple pair of pants and a shirt. Over that, I wore a hardened leather chest piece, which had been worn away on the inside. To everyone in the stands, it would look like a piece of simple armor, but it was paper thin and would do little to protect me.

Before it was put on, Golana punched me in the gut again. I'd been expecting something like this and reacted as I had the first time, several days ago, but this time, it was an act. The strike was more like someone's regular punch, not the organ-rearranging, dwarf-empowered hit it should have been.

Several helpers hauled me to my feet and put the armor on me, handing me a rusty short sword as my only weapon. Izzy had told me my opponent would be a troll. This small weapon would do nothing against their long-armed reach.

"Good luck," Golana muttered, then a heavy gate lifted and I was pushed out into the arena.

The crowd cheered as I staggered a few steps. Looking up, the stands were completely packed. I hadn't thought I'd be much of a draw, but then... if word had gotten out that I was secretly bonded to an elf, that might have peaked the macabre curiosity of some. Perhaps the troll on trial was famous as well?

I shrugged off those thoughts as the gate on the far side of the arena opened and a massive form lumbered out.

I sighed.

Of course the troll I'd be facing would be the biggest, nastiest-looking troll I'd ever seen. Trolls had been subjugated by dwarves generations ago, trained to help with mining and be front-line warriors and protectors. They were to dwarves what dragons were to the elves. As such, they were big and tough. But this one was over seven feet tall, with muscles bulging all over his massive frame and scars all over those muscles.

He wore no armor and had no weapons, thankfully. As much as Saldrea and her goons could cheat by hindering me, they couldn't break thousands of years of tradition and give weapons to a convict. Not that it mattered much, his long arms had a better reach than my little sword and his heavy fists would hit like hammers. Trolls also possessed some physical magic, so he might be able to enhance himself, assuming his binding collar wasn't working, which I wouldn't put past Saldrea. Some trolls also had the ability to manipulate darkness. That didn't bother me. I was quite at home in the dark.

A gong sounded, breaking my assessment of my opponent and starting the fight.

The troll charged, strong legs propelling him across the arena.

For a second, I debated whether to draw this fight out and play things up for the crowd, lose a little to have my win be that much more significant. I decided against it. I'd go with shock and awe instead.

When the troll reached me, one big fist descending toward my head, I spun in toward him, flashing out my wings and curving them around me like a shield. Pain surged from where my wings connected to my back, but I ignored it. My wings emerging had the side effect of cutting away my armor and tearing through my shirt, mostly shredding it, leaving me topless.

The troll's fist hit the steel shell of my wings around me, like a clapper hitting a bell, and he yelped in surprise.

I spread my wings wide, still spinning, and let the razor's edge Izzy had put on the front of my wings take the troll just above the knee. With my enhanced strength, plus that cutting steel, I sliced through both of the troll's legs with ease.

The big creature toppled forward, screeching in pain. I completed my spin and severed his head from his body before it even hit the ground.

I walked away from the massacre with my wings shining in the sun.

Silence filled the arena for a heartbeat... before everyone erupted in cheers and applause. Then, the shouts and ovations became a steady chant:

"Steelwing! Steelwing! Steelwing!"

Looked like I had a new nickname.

I raised my wings and arms in triumph, playing to the crowd, before flashing my wings away, because they hurt like hell. But I kept pumping my fists into the air.

Spirits! It felt good to win, to have my freedom back, to have tens of thousands of people cheering for me.

It was one of the rare times in my life when I felt truly powerful and admired, not a common feeling for me.

It didn't last.

Men came to clean up the dead troll. Six others came to collect me, and given they were a mix of dragons and titans, I knew who'd sent them: Saldrea.

No, no, no, no, no!

I couldn't fight all these guards, not dragons and titans. My enhanced strength and steel wings might take a couple down if I was lucky, but against six...?

To everyone else in the stands, it would look like an honor guard, but in reality, I was trapped. Even if I transformed into a bat to fly away, there was a magical barrier over the fighting part of the arena to keep flying creatures contained.

No, my only chance was to wait till I was in the dimly lit

confines of the preparation room, then I could shadow-step away.

But I never got the chance.

I had to be fully out of bright light to use my shadow-step and Golana was right at the entrance waiting for me. She grabbed my arm and some enchantment washed over me. I collapsed into darkness, unconscious.

And when I woke, despite being in an even darker place... I couldn't shadow-step for some reason. Also, Saldrea was right beside me.

Her smile was cruel, with a hint of curiosity.

"Tell me, you little shit, who helped you? How did your collar lose its binding? Who gave you those fancy steel wings?"

I couldn't move. I lay on a cold stone floor with Saldrea kneeling next to me and the rest of her crew close by.

Fuck. This wasn't good.

"Tell me," Saldrea hissed. "I've already bound you to this place unable to move. I could bind you to tell the truth, but if I have to do that, you're *really* not going to like it."

I believed her.

"Izzy," I said, my voice tight. It felt like there was an iron band around my throat pinning me to the ground. There might actually be, though I guessed it was the force of Saldrea's binding. "She snuck in, pretended to be the succubus, she altered me and broke the binding on my collar."

"That cheating little bitch," Saldrea spat the words as she rose. "Not playing by the rules, are we?"

I didn't point out that Saldrea *never* played by the rules, since I should be free right now.

"I'll make her pay for that," Saldrea murmured with a hint of glee. She looked down at me. "But first... you'll pay for your part in her treachery." She laughed. "If you thought those jailors were tough on you... I'm a thousand times worse."

I believed her. There were lurid legends of Saldrea's torture. Nothing could prepare me for what would come next.

IZZY

Myel was missing.

Everyone had been looking, even Rook, who'd found us after Myel had won the fight. The incubus had wished to congratulate Myel and also mentioned wanting to talk to me, but he hadn't yet had the chance. Myel hadn't been in the victor's room, where we'd expected. And when Koar had unsubtly "questioned" the arena staff, we'd found out Golana and a bunch of guards had hurried the shifter away.

After that, I'd turned inward, to my bond, seeking out my mate, even as a sinking feeling had filled my gut with cold dread.

West.

Myel lay somewhere to the west, among the many residences. I feared I knew exactly where he was, in a certain false princess' clutches.

"Fuck," I hissed, then told the others what I'd felt.

We all hurried in that direction, crossing a bridge over the river which ran through campus. Some other time, I might have stopped to admire the beautiful view off one side of the bridge, where the river almost immediately dropped off a waterfall, and beyond lay the sparkling ocean. But I barely noticed the view in my periphery, focused on Myel and the mounting sense of doom churning in my stomach.

Please God, don't let him—

A wave of agony hit me like a ton of bricks, stopping me dead. My momentum carried me forward, falling down the last few steps off the bridge to the hard stone path, where I writhed in the street, screaming.

Pain radiated through my bond with Myel, wracking my body, dominating my thoughts. I couldn't think, couldn't speak. Myel was being tortured, probably in Saldrea's dungeons. I knew it to be true but couldn't communicate it to the others.

Vyns collapsed to one knee next to me, teeth gritted.

"Izzy? What's wrong? I can feel…" Some of this raging agony must have transferred from my spirit to his. That's how all-consuming this torment was.

Just when the pain in one area began to lessen, some other place exploded in dazzling affliction.

It went on and on, for what seemed like an eternity. I became only vaguely aware of my surroundings, too focused on the torture consuming me. Vyns spoke to the others, Koar lifted me, trying to carry me, though I didn't make it easy, squirming and screaming and bashing at him.

And even though I hadn't been able to tell them my suspicion about Myel's location, they kept moving in that direction.

Then we stopped. There was shouting. Koar tensed, and I was set down. I felt more than saw everyone around me tense.

Somone — voices all seemed to blend together — said, "We'll fight through this and get Myel, don't worry, Izzy!"

Then... suddenly...

The pain ended, but *not* in a good way. I went limp, exhausted from the strain of thrashing, the tension of every muscle. Something was so very, very wrong. I let out the most pathetic keening whimper as a wretched, aching loss overwhelmed me. It felt like someone had torn out my soul and taken half of my body with it, including my lungs. I couldn't breathe. A massive weight pressed down on my chest, but somehow it came from inside me, an implosion, a compression. A black hole swirled in my soul, trying to suck everything I was into it.

"Izzy?" someone called, sounding concerned.

They should be. I was dying, slowly consumed from within. An oppressive emptiness ate at me. I couldn't think straight, so it took longer than it should have for me to realize what had happened.

Myel was dead.

Oh, God!

No!

Oh God! Oh God! Oh God!

Only now did I understand.

Madness or death.

They were my only options. There was no possible way to live with this sucking wound in my soul, which devoured everything around it. Either I lived in eternal, empty, agony, unable to cope with life or anything beyond this feeling... or I put myself out of this epic misery and died.

They'd been words before. Terrifying words, but still only words, with no real understanding of the truth.

Now I knew.

I lived with this horrid duality for a lifetime between the span of two heartbeats, despising both options unable to choose...

Then the bond was slammed back into my soul. It radiated through me so intensely a full-body flinch jumped me off the ground an inch or so. I landed hard. The pain stunned me, as did the sudden influx of *everything* inside me again.

It was too much for my body to handle, I threw up everything I'd eaten that day, but since I had no strength to roll over it came up as a fountain, covering my face and upper torso. Luckily someone turned me to my side as I emptied my belly in the most horrid fashion.

And yet, that disgusting embarrassment meant nothing next to the stunning realization that I could once again feel my bond with Myel.

He was alive!

I wept whilst continuing to be sick.

"Izzy? What happened? Are you okay?" someone asked. I had no strength to respond.

"We need to get Myel back." Another voice.

"I'll tear these guards apart!" said a third.

"Wait..." came a female voice. Then that same voice whispered into my mind. *That was quite a disgusting display.* The voice held a note of mocking glee. *Was that from the death of your lover or his revival, I wonder?*

"Step aside Hana," a rumbly voice said, sounding dangerous. "Or give us back Myel and we'll be on our way. If you don't, I'll happily rip you apart, as well as these guards."

Attack me at your peril, little dragon. For I am the only one who can help your lover end her suffering.

Yes, please, end this, I begged. I'd never given up so easily, but I had no choice. I couldn't take any more of this. The shock to my system of Myel's death and revival — if this woman was to be believed — had been beyond too much. I felt like I'd run back-to-back marathons across a blazing desert while someone had been disemboweling me. Even that didn't capture the full exhaustion and agony I'd endured.

What you just saw was Izzy experiencing the rather extreme torture of her bondmate, then his death, and finally his revival. And he will continue to be tortured to death, then revived until such time as Izzy complies with our wishes. Is that understood? the voice — I recognized it as that horrid sylph, Hana — stated.

I had finished emptying my stomach and was ever-so-slowly starting to recover, so I managed to catch the reply.

"What is it you want? State your demands." The deep voice sounded thoroughly disgusted. It was Koar, my dedicated dragon.

Izzy will submit herself to the authorities and admit she is a traitor who wishes to overthrow the existing elven government. She will tell them she has realized she cannot fight the might of the elven empire and is turning herself in for punishment.

"That's ridiculous!" Rook's voice, heated and furious. "She'll be executed for treason!"

"No fucking way!" Koar roared. "Why would we hand her over to you? What do we get in return? If you give us Myel back—"

Then we lose our leverage, now don't we? Hana hissed. *No! You will do this because you have seen what our torture does to the little whore. You will do this, because it's what Izzy wants. Isn't it? Tell them, slut. Tell them you'll do it.*

"I'll do it," I croaked, throat burning, voice raw, every muscle in my body still trembling from the ordeal I'd just gone through. I couldn't do it again. I'd submit. I didn't want to. I wanted to fight, but I couldn't. There was nothing left in me to fight. If they kept torturing Myel like this, I'd soon wish for death. "Just... don't hurt Myel."

Yes, exactly. We'll keep the shifter safe and sound and... mostly... unharmed. In return, Izzy turns herself in. And you're right, she will be accused of treason and executed, but as a final kindness, we'll give her a fighting chance. Izzy will fight Saldrea in the arena tomorrow morning. That's the deal... take it or leave it.

Everyone gathered close, huddled around me. Vyns was behind me, supporting me. He'd been the one to turn me to my side so I wouldn't choke on my vomit. You had to love a guy who was willing to help you at your worst, your most disgusting. Koar and Rook knelt in front of me. Safir and Zora were close by, they'd been helping search for Myel at the arena as well.

"Izzy?" Koar's voice was as soft as I'd ever heard it. I must look quite pathetic — have truly scared him — for him to treat me so gently. "Are you sure about this?"

I nodded, tears returning. "Yes." I didn't want to admit I'd lost, but I had.

The big man looked up, presumably at Hana. I'd curled in on myself and didn't really know where the sylph was, just that she was somewhere nearby.

"One condition," Koar growled. "One of us stays with her, to ensure she isn't mistreated."

"Fine, whatever," Hana said dismissively. It was one of the few times she'd spoken aloud... and I'd just figured out why. Saldrea's plan hinged on her remaining spotless in the eyes of the public. She'd said she wouldn't go after me personally, so she wouldn't. Hana giving us the instructions telepathically meant no one else would have heard it. It would look like I was turning myself in and admitting I was a traitor.

Anyone with half a brain would probably be able to

figure out that the false princess was behind all of this, but there'd be no hard evidence.

I had to hand it to Saldrea; it was viciously cunning. She had me over a barrel and I'd do as she wished.

There was one thing I didn't understand. I'd already bested Saldrea in a direct match of our magic. Why did she think she could beat me in the arena?

Then I recalled the suppression collar they'd put on Myel.

Fuck...

But I had no other choice. I'd do as these psychopaths wanted.

"I'll accompany you to the campus authorities," Hana said, now sounding bored. *Try anything and I'll send a command to Saldrea to continue her work with the shifter.* Because, of course, she couldn't say that out loud.

My guys helped me up, but I couldn't even stand, I was worn out. Koar carried me as we followed Hana toward the administration buildings.

This was it.

This was how it ended for me. Before I'd ever had a chance to change things. I hadn't even been in this world for two full weeks. That was how long it had taken the vile oppressors of this place to wear me down and get me to submit.

Who had I been kidding? I could never have won. I'd lost the moment I'd come to this world, and I was only realizing it now.

KOARTHANDRIS

IZZY TREMBLED IN MY ARMS. I'D NEVER SEEN HER LIKE THIS, SO small and vulnerable. In a matter of scant minutes, she'd been reduced to a quivering shell of a woman. And it made my fury rise like a tidal wave... only I had no place to put that seething rage. Izzy wasn't fighting this. She'd given up.

I wanted to fight for her, but what could I do? Barging into Saldrea's dungeons would be a great way to get Myel killed, perhaps permanently this time. I knew exactly where Saldrea's torture chamber was, below her residence, but I had to imagine those tunnels would be filled with guards, and that didn't count the half-dozen who'd been stationed outside her house. With this fury burning through me, I could take them all on... but some tiny — still thinking — part of my brain told me fighting would take too long and alert those within. Meaning someone would kill Myel before I got to him.

But then, what was there to do?

I'd vowed to stay close to Izzy, but now that felt like a chain around my ankle. If I stayed with her in the prison, I'd be useless to actually help her get out of this situation.

Safir and Zora ran off, probably to tell Olinara and Lhorine what had happened, and hopefully to activate their little spy network. I didn't know what good that would do, but at least they were *doing* something.

Vyns slipped up beside me.

"Just got a text from Rook. He's going to distract Hana so she's not focusing on our minds, give us a second to plan."

I watched as the incubus confidently strode forward to chat up the sylph, a rigid tension in his shoulders. He didn't like any of this, but he was doing his part and I'd not let his efforts go to waste.

"What can we do?" I hissed.

"I know you'll want to stay with Izzy, but in this instance, I think I should. Your destruction will be more useful than my light in whatever rescue plan the others come up with. Also, Izzy may need some bolstering in spirit, which I can do through our link. I'll make sure she's okay and keep her spirits up. You... do whatever you need to do to get Myel out of this mess!"

Vyns was thinking clearly. He was right about all of that.

And oddly, I wouldn't mind leaving Izzy in his hands this one time. He'd protect her with his life. And focusing on getting Myel out would provide some focus for this blinding rage coursing through me.

"Okay," I grunted.

"Really? That was easy."

"I really need to destroy something or someone and I can't do that if I stay with Izzy. You watch her, keep her safe. I'll ruin someone's life for the pain they've put her through."

Izzy shifted in my arms.

Could she hear me? She seemed only semi-coherent, mostly out of it.

"Good... Now freeing Izzy and Myel is only part of the

problem. They'll probably put Izzy in the strongest binding collar they have. We'll need some way to get her out of that, which may mean… finding some new allies."

I growled.

Vyns understood. "I know you don't like the idea, but I'm willing to bet Lhorine isn't strong enough to break a collar of that magnitude on her own. And I don't think we'll find many elves to help us."

"Dwarves?" I suggested. "What about Svokol?"

"As far as I know he has no ability with binding. Most dwarves aren't very good with bindings anymore."

Yeah, I'd known that. I just didn't like the other option. In fact, for me there was no other option, but Vyns brought it up anyway.

He lowered his voice. "We may need to see if we can find a friendly… titan."

I let out another low growl.

"I know, I know," Vyns whispered. "But listen… the ones on campus, as much as they're working for Saldrea, I get the distinct impression they don't like it, that she has something on them, forcing them to do her bidding. I wouldn't go so far as to say we can trust them, but we may have a common enemy in Saldrea. Perhaps we can convince them to help us with this so that together, we can take down the false princess."

I hated this idea. What I hated most… was that it made sense.

It had been ingrained in me since I was a hatchling that titans were evil, the enemy, to be destroyed. I'd fought them in the last war between our kinds roughly five hundred years ago. I'd killed their kind and they'd killed many dragons I'd called friends. I could never trust a titan…

And yet…

I ground my teeth, knowing Vyns was right.

"I'll talk with the others and see what they think," I said. It was the closest I'd get to conceding Vyns' point. "But if we come up with a better option, I'm taking it."

"Of course," Vyns whispered. Though from his tone I got the feeling he didn't think there would be any other options.

The angel changed the topic, for which I was grateful. "You know where they're keeping Myel, right? Where Izzy was headed, it could only be—"

"Saldrea's dungeons, yes."

"And she'll have way more guards down there than usual."

"I know."

Vyns sighed. "Okay, I just… I have no clue how we'll free Myel in time."

I didn't know either. But in case Izzy was listening I said,

"We'll find a way."

Vyns nodded to that.

By then, we'd reached the administration building and Hana was gleefully talking to the on campus security — more dragons — explaining the situation.

"Can you walk?" I asked Izzy. If not, I'd hand her over to Vyns.

But she nodded, the motion limp and lifeless.

I was about to set her down, when she squirmed and her gaze focused on me.

"Thank you," she whispered. "I know you want to protect me, I'm sorry I gave up so easily."

I clamped my jaw so tight it made my cheeks twitch. This wasn't her fault.

"We all do what we must to survive," I whispered to her.

She nodded, then sat up a little in my arms, one hand reaching for my face. I shifted her so she could cup my cheek, then she lifted herself and kissed my other cheek softly.

"For everything you've done for me," she whispered, voice weak. "From the moment you left Saldrea, you've never failed me. You've always been there for me. Thank you."

I didn't know what to make of this. Pride swelled and mixed with my fury, along with a deep longing and an aching sadness.

You've never failed me. Those were the words I'd waited to hear from the royals for over a hundred years, even though it had seemed impossible. Some part of me let go of a deep and abiding tension I'd been holding all this time.

Yet, I *had* failed Izzy, by allowing all of this to happen. I should have protected Myel... even if it was impossible to protect two people in different places at the same time. That didn't stop my self-recrimination.

I couldn't quite reconcile these words from Izzy. As much as they were everything I wanted to hear, they didn't make sense here and now.

"I..." I had no clue what to say.

Then, I lost my chance as the other dragons came to take Izzy away.

I set her down and she wobbled, barely able to walk, but she straightened her back, found some deep reserve of strength and followed them. Perhaps she was putting on a show for me, so I wouldn't worry.

It didn't work. I was so damn worried.

My hand drifted up to brush my cheek, where she'd kissed me. It had felt a little too... final, a good-bye kiss. My heart tore open at the permanence of it.

I'd failed.

I'd not been able to protect her.

And… I'd lost my chance to be with her. That kiss might be the only affection we ever shared. I'd denied myself up till now, which suddenly felt like the most idiotic thing in the world. At least with Mynrial, I'd had one night with her before I'd lost her, but with Izzy, I'd been so preoccupied with my duty…

And now…

I'd never be able to show her my true feelings.

Maybe I should have taken the opportunity to be with her when I'd had the chance, because now… it was far too late.

Somehow this felt a thousand times worse than having been distracted in my duty. I'd never allowed myself to be with her, and I'd still somehow failed… and lost her… all at once.

Vyns nodded to me before he disappeared down the hall, following Izzy.

They were gone.

My soul cried out.

And my rage boiled over.

Someone was going to pay for this… and pay dearly.

VYNSIEL

Izzy's spirit had always been blindingly brilliant... until now. Saldrea killing Myel and reviving him had destroyed Izzy, torn apart her spirit, soured it. The tepid glow of Izzy's broken spirit sickened me physically. It was everything I could do not to lose my lunch over how wrong she felt through our link.

This was why I had to stay with her. I'd be next to useless in the field, given this feeling, but even more important, I knew what Izzy needed to get through this. I could bolster and revive her spirit through our link. Hopefully that would return some hope to her eyes.

She needed to snap out of her current state to have any chance of beating Saldrea tomorrow.

I watched as a severe-looking elf administrator, with a hint of a sneer on his face, affixed the strongest binding collar they had around Izzy's neck.

Thankfully, my link to her wasn't hindered. I didn't know how or why, but I guessed it had something to do with our link being outside of us, not an internal power or ability.

She was taken to a cell. I was not allowed inside, but I sat in the cell next to hers, holding her hand through the bars as she sat there, a glazed-over look in her eyes, hopeless. After everyone had gone, except for the guards somewhere out in the hall, I whispered to her.

"Don't lose hope."

She blinked and looked at me. "How can I not?"

I lowered my voice even more, moving my face closer to the bars. "Even now, we're working on a way to get you and Myel out of this. Trust in Koar and the others. They'll find a way to free you both."

Izzy sighed heavily.

The look in her eyes sawed through my heart. It wasn't that she didn't believe me, more that... she didn't care.

"What use will it be?" she huffed. "Saldrea knows my weakness now. She'll continue to target those I care about. Even if we free Myel, he'll have to live in hiding, for fear Saldrea might find him and kill him and..." She shuddered so hard it looked painful.

She continued, voice barely there, quavering in fear. "Even if we hide him away, there are so many others I care for. She could target any of you. Your deaths wouldn't hit me the same way as Myel's, but it would still be horrible. How... how can I live like that? How can I go on?"

I had my work cut out for me if I wanted to snap her out of this.

"We'll find a way." It was all I could think to say.

Because the truth was, we *had* to find a way. Izzy needed to keep going. She had the power to fight against the systemic injustice of this world, to make a difference. If she became queen, she could change so much, but first she had an uphill fight on her hands. One she could win, but only if she fought as hard as she could against Saldrea and her mother. She couldn't give up.

I squeezed her hand, trying to give her some of my strength. Over the last few days, watching her train like mad, I'd seen how strong she was, but right now, she needed me to be strong. And I was ready to be there for her, fully.

I'd realized some things over the past few days as I'd witnessed Izzy's miraculous transformation from a mostly powerless nymph to a stunningly strong elf. I'd been impressed by her work ethic and dedication to changing herself, becoming what she needed to be.

It had inspired me...

...to forgive myself.

As long as I'd known Izzy — and admittedly it hadn't been that long — I'd held out hope that she could heal the wound in my soul, caused by the horrors I'd inflicted on others while serving Saldrea. But over the last couple days I'd realized that wasn't her job. It was mine.

She couldn't heal me, only I could do that, though Izzy had been the catalyst for my healing. She'd given herself to me freely — once I'd gotten passed my need to have her all to myself — with such love and joy and passion that I'd been overwhelmed by it. She had her own issues from her past, but she never let them bog her down. She shone so brightly and loved so deeply, that I'd been stunned by the wonderful sensation of someone actually caring for me. It wasn't something I'd ever felt, not from my family, nor anyone else.

Izzy cared.

She cared for me, and Myel, and Koar, even Rook. She cared for this world, which hadn't even been her home two weeks ago. She had enough devotion in her heart to help everyone in the three realms, to bring peace and equality to lands which had never known either. That was the Izzy I knew and loved.

This past week and a bit, basking in the radiance of Izzy's spirit, I'd finally started to live a life where my moral convictions no longer warred with my duty. I'd experienced true peace in my soul and that had finally allowed me to come to terms with everything I'd done in the past. I'd begun the process of healing, of forgiving myself for the atrocities I'd committed. Eventually, I'd seek out those I'd hurt, or their loved ones, and make amends, but first I had to be true to myself.

And forgiveness didn't mean an absence of guilt, only that my guilt fueled accountability, not shame. I vowed to do better, be better, live a life which made me proud of myself. Watching Izzy's determination to learn and grow had inspired me to change myself for the better as well. And ever since I'd forgiven myself, I'd been able to access a deeper well within my spirit. And I used that now to help strengthen and support the woman I loved.

Because she needed someone to care for her, while her care for this world flagged. She needed to get her spirit back, needed to stand strong against Saldrea, against oppression, and to do that, she needed to find her fire once more.

I closed my eyes, feeling my own blazing spirit, and sank down into that bonfire to find my connection to Izzy, where sour sickness seeped in.

I stopped that flow, then began to reverse it, pushing my light and spirit through our connection, into her.

She gave a long, slow intake of breath, then an equally long sigh.

"Was that you?" she whispered.

I smiled as I opened my eyes to meet her gaze through the prison bars.

"I'm only giving you back some of what you've given me since our link formed."

She smiled at that. It wasn't a big thing, and it didn't last long, but it gave me hope.

I went on. "Not only have you literally saved my life, bringing me back from the brink of death, but you've inspired me to change myself, better myself. You mended my body and your example — your work ethic, your indomitable spirit — gave me the strength to mend my soul. So yes, I'm giving you some small part of what you've given me."

A tear left her eye and traced her cheek.

"Oh, Vyns, thank you." Soul-weariness edged the hope of those four simple words.

She drew in another deep breath. And though she trembled as she let it out again, her back straightened, head once again held high.

"Sorry, I lost myself there, for a moment."

"You experienced something far worse than any of us could ever imagine, so don't beat yourself up for it. I'm glad you're back with us again."

"I am." Another deep, long breath. "So, what's the plan?" She was still far from her full strength of spirit, but she was trying and that's what counted.

"For you? Stay strong. The trials you'll face here aren't done. The authorities will return in a bit for your confession, to be broadcast across campus and all of El'Arias. You'll need to go through with it and make it sound good, so as to please Saldrea... but you have a chance here as well. You'll have to be subtle, but Saldrea has essentially given you a platform to tell this world what you'd hoped to achieve. Your confession can also be your manifesto, since what she's asking you to say is essentially the truth. You *do* mean to overthrow the government here and change this world. So say it proudly."

"Huh... I hadn't thought of it that way, you're right."

"And secondly..." I lowered my voice even more. "You need to fight... in secret. You're stronger than that binding collar. I heard what Lhorine told you: *all bindings can be undone, if you're powerful enough...* and you are. You have to be. No matter who made that collar, you're stronger, I've seen it, I know it. Everyone knows it. You're your mother's child. You hold her legacy. You beat Saldrea and Golana combined. You can do it. Lhorine taught you how to wear down a binding, like a slow river carving a gorge. So, even if you only have access to a tiny bit of your power, that's enough. Wear down the collar. It may not be easy, nor quick, but you can do it."

She smiled.

"You've thought of everything, haven't you?"

"I'm more than just a pretty face," I quipped.

"So much more," she breathed, then we both leaned in close for an awkward kiss through the bars.

She blew out a breath.

"Okay... I can do this."

And it was just in time, as the authorities then returned, ready to take Izzy's confession and broadcast it out to the world.

VYNSIEL

THANKFULLY THE ELVEN OFFICIALS HADN'T WRITTEN A verbatim script they wished Izzy to recite. They'd come up with a bullet-point list of items for her to touch on as part of her confession. That gave Izzy some leeway in how she communicated to the public, and she used it brilliantly.

She began formally.

"My name is Sa Brown Izzy and I am guilty of conspiring to overthrow the righteous elven authorities of this wonderful land."

I had to smile as I watched her. Her expression spoke only of submission and remorse, but a fire blazed in her spirit as she spoke. And she'd already chosen some rather on-point words.

...righteous elven authorities... could mean they had the high moral ground, or it could mean they were pompous and hypocritical.

...this wonderful land... showing her love and support for Seial while seeming apologetic.

A good start.

"I am a traitor, guilty of sedition and treason. I had

hoped to abolish the rule of elves and bring equality for all people." And the way she shook her head after saying this was inspired. It could be seen as apologetic and contrite to those who wished to see her fall, or... it could show her empathy for the plight of the oppressed, garnering her support from those who wished for change. A brilliant double-edged sword of a gesture.

"And now I see the error of my ways. I shouldn't have even tried. This is not something I could ever have done alone."

And it was that mostly innocuous little word tacked onto the end of that sentence, which gave it so much power.

Alone.

Izzy admitted she'd tried and failed to overthrow the government, but only because she hadn't had the support of the people, the masses behind her. And the way she minimized those two syllables meant most people might not notice the word. But for those who did, it suggested that united we could fight the power of the elves.

"I accept my punishment: trial by combat against Princess El Tyrianel Saldrea. I will face her, knowing I'll find justice and peace. May my fate be an example to all those who might challenge the rule of the elves."

A single tear fell, tracing Izzy's cheek.

A stunning finish.

She'd thrown the door wide open for a rebellion, and it was possible none of her captors were even aware of it. She seemed to be accepting her fate, but her words could also be taken another way. She'd *find justice* against Saldrea... if she won. And if she did, her fate would *be an example to all those who might challenge the rule of elves.*

I had to stop myself from applauding.

The authorities, satisfied with her confession, gloated and left.

I had to force myself to wait until I was sure no one would overhear before I quietly congratulated my love.

"That was brilliant!"

A tiny smile crept onto her lips. "You think so? I was so sure the elves were going to see through my ploy, but... they all seemed to think they'd won at the end."

"It's because they've always been superior. Your subtleties were lost on them because they heard what they wanted to hear, what they always hear. They're so arrogant, they can't see or hear anything other than what they expect."

"How?" Izzy asked baffled. "How can they be so blind, so... dense?"

"When you live for thousands of years, and everyone has always submitted to you and told you what you wanted to hear, it becomes the norm. To them it's utterly impossible that anyone would even try to rise up against them. And frankly, it *has been* impossible for so long. Your existence changes all of that, but they can't see it, probably because they don't know... who you really are."

I wouldn't say she was a royal out loud, even whispering as we were.

"They see a half-blood, who may be strong, but has now learned her place and who they'll soon be rid of."

Izzy frowned at that.

"That's what they see, not what I see. I know you'll get out of the collar and beat the crap out of Saldrea tomorrow."

"After the other's free Myel," she breathed, some uncertainty creeping back into her voice.

"Yes, of course."

She nodded, but I sensed a resurgence of her trepidation. She'd been so strong, a stunning actress, for that confession, but it had taken a lot out of her. She was already drained, and exhaustion never helped to keep up one's spirits.

I gave her more strength from my spirit, and she smiled.

"Thank you," she said again. "For being here, for... keeping me strong."

"Maybe you should rest for now, you've been through a lot, I'll watch over you and make sure you're safe. Sleep, if you can, then wake refreshed and tackle the binding on your collar."

She nodded to that and lay down on the simple cot in her cell.

I remained as close as I could, watching over her, as I'd promised.

My phone rang a little while later. It was Koar.

"We've had a meeting," he said, voice clipped, unhappy. "Lhorine is quite certain she can't break Izzy's collar on her own and we have few other options... so we're going to do as you suggested and reach out to the titans." Strain lay heavy in his voice. He didn't like it, but he'd go along with it... for Izzy.

And I was thankful. As much as I believed Izzy could break the binding on her collar, the question was: *could she do it in time to face Saldrea*? If someone else could break the binding for her, Izzy could save some strength for the fight with the false princess.

"Safir and Zora have confirmed that Myel is in Saldrea's dungeon, guarded by ten dragons when Saldrea isn't around. We can't take on a force that size without help. We're reaching out to other contacts, but... it seems we may need the titans for that as well."

Yeah. Ten dragons comprised a significant force. Ten

powerful dwarves could take them, but I didn't think we had the connections for that. Otherwise, it would take a small army to take them on. In the limited confines of the dungeons, the ten defenders would have the advantage, since only so many attackers could come at them at once. But a single titan, depending on how strong they were, could take a dragon or two.

"That's it for now. We're looking for the leader of the titans, a man named Bayn. Haven't found him yet. I'll keep you in the loop."

"Thanks, old friend. Keep up your resolve. We can do this. Izzy is strong and will survive this. Remember that."

He grunted. I don't think he doubted me. I assumed the non-committal response was from his dislike of the whole situation.

He hung up and that was that.

Now, it was a waiting game, at least for me. I'd keep Izzy strong in here, while the others did what they needed to, to free us and Myel.

Heavens, I hoped they could do it.

Time was so short.

Honestly, it would be a miracle if we pulled this off.

BAYN

I DIDN'T GET MUCH TIME AWAY FROM SALDREA, SO I TOOK advantage of any breaks I got. Nearly always, my first stop was the campus stables, to visit the only things in this world which brought me joy: my creations.

Other races referred to them as abominations, but only because they couldn't see the beauty in what we titans created. A horse could be strong and proud and beautiful, so could a dove, but a silvery-white horse with gleaming feathery wings… no, that was evil.

I patted Skycleaver's neck bending my head to lean against his.

"They're all fools," I whispered. He couldn't understand me. Even so, I talked with my creations more than anyone else. At least they listened. Some days I felt like Skycleaver was the only one who truly understood me.

In many ways, I was more animal than man. Animals were simple creatures. They lived in a complex hierarchy of predation, sure, but I was an apex predator, and at that level, there was peace. All I needed was to hunt, eat, rest, and fuck. Not that I'd done a lot of the latter since… Osserime. I hadn't been able to trust any woman since my betrothed had betrayed me. Perhaps that was why I trusted beasts more than people.

Unbidden, an image of the half-breed woman came to mind. Izzy. She was strong and durable. She could probably take my affections. My arousal stirred.

I shook my head. Why was I thinking of her? I barely knew her. How could she arouse me, when no woman had... since Osserime? Perhaps it was her nymph side? Nymphs could become whoever you desired. And with her elven side, she'd be tough enough to endure my... aggressive nature.

I grunted and pushed thoughts of the woman from my mind. They were a distraction. What I needed was to focus on the problem before me: freeing my sister from Saldrea's clutches.

My titan companions had finally found where Wensuria was being held, or at least, they were mostly certain. They'd located an underground compound well off campus. The trouble was their earth-sense couldn't penetrate its walls; some magic protected the place from outside senses. The only reason they believed my sister was there was because they'd tracked Saldrea to that location before my last check-in with my sister.

Given all of that, we were nearly certain that's where Wensuria was being held. But I had to assume that the physical guards on the place were as strong as the metaphysical barriers keeping us from sensing inside.

Saldrea had ten dragons on that little shifter in her personal dungeon. There wasn't room for many more down there. I had to assume, given the size of the hidden complex off campus, that it held a hundred guards or more.

I'd never be able to get my sister back on my own, even if I got all the titans on campus to help.

It infuriated me.

I hated that I needed help. Only weaklings needed help. I should be in control. I should be strong enough to deal with anything!

Skycleaver whinnied and brought me back to reality. Even though he wasn't sapient, sometimes I wondered if he was somewhat empathetic. He seemed to know when to nuzzle my shoulder, or whinny, or stomp, breaking my melancholy.

I ran a loving hand down his silky mane and sighed. "Thank you, friend."

I quickly saddled Skycleaver and mounted up, taking him for a flight. I'd brought one other creation with me, but it had been so anathema to the senses of the elves they hadn't even allowed it on campus. I'd created a pen for it some distance off campus, hidden by trees and wilderness. Landing and dismounting I strode through the forest to the large cage of stone I'd surged up from the earth to house Prideaon. If Skycleaver was beauty and grace, Prideaon was power and passion. Of all my chimeras, Prideaon had been my crowning achievement, the blending of a dire lion and a wyvern to stunning perfection.

The body was mostly lion, with a large head and shaggy mane, it retained all the proud heritage of — what the human-realmers called — the king of beasts. In Seial, lions were far from the strongest of beasts, but dire lions were still proud and powerful creatures. Leathery wings emerged from behind the shoulders and were currently folded back along the sandy-colored flank. Two stripes of spiky scales trailed along the bottom sides of the beast, and another along its back, all meeting at the hind quarters. The back legs were scaled, like a wyvern, and a long serpentine tail, barbed with heavy spikes, swung casually behind my creation.

I lowered the stone cage and Prideaon came to me, I hugged that massive head close and breathed in the earthen scent of the beast.

"Shall we hunt?" I whispered to Prideaon and though he didn't understand my words, he seemed to know my intent, frisking at his freedom and ready to feed.

I mounted Skycleaver and launched into the sky with Prideaon close by. Technically, this was illegal. I'd been told Prideaon could be fed with meat but couldn't hunt freely. I used the flimsy loophole that he wasn't "free" but guided by me. I'd done this a few times, and we were far enough from campus that killing a few of the forest beasts didn't seem to bother anyone. Eventually some dryads would find out and protest, I was certain, but I didn't much care. These were the only real moments of joy I had anymore, and I'd not give them up.

Prideaon was a masterful hunter from the skies, taking down a massive bull moose and a large sow bear. I gathered the two carcasses in one spot and let Prideaon feed as I sat nearby, wishing this could be my life.

Eventually, however, I erected a new stone cage around the area, leaving Prideaon to his meal — those two kills would last him for a week or so — and returned on Skycleaver to campus.

I landed, brushed down my beautiful mount and was about to leave and return to the despicable princess... when someone called my name.

"Bayn?" The voice was strong, male. Not one I'd heard before. "Leader of the titans here on campus?"

I turned to see an odd group approaching me. The big

one was a dragon. Of all those on campus, dragons were the only ones who came close to the size of us titans. With him was an incubus. I could tell his race more by the way the man walked than anything else about him. Concubi had a way of moving — whether they be male or female — as to draw the eye to them, accentuate their masculine or feminine forms. Though, when I took a closer look at the man, I reassessed my initial guess. He was also part salmaeri, as witnessed by his fiery eyes and red hair, which were not common concubi traits. I recognized him as one of the three who'd fought beside Izzy during her dominion match against Saldrea.

Curious.

The last was a buxom nymph, who looked like some young and nubile wench, but I knew better. Nymphs were rarely what they appeared to be. The eyes of this one spoke of experience, and probably a much longer life than her form suggested. Also, something about her look vaguely reminded me of that half-breed, Izzy. She might be a family relation, on Izzy's father's side. If my intuition was correct and Izzy was the lost princess, then her father would have been a nymph. Which meant this was most likely an aunt or grandmother, probably the latter, given the depth of experience in her eyes.

This didn't bode well.

If they were friends of Izzy, they could only be here for one reason, to enlist my help in freeing the half-breed, or the shifter, or both. I couldn't. Betraying Saldrea would mean the death of my sister...

Although...

An idea began to form in my mind as the three drew near. Perhaps I could use these folks as they wished to use me.

"Yes, I am Bayn, leader of the titans. What do you want?" My tone was blunt, harsh. I'd never been one for niceties.

The dragon bristled but calmed himself. Good, he wasn't easily goaded, perhaps he had a decent head on his shoulders, rare for a dragon, most of whom were hot-tempered blowhards.

The dragon looked back at the nymph.

She seemed to concentrate, then said, "We're alone. The only creatures around are these horses." It wasn't a common ability among nymphs, but some could feel the water in creatures nearby. It seemed this one possessed such a gift.

"I'll keep an eye out, just in case," the incubus said, and slunk off.

"As much as I hate to admit it, we need your help," the dragon began. I was curious why he was doing the talking, not the nymph, who seemed far more self-possessed and controlled. "I have it on good authority that you hate Saldrea as much as we do, that you're being forced to serve her. Is that correct?"

Straight to the point. I liked it.

But I'd not give anything away easily. "*If* that were the case, I'd clearly not be able to help you, now would I?" This was where my burgeoning idea came into play. "Unless... *you* remove whatever it is Saldrea might have over me."

The dragon bristled.

Good. Let him get up in arms. I had a feeling he'd hoped to bully me into helping them, but I'd never agree to such a thing. I hated all these beings nearly as much as I hated elves. Why should I help them? Even if it was to fight against each other. BUT... *if* they could free my sister... *then* perhaps I could ally with lesser enemies to defeat a greater one.

"Now, listen—" the dragon began, but the nymph sighed and laid a hand on his shoulder, stopping him.

"What might that be?" she asked, voice level. "Our time is short, but if we need to help you, to get you to help us, that seems only fair."

As I'd thought.

It was clear they were desperate.

Still, I hesitated for no small amount of time before telling them the truth. As soon as I did, they'd have power over me, which I despised. How could I turn this to my advantage?

"First, tell me what you would have me do. How could I help you?"

"Two ways," the nymph replied, taking over from the dragon who clearly didn't want to give away their secrets. "First, by breaking the binding collar on Izzy, or loosening its control enough so she can overpower it before she fights Saldrea tomorrow. If she kills or subdues Saldrea, wouldn't that help your cause?"

"It might."

The nymph nodded.

"Second, would be to have your allies on campus help us raid Saldrea's dungeon. We'd do it when she wasn't there, to minimize casualties, but we need a strong force to overpower the dragons she has guarding our shifter friend."

This was no surprise.

"You'd kill your own kind?" This I said straight to the dragon.

"Any of my kind who cannot see the truth about Saldrea deserve what they get." He spoke so quickly and with such heat, it took me by surprise. I hadn't expected that level of betrayal for his own kind.

Which spoke of something much deeper.

He was in love with the half-breed. And — it was a guess

— but he also knew her true heritage. Something in how he'd said "the truth about Saldrea," made me think he knew Izzy was a royal and Saldrea a false princess.

I smiled. Oh yes, they were desperate. There was no way they could achieve what they desired on their own. They *needed* me.

Which meant I could trust them... a little. "Betray me — tell anyone what I'm about to tell you — and I'll kill that half-breed wench myself," I said by way of warning.

They both bristled.

Yes, this nymph had to be related to Izzy, given how her anger flared.

"Your *friend* is safe," I said with a more sedate tone, "as long as you keep my secret. Agreed?"

"Agreed," the nymph said quickly.

I looked at the dragon.

His jaw twitched, clenched so hard, ire in his eyes. But he blew out a huff through his nose and slowly unclenched. "Agreed."

Hopefully I could trust them, if only for this one venture. We both needed each other with an egregious desperation.

"Saldrea has my sister," I said, the words pulled from my soul. Never would I have imagined sharing such a thing with the enemy, but in this case... they were the lesser of two evils. "She tortures her and makes me watch. It's not bad, nothing a titan can't endure, but it's enough for Saldrea to show her dominance. That's how she controls me. Free my sister, and I will help you."

"We'll free her as soon as Izzy is safe," the dragon said, easily accepting my dire secret it seemed.

"No. You need me more than I need you," I asserted

control. "Free my sister first, then I'll help you, not a moment before. Once I've seen my sister is safe and no longer in Saldrea's dungeon, then I will do as you ask."

"There isn't time!" the dragon hissed. "Izzy's trial is tomorrow morning!"

"Wait," the nymph said, once again laying a hand on the dragon's shoulder to calm him. "You said your sister was in Saldrea's dungeon? Then this works perfectly. We can all go in and free her and our shifter friend, then you can weaken Izzy's collar, and she'll defeat Saldrea."

I gave them a sour smile.

"If only it were that easy. Your shifter is no real threat to Saldrea, so she has him in her personal dungeon, at her residence. I, however, pose a much more dangerous hazard to the false princess. Hence, my sister isn't in her normal dungeon, but a fortified bunker well off campus." The nymph's shoulders slumped, her hopes falling. She was about to say something when I spoke over her.

"I know where she is and can give you the location, but you'll have to find some way in to free her. I do not doubt it will be dangerous, probably far more so than freeing your shifter friend. But I will not move a muscle to help you until my sister is safe. That is my condition and I will not move on it. Take it or leave it."

As much as I wanted to get my sister out of that place as soon as possible, I didn't *need* to free my sister right away. Yet these folks needed help this instant. I could make the terms as amenable as I wanted. They had to accept them.

"Fine," the nymph hissed. "Tell us where and we'll free her tonight. But you'd better be available to do everything we've asked as soon as we free your sister." Her voice grew cold and vicious. "Betray us and trust me when I say there will be no place in any of the three realms, or the human realm, where you can hide from us. You may be strong, but against all of us together, you'd have no chance. If my granddaughter dies because of you... If you betray us..." A nasty smile spread on the nymph's pretty face. "Then your life will be measured in hours, not days."

So, I'd been right, this was Izzy's grandmother. And I believed her threats. If all of Izzy's followers — or her family in this case — were as devoted as these two, then I'd be in trouble. Not that I was truly worried, but still, I took her threat seriously.

"Someone's coming!" the incubus said, rushing back toward us. "We've got maybe a half a minute."

"Deal," I said to the three of them, and I quickly explained where the fortified prison was and what little I knew of it. Lastly, I let them know how to contact me, putting their information in my phone with a special ring tone. All they'd have to do was send me a picture and I'd know they'd freed my sister. Once I'd verified it, I'd help them with their plans.

"Now go, you don't have much time before your friend dies," I said, and saw how much the three of them knew it.

They hurried away.

Soon after, Golana, with two dragons as her escort, found me in the stables.

"Saldrea wants to see you," the dwarf said with little emotion.

"I still have some time off, can it wait?" I said, paying more attention to Skycleaver.

"No. Come."

I bristled at the command, but just like I had Izzy's friends over a barrel, the same was true of Saldrea and myself. I went with the dwarf, wondering what was so important it couldn't wait.

When we didn't head for Saldrea's residence, I asked, "Where are we going?"

Golana gave a grim smile.

"The administration building... to torture a certain half-breed."

BAYN

"You can't do this! You promised you wouldn't hurt her!" the ineffectual little angel protested from the cell next to Izzy's.

Everyone was here, Saldrea had brought her whole gang, plus a few guards, and me. One of the guards locked the angel in his cell as Saldrea responded to him,

"*I* never made any promises. Hana promised one of you could come along to ensure the half-breed wouldn't be mistreated, but she never actually promised we'd not hurt her. And you're here, so... go ahead, *try* to ensure Izzy isn't mistreated, I dare you."

"You filthy, lying, bi—" He only got that far, raising his hands to attack with his light powers, before Hana took hold of his mind. The angel fell back with a wide-eyed gaze, trapped in some vision.

Hana chuckled. "I really love torturing seraphim. Their spirits are so strong, but their minds are so weak."

I almost felt bad for the man, but he should have known Saldrea would betray him. She never kept her word.

But then... why did I expect her to keep her word?

Because she had so far. My sister was "safe," and unharmed most of the time. Saldrea hadn't killed her... yet. But I realized then, she would. Saldrea would kill my sister and laugh at me while she did it, call me weak and helpless. It was in her nature. Once I was no longer needed, she'd dig her dirty little fingers into my largest wound and squeeze my pain.

Which only reaffirmed that I'd done the right thing by agreeing to help those others. They'd free my sister and I'd do what I could to help them.

After my talk with them, I had considered taking my sister and fleeing once she was free, not helping them. But a man was nothing without his word, his character. It might get me killed, but I didn't much care for my life anymore. If Wensuria was free, I'd gladly face down Saldrea and die knowing my sister would live.

I'd done the right thing, but I still had to play the part of Saldrea's lackey until my sister was free.

Thankfully, Hana was preoccupied with tormenting the angel and wouldn't have overheard those thoughts. I stilled my mind and put all of that away for now, going hard once more, enduring what I must, until I was free to act as I wished.

"Now, Bayn," Saldrea said. "I want you to pay attention. I see how you look at me. I've tried to beat it out of you. I've tried to beat it out of your sister, but you haven't changed. So... consider this an object lesson. This is what I do to people who go against me." She smiled, a twinkle in her eyes. She was happiest when inflicting pain on others.

I nodded, not sure why she thought hurting someone else would change my mind. Though the fact that she knew how I felt was worrying. I'd need to calm my emotions even more for the next few hours; after that... with luck,

Wensuria would be free and I could repay Saldrea a debt of pain.

Saldrea turned to Izzy. I gave my attention to the half-breed woman as well. She had been sleeping when we arrived, but a warning from her angel had roused her. She stood, arms crossed, boldly facing us down. Her eyes darted toward the angel, showing her concern for him. I found that fascinating. She was about to be tortured and was worried for another. I didn't think any elf could be that compassionate. And her defiance in the face of Saldrea's impending torment was admirable.

I had to respect the woman's strength.

I'd seen so many others fall apart at the mere mention of Saldrea's torture.

Izzy didn't flinch.

Which only angered Saldrea even more.

"Resist all you like," Saldrea hissed, "but I swear I'll make you scream. I won't kill you. That honor I'll save for tomorrow, but I'll make sure you're in so much agony from now till then that you can't rest, can't sleep. I'll heal you... mostly... before the fight tomorrow, so it looks like a fair fight, but it won't be. You'll be an exhausted mess, still suffering on the inside while I slowly kill you."

Saldrea's words had no effect. Izzy stood there, resolute. In fact, a small smile crept onto the woman's face.

"You've made a mistake," Izzy said.

"Have I? Tell me?" Saldrea was quickly losing her shit.

"No." Izzy said simply. "I know, and that is enough."

"Gah!" Saldrea screamed. If this had been a contest of which woman could make the other scream first, Izzy had won. But I doubted Izzy would like what came next.

Stone rose up from the floor to encompass Izzy's feet. At the same time, two arms of stone reached out from the wall behind her to grab her shoulders, restraining her. Then the earth at her feet moved her back while the arms dragged her toward the back wall. There was a bed in the way, but Saldrea paid it no mind forcing Izzy's body back even as her legs hit the small cot.

Izzy grimaced, eyes wide with pain, but managed to restrain any scream as her body and the bed fought against each other. Izzy's body won... mostly... The metal frame of the bed was crushed sideways as the bones in Izzy's legs broke. It was a testament to elven durability that the bed had collapsed before Izzy's legs had been torn apart. Any unenhanced race would have two bloody stumps below the knee right now.

Saldrea laughed, a gleeful noise, clapping her hands together.

"Wonderful! Oh, look at your face. I'll make you scream, I promise."

The stone around Izzy shifted and moved, a band at her hips kept her pressed to the wall while her arms were pried away from her chest by grasping tendrils of rock. Her arms and legs were pulled out to the sides, till she was spread-eagle against the wall. This caused more of the bed to collapse and more pain to Izzy's already injured legs.

Izzy gave a gasp of pain, but that was it.

Tough woman.

I couldn't see what Saldrea did next, but I felt it with my earth powers, and saw its effect on Izzy. The half-breed's eyes went wide, and her entire body went rigid, she bared her teeth, hissing, eyes watering at the pain... as a dozen thin spikes of stone were — very slowly — driven through her body from back to front. Two pierced her upper arms, two penetrated the soft spot inside of each shoulder, below the collarbone. Four sprouted from her stomach and two more bored their way through the soft portions of her hips, finding the gaps in her hip bones to come out close together low on her abdomen, probably just missing her reproductive organs. The last two slid through her thighs. Saldrea's placement was perfect, inflicting maximum pain with little to no damage to any vital organs.

Izzy let out strangled little noises, but no scream. She drew in a shuddering breath then gave a hard, teeth-gritting smile.

"Nice... try," Izzy muttered, clearly in pain, still fighting Saldrea.

For the first time in what seemed like ages, something stirred deep within me. Seeing this woman fight with nothing but her willpower sparked a passion I'd thought long gone. I'd been dead emotionally ever since Osserime's betrayal, feeling little more than rage and emptiness. I'd never expected to feel much ever again. My grand plan was to get my sister back, make sure she was safe, then take her away from the horrors the elves — and our own family — had inflicted on us. Beyond that I'd expected nothing for myself, no joy, except insomuch as I got from seeing my sister free to live her life.

What I felt now wasn't joy. If I experienced such an emotion while watching someone in pain, I'd be a monster. I'd be Saldrea. No, this was a feeling of interest, of curiosity tinged with awe, maybe a little pride. I couldn't fight Saldrea the way I wished. Currently, I fought by doing as little as possible for her, but this woman — Izzy — she fought with everything she had, all the time.

I respected the hell out of that.

It had been a long time since I'd admired anyone for showing such strength of character and determination. Izzy shone with pure defiance, rebelling against everything this world stood for. A part of me found that fascinating. It made me want to see her live, see what she could do if she had a chance. Hell, if she became queen of the elves...

No, best not to think about that.

Nor let my respect for her turn to anything more. She was strong and stunning, yes, but she and I... there could never be anything between us. I'd never allow another woman into my life, not unless she was willing to bow and scrape and worship me as a god. I needed full and utter control, or I wouldn't trust them. And Izzy wasn't one to submit like that.

Though, for an instant, my mind betrayed me. It imagined Izzy spread-eagle in a very different scenario, open to me, receptive, yielding. I crushed that thought, but not before it stirred a certain physical part of me.

Stone and Bone! Was I truly aroused by seeing a woman in pain? No, it hadn't been her pain that had stimulated me, but her fight, and imagining her giving up that fight to me.

"Scream, damn you!" Saldrea shrieked, spittle flying from her lips. "I can't do anymore to you without permanent damage and I'm not willing to do that till tomorrow. You have to look healthy enough for the crowd before I crush you!"

"Then... I guess... I win," Izzy said with that same pained grin.

"No!" Saldrea turned to Hana. "Stop messing around with the angel and focus on Izzy. I want to know everything, all her secrets, every weakness!"

Hana sighed and shrugged. The angel went limp after having been tense, wracked with some imagined, horrible scenario playing out in his mind. The sylph turned to Izzy and seemed almost bored as she cleaned out the woman's mind.

"Titania's tits!" Hana gasped. That was pretty much the worse curse there was. A non-elf saying it could get them killed.

Saldrea went pale at Hana's vile expletive. "What?"

"She's a fucking royal!"

Well... yeah. I'd known that for a while now.

"No!" Saldrea gasped. I watched as it hit her, every clue sinking in. "No," she breathed, horrified. "The lost princess?"

"You can bow now," Izzy stammered through her pain.

It was the wrong thing to say. Saldrea had only been holding back against Izzy to keep the real pain for tomorrow, but Saldrea's world had just been shaken. She snapped.

The false princess let out a wordless, hysterical scream. Stone reached out from the wall and wrapped around Izzy's neck, forcing her head up at an odd angle as it squeezed back in, crushing her throat. Then more stone wrapped around the poor woman, constricting, breaking bones, compressing muscle, bursting open skin, blood flowed like a waterfall.

I didn't know what prompted me to help her, except perhaps that I'd found someone worthy of my respect, and I didn't wish to see her die like this. Using my own magic, I pulled the stone away from Izzy. As much as I hated to admit it, Saldrea was usually stronger than me, but she was in a fit, her power wild. I had control, fresh and unspent. I freed Izzy from the stone slowly killing her.

The woman fell limp to the floor, dying, far too much blood flowing out of her.

"Who?" It was a testament to how far gone Saldrea was, that she didn't even think I could have done this. She turned to Golana and slapped her instead. "Why?"

"It wasn't me," Golana said, glaring in my direction and trying to fend off Saldrea.

Saldrea turned to me. "You? You dare go against me?"

"I only wish for you to have your day tomorrow, killing this wench in front of the world," I lied.

Saldrea blinked.

"Oh... yes... of course. I just... I can't... this little whore is the true princess? I... I..." Saldrea floundered, lost and disoriented. Not for the first time, I marveled at how broken and unbalanced Saldrea was. I hadn't really expected my words to sway her. There was no good reason for Saldrea to keep Izzy alive, now that she knew Izzy was a royal. Any sane person — who was as evil as Saldrea — would have realized Izzy was an imminent threat and killed her here and now instead of waiting for tomorrow. But Saldrea was so unstable I'd been able to convince her to keep to her original course of action.

Time to see if I could use her madness against her again.

"Which means you need to heal her, before she dies."

"What? Oh... yes... I suppose. Golana!" Saldrea was losing it, gaze unfocused, twitching. I couldn't believe that had worked.

Golana huffed and got one of the guards to open the cell, then went in and tended to the dying Izzy.

"Don't heal her too much," Saldrea ranted. "She has to suffer, heal her only enough to live through the night." She must have convinced herself her original plan was best. Perhaps it was ego, which Saldrea had in spades. She needed the world to see her kill Izzy. It was stupid, but for now, it was keeping this half-breed alive, which was what I needed, so her friends would free my sister.

"Yes, I know," Golana hissed. "There." She got up and

left the cell. Izzy hadn't roused, but some of her wounds had closed. I had to hope it would be enough.

"I can't believe..." Saldrea said shaking her head as she made to leave, clearly done here.

I followed, but a part of me wanted to go back and check on Izzy. I wasn't sure why I needed her to live. Except... she was unlike any woman I'd ever known, strong and resilient and fierce, but without the usual arrogance which went with those traits. Perhaps it was an act, but I had a feeling what I'd seen today was Izzy's true nature. It was hard to put on airs when you were being tortured.

And once again, I couldn't help but wonder how different this world might be if Izzy was queen. A world of acceptance, restraint, moderation, and equality? A world where my sister and I would be safe.

It seemed preposterous.

Impossible.

But as long as Izzy lived... there was hope, however faint. Maybe, once my sister was safe, I'd do more than free Izzy and her shifter. If her goal was to overthrow Saldrea and Valnea... I just might help.

AMARHUK (ROOK)

"IZZY? FUCK. IZZY? WHAT'S GOING ON? IZZY!"

"What's wrong with you?" Lhorine hissed, voice low. "Quiet!"

I hadn't realized I'd been speaking aloud till the elf pointed it out, but I couldn't help myself. It was this damned mental link with Izzy. A part of me was glad I didn't share a mate bond or spirit link, as then I might have felt what the woman had just gone through, whatever it had been. Instead, I'd caught her thoughts, but they'd been so jagged and disconcerting and horrible that I'd still been confused, filled with mental anguish.

Not all of her thoughts reached me, but when they were screamed at me with such distress, they rang through my mind so loud it was hard to concentrate.

The horrible part was, I had no context. I assumed Saldrea was doing something to Izzy from the scattered thoughts I'd received, but I had no clue. And whatever it was, it had been dreadful and painful and terrifying.

There had been some snarky mention of Saldrea earlier in Izzy's thoughts, which was the only reason I knew the false princess was involved. But… wasn't Vyns supposed to be ensuring Izzy wasn't hurt?

Though, come to think of it, if Saldrea and all her goons showed up, there wouldn't be much Vyns could do to stop them. We probably should have considered that.

Too late now.

And there was nothing I could do to help Izzy. Lhorine and I were far from campus, staking out the prison compound Bayn had told us about, where his sister was being kept. I still couldn't believe the big titan wouldn't help us until his sister was free, but then… if it had been my family… I might have done the same.

The prison was hidden in the woods, far from prying eyes, about a half-hour's walk from the city of Yrensil. Veilblood Academy was in the opposite direction, miles and miles through dense woods. The easiest way to get here would be to take the campus sigil point to Yrensil, then walk into the forest, but we'd wanted to avoid the known routes. So, Lhorine and I had walked through the forest. Luckily, Lhorine had an earth-based enhancement which allowed her to move extremely fast through nature while seemingly only moving at a walking pace. She'd gotten us here in just a few short minutes.

"Rook? You with me?" Lhorine whispered, intently. "Here comes a guard, you ready?"

Nope, not remotely.

We'd stationed ourselves along the simple path from the prison compound to Yrensil, in hopes of capturing a guard on his way home after his shift. Lhorine would then bind him and get him to tell us any passwords or other security measures inside the underground bunker. But after what I'd just experienced, I was distracted as hell. It didn't help that, after all that screaming, Izzy's mind had suddenly gone silent. That could mean she'd passed out, but what if Saldrea hadn't waited for tomorrow? What if she'd killed Izzy and none of us had been there to help?

I couldn't get that thought out of my head as Lhorine took action.

"We need to go now!" she hissed at me, then leaped out from the bushes. She tackled the surprised guard, but he was quick, and an elf like her, so he fought back with everything he had.

I should do something, but given the frenetic chaos in my head, I couldn't concentrate, and I might hurt Lhorine instead of helping her.

"Rook! ROOK!" Lhorine hissed as she struggled with the guard.

I reached out to Lhorine, hoping to enhance her spirit to help her fight... only I was muddled, and I didn't use the right power. I did what came more naturally to me and surged her lust.

"Fuck!" Lhorine gasped, low and heated. "Not helping!" The guard had the upper hand now and was about to get free.

I sapped her lust and surged it into the guard instead. The guard gave a startled moan. We'd see how well he fought with the world's hardest erection in his pants. Then, I leaped out of the bushes and managed to clock the guard, stunning him. After that Lhorine overpowered him and subdued him easily enough.

"What was that?" she asked, out of breath, as she dragged the guard's body into hiding. "What happened to you?"

"Sorry," I said with a heavy sigh. "I'm connected to Izzy's mind and she just endured something horrible. I was distracted."

Lhorine huffed.

"What is it with that woman and binding herself to men?"

Yeah, tell me about it.

"And... I can't sense anything from her now," I voiced my concerns. "Given what she just went through I can't be certain she isn't..."

"You'd know," Lhorine whispered as she settled the guard against a tree trunk. "It doesn't matter what sort of link you have, if they die, you'd know, you'd be certain."

I breathed a little easier, but I was still worried. Izzy had endured something which had made her scream in agony, swearing like a sailor. And the snippets of coherent thought I'd managed to catch hadn't been great:

Oh God! My legs!

Or...

How in the blazes am I still conscious after that? Damned elven endurance!

Or the most horrifying one of all, just before Izzy had succumbed to wild and horrified screaming...

Oh shit, they know! She's lost it!

What did they know?

If Saldrea had "lost it" then that would explain the horrified screaming afterward. That woman was insane and had no compunctions about ripping people apart when she was angry.

"Sorry," I mumbled again.

"Don't worry, we got there in the end."

Lhorine put a binding on the guard to hinder his movement and magic, then we woke him and she used a second binding to make him talk. We got the information we needed, but none of it was good. Our plan wouldn't work.

With limited time and information, we'd come up with

the idea to use Saldrea herself to get us in. Olinara would take Saldrea's form — she and Koar were still back on campus trying to get close enough to the false princess to do so — while Lhorine and I found and interrogated a guard to discover the security measures inside the compound. We'd hoped to use the false princess' influence — with an illusion over the rest of us, posing as Saldrea's crew — to walk right through the front door. It was the only way in, since tunnelling wouldn't work. Whatever magic kept earth-wielders from sensing inside also made the walls immutable, the stone couldn't be shaped or altered.

But, according to the guard, even someone as influential as Saldrea had to submit to all security measures, which required their ID, and a pass phrase, different for each person. This guard didn't know the pass phrases, only the head guard at the door did, and we didn't have any ID for the princess, nor did we have time to try and steal it from her. So, our plan to have Saldrea bully her way in... wouldn't work.

We needed an alternate... and fast.

When Koar and Olinara arrived, over two hours later, we told them the bad news. Though, given how upset Koar looked, I wondered if he and Olinara had some bad news of their own. The dragon radiated fury: jaw tense, brow furrowed, eyes tight, mouth set in a grim line.

"What happened?" I asked.

Olinara spoke, voice strained, taut. "I witnessed something I hope I never see again." She took a long breath, and that's when it hit me.

If Izzy had been tortured by Saldrea and Olinara had been close to the false princess, then she'd have witnessed her granddaughter's torment.

She confirmed my suspicion, talking through clenched

teeth. "Saldrea was in the middle of torturing Izzy when I found her. Everyone was distracted, so it was easy enough to slip in unnoticed and get a good read on Saldrea. But..." Olinara's fury rose, speaking in a vicious hiss, "... she nearly killed Izzy! So, I had to stay until they'd all left. There was no way I was leaving my granddaughter like that. I healed her once they were gone, but that meant the whole thing took longer than anticipated."

Olinara looked at Koar. "He's even more upset about this than I am. He's furious Saldrea stooped so low, angry at Vyns for not defending Izzy, irate at me for not stopping it, and beside himself that he couldn't protect Izzy. I debated whether or not to tell him at all, but there were things we all needed to know: mainly, Saldrea knows Izzy is a royal."

Oh shit, they know! She's lost it!

That made a lot more sense now.

"And it was all for nothing, since our plan is toast!" Olinara spat the words. "Though... I am glad I was there to help Izzy. I can't imagine how she would have fared otherwise."

Yeah, spending a night on the verge of death didn't sound relaxing.

"Did you two come up with any other ideas?" Olinara asked.

In fact, we had, but it wasn't great.

"If we need IDs to get in, then we'll have to steal some. We ambush some guards heading to the compound for the next shift, take their IDs, then Olinara takes one of their forms while using the illusion to make the rest of us look like the others."

"That... could work." Olinara bobbled her head from side to side.

"And if we need pass phrases, we can use a binding to

get them from the guards, assuming we take them alive," Lhorine added. "There's only one problem, and it's a big one."

"What?" Koar growled.

"The next shift change isn't until five o'clock," I stated. "Which leaves us only three hours to get in, find Bayn's sister, get out, get back to campus, find Bayn, then free Izzy and Myel."

"Fuck," Koar swore.

"Exactly," I agreed.

"Three hours isn't a lot of time, but it should be enough," Olinara said, her hopeful tone sounding forced.

"But it also means we're doing everything in broad daylight, not under the cover of night," Lhorine added.

It wasn't great, but it was the best plan we had.

As we waited, we came up with contingency plans and alternates for various scenarios. Then we tried to get some sleep. I couldn't rest. My thoughts wandered down morbid alleys. I had to believe our plan to save Izzy would work, but a part of my brain kept toying with the what-if's.

What if we didn't get there in time?

What if Izzy had to fight Saldrea?

What if she... failed.

What would my mental link do then?

It had been hard enough hearing her thoughts when she was in pain. Hearing her dying thoughts...

Anyone who thought mind-reading might be fun or informative, was sorely mistaken. Most thoughts were mundane and trivial. On the rare occasion when they weren't, it was often intimate details that you really didn't need to know. And hearing someone's final thoughts...

Well, I tried very hard not to imagine what that might be like.

THOSE WHO HAD SLEPT WERE AWAKE BEFORE DAWN. WE SET up our ambush and waited. With the four of us, and the element of surprise, we managed to capture four guards before they could shout for help. Once again, Lhorine used a binding on each of them to get what we needed.

Olinara took the form of one and put a very convincing illusion over the rest of us. Then, we headed for the compound.

Given the men we were impersonating worked here — and we had their faces, and IDs and pass phrases — it was surprisingly easy to get in. I had a feeling after this, once it was discovered someone had escaped, security was going to get a lot tighter.

Fuck, no, not again! Izzy's thoughts echoed in my mind. I stumbled, nearly falling down a flight of stairs as we made our way deeper into the underground complex. Thankfully, Koar caught me.

"Izzy," I hissed to let the big man know why I was suddenly out of sorts.

His eyes widened with concern.

"Catch me if I stumble again, I'm going to try to talk to her."

He nodded and we continued on down the stairs.

Izzy? I sent to her.

Rook? Oh... right... your mind-link-thing. Now's not a good time.

Me neither. But I wanted you to know we're coming for you, we just need a little more time. Are you okay?

I was, but Saldrea and her crew just returned. I didn't think they got up this early. They weren't happy that I was completely healed. Not sure how that happened. Saldrea is blaming Golana, but the dwarf doesn't seem to know anything about it.

Your grandmother did it, afterward. She's with us now.

Tell her thanks for me, allowed me to get a decent sleep. Still... it looks like I'm in for another round of roughing up before... nope... huh...

What?

They're letting me out of the cell... I'm... they're taking me to the arena.

Fuck! It'll be harder to get to you there.

Yeah, sounds like they suspect someone got in and healed me and are taking me to a more secure location.

Once you're there, reach out, let me know where you are, we're coming for you.

I will, she said, but behind her strong facade there was fear in her voice. *I'm working on freeing myself from this collar, but I don't know if I'll get it off in time.*

Huh... she could do that? I didn't think it was possible to break a binding collar while wearing it. But if anyone could...

We're coming, I repeated. I didn't know what else to say. Then I relayed what Izzy had said to those with me.

Koar swore.

Olinara let out a long, frustrated huff.

"Our plan doesn't change," Lhorine said. "Let's get Bayn's sister and get out. Then we can help Izzy... somehow."

She was right. Though the uncertainty behind that "somehow" bothered us all as we crept farther into this secure facility.

So much of our plan had already gone wrong. We were well past "the other shoe" dropping. It was raining shoes, and I just hoped we could make it out of this storm before we were trampled.

KOARTHANDRIS

I WAS BESIDE MYSELF, ITCHING TO BE GONE FROM THIS PLACE. I was too far from Izzy. I hadn't been able to protect her last night, when Saldrea had nearly killed her, and I wasn't there now. I needed to do my duty to the crown, to Izzy, but I couldn't because of that damned titan's stubbornness.

I could understand why he'd want his family freed, but didn't he see the imminent danger Izzy faced? What a callous bastard.

And now Izzy was being moved to the arena, where it would be even harder to get to her. I certainly hoped that damned titan had a way in, otherwise this was all for naught. If we couldn't reach Izzy in time, couldn't break the binding on her collar, then Saldrea would kill her in the arena.

Everything balanced on a razor's edge. We needed to do what we came here to do and get back as quickly as possible. Our plan was to tell the men guarding Wensuria that we were their replacements, but it seemed we were too late.

"We just started our shift here," the one guard said. "You must be mistaken."

The guards were dwarves, not elves, but I had a feeling they'd still be a challenge to fight. You didn't make it into the queen's secret dungeons if you were a slouch. We'd have to deal with them quickly since there were other guards not far away, just around a corner, down the next hall. We'd seen them when we passed. Lhorine had a spell to engulf an area in silence, but she'd need a moment to cast it.

"Ah, sorry, my mistake," Olinara said... and Lhorine began casting.

I charged in, followed by Rook.

"What the hell?" one of the guards managed to get out before we were plunged into silence.

The basic attack strategy we'd worked out during the night was for Rook to arouse them as a distraction. Then I'd keep the guards occupied while Olinara cast spells.

That all went as planned. The two dwarves cringed awkwardly as lust filled them. Even two on one, I'd taken one down by the time Olinara's spell went off and ice cut through the other one.

The problem was the guards from the other hall, who must have heard the one guard's startled words, before the silence, and came to investigate.

Lhorine couldn't get another silence spell off fast enough, and one of the guards gave a loud shout, alerting all the other guards on this level. We'd counted ten on our way to this cell, but from what we'd gleaned from the guards captured last night, any given floor could have as many as two dozen men guarding it.

I cursed, but no sound came out, we were still silenced. I pointed at the door to Wensuria's cell, hoping the others got my point to get her out. I'd take care of the guards.

I marched toward the two dwarves and brought forth my destruction. Dwarves were usually resistant to fire, many of them having spent time in Urval, so neither my burst of flame power, nor my fire breath would do much. So, I used raw destruction. It was the same power I'd used to destroy Izzy's room.

The wave of raw destructive power I unleashed flowed down the hall and ripped apart the two dwarven guards where they stood. It wasn't quiet.

I quickly looked back to check on the others. Rook was helping a large titan woman — Wensuria — out of her cell, she looked weak. But what caught my attention was that Rook and Lhorine looked like themselves. Olinara's illusion had failed, probably when she'd cast the other spell. Olinara herself still looked like a guard, since that was her nymph ability.

Booted footfalls came from seemingly all directions.

"Come on, let's get out of here," Olinara said as the others reached me.

We'd known going in that if things turned bad, our escape wouldn't be easy. In any normal underground complex, Lhorine could have moved earth and stone to create a diagonal tunnel for us to climb out, blocking anyone behind us. But this place had special enchantments on all the surfaces, walls and floors, reinforcing them. That meant earth magic was no help in here. It hindered Lhorine, but it also meant the dwarven guards could only use their physical enhancement and mundane weapons against us. We, however, had three non-earth-magic users, and Lhorine had smuggled in a few small stones, which she' reworked into long thin spikes, throwing them with precision. I used destruction liberally. Rook threw fire and Olinara summoned water, encompassing guards' heads in swirling pools, drowning on dry land.

In that manner we managed to fight our way back up six

floors, but we found ourselves trapped in the stairwell below the ground-level. The guards there were ready for us.

Olinara froze the stairwell below us in solid ice, stopping anyone from coming up behind us, but we were trapped. The dozens of guards on the main level didn't rush in, which might have served us better, fighting them in a bottleneck at the door. Instead, they waited for us to come out.

They had all the time in the world.

We didn't.

"Can you send a flood over them?" Rook asked Olinara.

She answered with strain in her voice. "I'm not sure if you've noticed the twenty-foot-thick block of ice below us? That's not easy to maintain. I'm a bit busy keeping us from being flanked."

Rook swore. "My fire won't do much against a bunch of enhanced dwarves and elves."

"I could probably get most of them with my destruction," I said. The trouble was, I'd been using that power a lot and was starting to feel the strain. And we still had to get back to campus and potentially fight again once we arrived.

I looked at Lhorine. This little lull in the fighting had given her time to break the binding on Wensuria's collar.

"There, you're free."

The titan woman massaged her neck. "Can we not... oh..." She grimaced. I guessed she'd tried her earth magic on the walls. "I'm afraid I'll be of little help. This stone resists my magic."

"Any ideas?" I asked Lhorine.

The elf shrugged. "Like Wensuria, there is little I can do. But I'll fight." She hefted the sword which had come with her guard's gear.

"Can you use a sword?" I asked Wensuria.

"Not well."

"Good enough." I tossed her mine. "I'll lead, destroying what I can, you four clean up the rest." I wouldn't call it a plan, but it was all we had.

I burst from the stairwell and blasted my destruction even as weapons were hurled my way, arrows and axes flying. They were blown away, as were most of the men before me. But that large blast left me staggered.

Luckily, it seemed to have dealt with the majority of the guards. We bolted for the door as a few guards filed in from other locations. But it was too late. As soon as I was outside, I transformed, with no care for my clothes.

Yet... I'd forgotten something. All those earth-wielders inside couldn't shape the structure they were in... but the stone outside...

Spikes of earth shot up from the ground. My hide was tough, but the sheer number of spears still hurt like hell, and that wasn't the worst thing. Most of the others managed to avoid the shards of stone, but Lhorine was skewered on one just as she exited the building.

Fuck!

Wensuria dispelled the spike — catching Lhorine as she fell, lifeless — and put a massive block of stone up in front of the doorway to stop any others from getting through.

Then everyone quickly mounted on my back and I launched myself into the sky.

Lhorine's earth-walk would have gotten us back to campus quicker than my flight, mostly because I had passengers to worry about and couldn't go as fast for fear of losing one of them. Still, I went as fast as I could.

We'd traversed perhaps half the distance back to campus when Rook shouted from my back.

"Izzy contacted me!" I could barely hear him over the rushing wind. "Someone at the prison must have called

Saldrea. She knows something happened, and she's moved up Izzy's trial. They're going into the arena now!"

Fucking hell!

Of course our attack would get reported back to the princess. Why hadn't anyone thought of that?

There was no way we'd get back in time to help.

Unless...

I used the telepathic communication I had in dragon form to reach out to Rook. Curiously... his mind was blocked to me. I tried Olinara and reached her.

Contact Bayn, let him know we have his sister. Now's the time to act!

I had to hope that damned titan lived up to his word. Right now, he was our only chance to free Izzy.

And tell everyone back there to hold on!

I put on speed as my soul cried out in pain, a twisting anguish which had nothing to do with failing in my duty and everything to do with losing someone I cared for.

If Izzy survived this, I swore I wouldn't hold myself back from her affections any longer. I'd been a fool, a complete idiot, ignoring my feelings for that perfect woman. I'd been so intent on protecting her that I hadn't understood *why* I'd needed her to live. It wasn't to uphold my duty, not anymore. No, I needed her to live, because I loved her.

BAYN

"Wake up!" As frustrated as I was, I restrained myself from slapping the unconscious angel too hard. Hana had knocked the man out when Saldrea had come for Izzy that morning, so he wouldn't put up a fuss. But she must have stunned him well, since I was having trouble rousing him.

And we didn't have time for me to linger here.

I'd received the call that my sister was safe as Saldrea had dragged Izzy — by the hair — into the arena. It was too early, even with a campus wide announcement, barely any crowd had gathered to watch. But Saldrea had been spooked when the prison called, telling her someone had escaped. She didn't know who, not yet, there had been too much chaos at the prison for them to be certain who'd been liberated. Still, it had infuriated Saldrea, who'd pulled Izzy into the arena to start her deathmatch.

The little shifter the others had wanted me to rescue from Saldrea's dungeons had been brought to the arena as well, unconscious and well-guarded. I couldn't get to him, nor Izzy, not without help.

So, I'd slipped away to get this angel. Even with my titan

friends we wouldn't be able to overpower Saldrea's minions and the guards at the arena. Though how much one little angel would help, I didn't know. I'd hoped he still had a few friends here on campus to join us.

I slapped him again, harder.

The man roused and groaned. I shook him till his eyes focused on me.

"They've taken Izzy. Can you fight?"

Instantly his eyes snapped open. He looked around, frantic, then returned his gaze to me.

"Yes, where is she?"

"In the arena. We need to take out the guards and Saldrea's cronies. I have four other titans who will aid me. Your friends, the incubi, the dragon, and the nymph are all off campus. Is there anyone else you know who can fight?"

The man blinked as I set him on his feet. I could see him assimilating what I told him.

"A shifter... maybe."

One shifter?

That was it?

"Call him," I said as we began to run across campus. As soon as we were out of the admin buildings the angel brought out his wings and flew, calling his shifter friend. I sprinted, enhancing my speed and the two of us reached the arena at about the same time.

An old man met us.

"I know what's happened, how do you need me to help?" the man asked.

This was the shifter friend? He looked ancient.

We made our way inside and joined up with my friends.

"It's us seven against Saldrea's friends and... how many guards?" the angel asked me.

"Ten dragons."

"Fucking hell," the shifter swore.

"Heavens!" the angel said at the same time. "And Myel?"

"The shifter? He's in there too, well-guarded by Golana, behind all the rest."

More swearing.

Yeah, I didn't like this either.

"I hope you're ready for the fight of your life," I said, heading deeper into the bowels of the arena.

The old man squared his jaw. "If I die so that Izzy can live, so be it!"

Ah... a fanatic. Great. Though perhaps that was what we needed right now. Someone willing to face death head on, because we didn't stand a chance. Still, I'd promised the others I'd fight to free their friends if they liberated my sister and they had. So, the seven of us marched into the well-guarded marshalling area in the arena.

I had to give credit to that angel and the ancient shifter. The angel instantly blinded our foes, then rose up on his wings and began a barrage of light rays so intense it seemed to fill the room. The shifter surprised a dragon and nearly took the big man down with one attack, his half-tiger form quick and agile as he slashed with claws and tore with teeth.

One on one, titan versus dragon wasn't much of a contest, but two dragons each was a challenge. We all fought with everything we had, but I didn't think it would be enough.

Cheers erupted from outside, in the arena proper.

I didn't know how long Izzy — bound by a collar — could last against Saldrea going all out on her. And if Izzy died, my life was forfeit. Izzy's grandmother had been clear about that. I didn't fear the nymph on her own, but given how savagely those around me fought, I had a feeling Izzy's allies would indeed tear me apart if I didn't save her now.

And a part of me didn't want to let that strange, intoxicating woman perish either. I wanted to know more about her. She defied Saldrea at every turn, even while being tortured. Her strength and determination was unlike anything I'd ever seen.

I had to hope those qualities would keep her alive now, because the foes before us, despite outnumbering us, were digging in to fortify their position. All they had to do was wait. They had the luxury of time. We didn't. We'd taken down three dragons, but that still left seven, not to mention a powerful dwarf, a fiendish sylph, and a nasty undine.

We fought with stone and light, and shifter's claws, but they matched us move for move with ice and wind, mental attacks, and swirling pools around our heads to drown us, all while dragons blasted fire, safe behind walls of stone.

We titans should have been able to tear down those walls, with five of us earth-wielders to Golana's one, but with the other attacks on us, it was everything we could do to defend and attack at the same time, distracted enough that Golana could rebuild their defenses quick enough if one of us did manage to tear them down.

And trying to reach past them with my earth magic was useless, the arena floor was protected by a powerful binding to ensure no one outside could help those within.

Izzy was on her own.

IZZY

I FLEW BACKWARD THROUGH THE AIR, LANDING HARD AND rolling, sending up a cloud of dirt from the arena floor. It was a good thing I was tougher now. The collar around my neck didn't seem to have diminished my natural durability as an elf, at least not much. I'd taken several full-strength hits from Saldrea, which would have killed me before my mother's binding had been removed.

Still, I wasn't in good shape. Cuts marred most of my skin, though few of them were serious. No, it was the massive welts from where Saldrea had hit me which really hurt. They seemed to be everywhere, radiating a throbbing pain.

I'd taken several hits while distracted, focused on breaking the binding on my collar. Having had a decent sleep last night, thanks to my grandmother healing me, I'd woken early this morning, before Saldrea had come to get me, and worked on freeing myself. But I had no idea how close I might be to breaking the binding. There was no lessening of resistance, the collar was an all or nothing thing, full strength until broken. But that meant I had no gauge to mark my progress. I hoped I was close. Every moment since I'd woken — through being moved, then held in the prisons below the arena, then finally dragged by my hair out to fight — I'd kept working on the collar. Even as the fight had started, I'd focused on breaking the binding on me instead of defense. I'd thought I'd been close. But it had cost me... in the form of these welts.

Then I'd figured something out, after Saldrea had hit me so hard I'd flown into the wall of the arena and crumpled to the ground. As the insane princess had sauntered leisurely over to me, I'd remembered the trick Grandma Oli had taught me, about how to lock my form when changing shapes as a nymph. I'd initially assumed it only worked on shape-changing, but perhaps it didn't. Maybe I could "lock in" my work on the collar, so I didn't have to focus on it constantly and it would continue on its own. It had taken a couple tries, but it had worked! That had left my mind free to focus on this fight. Since then, I'd led Saldrea on a merry little dance around the arena, evading her strikes, mostly...

It helped that she was toying with me. And if it meant prolonging this fight, then I was happy to play into her superiority fantasy. Every time I groaned louder, got up a little slower, she smiled all the wider, getting off on my suffering.

As an elf, she could have enhanced her speed, been much faster, nearly impossible for me to avoid without greater enhancements myself, but she'd only done that a few times, when she'd gotten frustrated at not hitting me. That's how I knew she was playing with me. Which I found odd, given that she'd rushed into this fight.

She'd dragged me out here, saying, "I don't know who your friends freed from my secret prison, or what they hoped to gain by it, but it means you'll die all the sooner."

I'd assumed that meant she'd end things quickly... but she hadn't.

She reached me again, launching a quick series of attacks, which I managed to avoid, taking only a glancing blow to my arm and leg before she finally sped herself up and hit me square in the chest, sending me flying once more.

I was pretty sure a rib cracked. It hadn't been the first time she'd hit that spot. My chest felt like I was half-run over, with the car still sitting on top of me, getting harder to breathe.

The crowd cheered. Saldrea raised her hands and turned slowly as I got up once more. That was when I understood. She'd taken her time with me, to wait for more of an audience. There had been hardly anyone in the stands when we'd started, but they'd been filling in quickly and were about a third full now.

But if that was her only reason for stalling... how much longer did I have? Would this be enough of a gallery for her to start fighting in earnest? Maybe half-full? I could only hope she was waiting for the stands to be packed, but I didn't think I'd be that lucky.

I didn't waste any energy trying to check on how the collar was coming. It wouldn't do me any good. I needed to focus all my attention on Saldrea and surviving as long as I could. The collar would come off when it came off, I had to survive until then.

The cheers of the crowd died down, and Saldrea turned to me again.

And this time, she enhanced herself, zipping to me faster than I could see. She grabbed my neck in one hand and lifted me, not stopping till I slammed into a wall. The air whooshed out of me and I was stunned for a second as Saldrea pinned me there.

"I don't know how you've survived this long, but I'm glad we finally have a decent crowd to see you die."

Fuck. We'd apparently reached enough people for her to fight for real.

"I'm an elf," I gasped in response to her first question. "We're tough."

Saldrea's brow furrowed. "The collar should suppress your elven nature, make you weak."

Oh...

Huh.

So, I was that much stronger than this collar? Not only did I have a modicum of magic to work with, attempting to break the collar, but my body was nearly as strong and tough as normal.

Saldrea caught on quickly.

"You're stronger than the collar," she hissed. "That was the strongest collar we had! It would have suppressed..." I could guess the end of that sentence: *my powers*.

I couldn't help it. I shouldn't have smiled, shouldn't have pushed her over the edge, but my damned fight-the-power nature decided to rear its ugly head, and I gave her a little grin.

"You little shit," she sneered, wrath twisting her face. This was the real Saldrea, her ugly inside coming to the surface. "You may be stronger than that collar, but it's slowing you enough. Time to end this!"

I can't say exactly what happened next, except that Saldrea beat the shit out of me. The hits came too fast, too hard. She used only one hand, with the other still around my neck, but that one hand was more than enough. Bones broke, skin tore, blood flowed.

Since I couldn't fight back, I retreated inward. I tried sapping power from my body to aid in my attempt to break the collar. It meant my wounds piled on all the quicker. The pain was like nothing I'd ever felt before. No, that wasn't true. The pain yesterday — after she'd lost her shit and gone all out on me — had been this bad. And nothing would ever compare to the agony of Myel's torture, then death.

And when she was done, she threw me toward the center of the ring. I landed in a heap, unable to do anything other than bleed on the dirt. My body was broken, useless. I clung to life by sheer force of will and spirit. Vyns had told me stories of how seraphim could push past physical limits with spirit alone. I understood that now. My very life essence suffused me with enough strength to keep taking one more breath.

Come on, you damned collar, break!

Though even if it did, it may be too late now. Even with my power back, what could I do? It might take all the power I had just to heal myself.

Even so, I fought with every shred of spirit that remained.

"You're still alive aren't you?" Saldrea said as she reached me.

I expected her to be furious, but instead she chuckled. "Fine. If you insist on living, I'll break your spirit too. This should be fun. Wait here... not like you have a choice."

She sauntered off.

Where was she going?

What did she have planned?

How would she break my spirit?

But then I knew.

Dread filled me as I sensed Myel's fear spike through our bond. Saldrea had gone to get him.

No, no, no, no, no!

Feeling Myel die the first time had been anguish beyond anything I'd ever endured. Nothing could be worse... or so I'd thought. Yet lying here, knowing I'd feel that epic agony *again*, so close but unable to stop it, *that* filled me with a dread horror, which shredded my soul and eviscerated my mind.

I wasn't strong enough to survive Myel dying again.

This time, if he was killed...

I'd die with him.

VYNSIEL

I'd never fought this hard before, never pushed myself to my limits this long, but I couldn't help it. I sensed Izzy's pain and her flagging spirit. She was dying, and I was so damned close but too far away to help her.

I fought with everything I had, blasting dragons and defenses and anything in my path with searing beams of light over and over, an unending barrage of lasers as I screamed my fury and frustration.

I'd grown wise after the first time Hana had hit me with a mental attack, stunning me, then Neyalim had surrounded my head with water attempting to drown me. I'd blinded them and fled, regrouping. My mistake had been having my beams originate from me, which gave them a target. Now I launched my attacks from all over, while adding blinding flashes to disorient them and hiding behind a shield of light, of which I kept three going at all times, alternating which I hid behind.

Never before had I attempted to do so much at once, surprising myself with my aptitude and strength. Even the hard-faced titans gave grunts of approval.

Then, as I flew from one shield of light to another, my enhanced vision caught something back amongst the enemies.

The heavy grate blocking the entrance to the arena floor was open. Saldrea stood just inside. For an instant I panicked, thinking she was finished and Izzy was dead, but no, I was still in contact with Izzy's spirit, strong but waning.

It was the other thing I caught in that quick glimpse which spiked my fear: Golana handing Myel over to Saldrea.

Fuck.

No!

Saldrea would use him to break Izzy's spirit.

I'd seen what his torture had done to Izzy the first time, how it had broken her. I couldn't let Saldrea take him into the arena. My life was worth nothing if Izzy died, so screw it. I braced myself for all manner of nastiness and flew straight into the enemy...

...or I would have if a hand hadn't clamped on my shoulder and stopped me.

"Let me go! Saldrea has Myel. She'll take him into the arena and torture him to break Izzy. We have to—" That's when I noticed who was holding me. "Koar?"

"We're here, we can help," the dragon said. With him were Rook and Olinara, Lhorine and a titan woman I didn't know but I assumed was Bayn's sister. This was confirmed by the big titan giving her a brief hug when he saw her.

Huh.

I didn't think titans had feelings.

That didn't matter; reinforcements had arrived and with their help, we could turn the tide of this fight!

"You heard what I said, though, right? We need to get in there now!" I reiterated.

"We'll break through their lines," Lhorine said. She

looked wan, rough, drained, but her words and tone were determined. "You need to focus on Izzy, on her spirit. Give her everything you have, support her, be her rock. She'll need your strength to survive what is to come. Give her time. Give *us* time."

She was right, but I balked at the idea of sitting back and not fighting.

"We've got this," Rook said, balls of fire in his hands, which he threw at the enemy.

"*The rest of us* have this," Olinara said to Rook. "You need to stay back too. Use your connection to Izzy's mind, keep her sane, keep her going." The nymph looked at both of us. "She'll need *both* of you."

I looked at the demon.

Not that long ago, I'd hated demons. I'd been told since birth that they were depraved and evil, vile beings. I knew better now. Rook may not be my favorite person — he'd left Izzy for a little too long when she'd needed all of us — but I could see now that he was as dedicated to her as I was. His eyes burned with devotion. He was all in for Izzy and I think that terrified him, but he was still here, helping, driven.

I nodded to him.

He nodded in return.

The two of us stepped back, out of the fight.

"For Izzy," I said reaching out to the demon.

"For Izzy," he repeated, taking my hand. The connection wouldn't really help either of us, but it felt good to know I wasn't alone, that we were all fighting in our different ways.

Then I dove into my spirit, seeking my connection with the woman I loved. I found her radiant spirit floundering. So I sent her strength through our connection, as I'd done last night. I couldn't communicate with her, but I hoped Rook would explain what was happening. I needed her to *feel* my love and support, to know she was strong enough to endure what was to come.

Because she was.

I'd seen it time and again.

That woman had taken nearly everything this world had thrown at her, trying to break her, and she'd remained standing, strong. Her strength had inspired me to change, to forgive myself, to be a better person. In doing so, I'd unlocked a deeper well of spirit, a font of power I'd blocked my entire life because I'd known what I'd been doing was wrong.

And I used every last drop of my spiritual strength to bolster Izzy now.

In return I felt something from her, a pulse of warmth through our link… like squeezing my hand. She knew I was here and helping, and appreciated it.

I smiled, then lost myself in spirit, giving everything I had to her. She'd need all of my power to survive what Saldrea was about to do.

AMARHUK (ROOK)

IZZY'S THOUGHTS CHURNED, DARK AND DESPAIRING, YET EVERY now and then, some small shred of light peaked through and she'd think of Vyns. His spiritual connection kept her going.

Now to do my part.

Stay strong, Izzy... I... I love you. You need to fight! I'd rushed through that middle part, even within my own mind, it hadn't been easy to say those three words. I wasn't ready to say them out loud, but here and now, connecting with Izzy in this way, it was what needed to be said, what she needed to hear.

Rook... That one word was filled with so much anguish and desperation, reaching out to me for support.

Let me take your suffering, I whispered, and with a long breath, I deepened my connection to Izzy's mind. It was something I'd never tried before. I'd never wished to get this deep, this intense with any woman. I'd assumed it was possible but never wished to go there... until now. I linked fully to Izzy's mind, a chaotic whirlwind of images and impressions, reflections, speculations, slivers of hope, and inferences of doom. I couldn't make her feel any better, this wasn't a domain of emotions. Vyns worked with her there. What I could do was calm her thoughts and help her find peace, so she could fight with greater strength and clarity.

Despite having never done it before, it took little effort. It was as if some greater force wished for us to be connected in this way, encouraged it. I didn't question it.

I took her horror and confusion, bringing it to my mind. I didn't know if Saldrea had started punishing Myel, or if these thoughts were imaginings of what the false princess *might* do, but I watched Myel being ripped and shredded, disemboweled slowly.

My gorge rose and I would have been sick... if it hadn't been for a faint calming influence, just a trickle, from where Vyns' hand clasped mine. He kept my emotions in check so I could endure these thoughts on Izzy's behalf.

And in return, Izzy's mind cleared, calm and settled.

Wow... Izzy breathed. *Rook... thank you. I... I can't... It's horrible, but now... I can focus. Thank you.* The raw pain in her mental voice tore at me, even as I sensed her strength building. She could focus on what she needed to do, not the horrors around her.

I'd done what I could. I'd do anything for the woman I loved, including enduring this torture and taking her pain, so she could fight.

And fight she did.

IZZY

I COULDN'T FIGHT PHYSICALLY, BUT I STILL FOUGHT. I FOCUSED all my strength — including a massive influx of spirit from Vyns — into breaking my collar. Maybe, if I got rid of that, I could do something to stop Saldrea?

And I *had* to stop her.

She had Myel on his knees, slowly pulling out his intestines. With one punch she'd punctured his abdomen. Now she laughed with sick glee as she reached in to pull out his guts. Her eyes were glued to me, where I lay helpless, watching. My gaze never left Myel's. His eyes had glazed over, his body limp. I had no clue how much longer he could hold on.

Stay with me! I sent to him through our bond.

He didn't reply.

I felt his pain, his weakness, his sorrow. He was in there somewhere, but I couldn't reach him. I hoped he'd heard me, since I couldn't spare the energy to deepen our bond. Everything I had went into breaking my collar.

Rook's mental assistance had cleared my mind, a

godsend. Being calm wasn't entirely possible in my current state, but I was able to focus on freeing myself.

And while I did, I played Saldrea's game.

I didn't look away, didn't talk back, didn't show strength. She wanted to draw this out and see me suffer, so I showed her all my anguish. Because the more I gave her, the slower she worked, savoring my defeat, and the longer Myel survived. A tear leaked from my eye and traced over a broken, swollen cheek. Saldrea drank it in. It was easy enough to do, since Myel's suffering was my own.

He began to slip away, death closing in, our bond faltered.

No, no, no!

Inwardly I screamed, a war cry, filled with raw defiance and resolve. I pulled more from Vyns, our connection straining as I siphoned his spirit, greedily taking everything he offered and pouring it all into breaking the collar.

Allies are coming, they've nearly broken through! Rook sent into my mind.

My heart filled with hope. And whether it was that surge in determination or the culmination of all the work I'd done, the suppression collar around my neck gave a loud snap as it cracked and fell away.

I was free.

Don't miss the next book in the series!

Clash of Queens
Veilblood Academy: Book 3

Out of the frying pan into all-out war. If I want the throne, I'll have to fight for it.

It took everything I had, and all my guys working for me and helping out, to defeat the false princess Saldrea and her henchwomen. But I barely have time to recover before her mother, Valnea, declares war on me.

Luckily the queen regent isn't in a hurry to start that fight, but only because she plans to gather the entire might of the elven empire to ensure she crushes me and my little rebellion completely.

I need help now, but where can I turn?

My dashing angel Vyns, with whom I'm bound in spirit, says he'll rouse the seraphim to aid me. Rook, the sinful incubus, who had been distant, is once again at my side. He can return to Urval, the fae realm's version of hell, to see if the people there can help. Though first, I think I need an apology and an explanation for why he's been a dick lately.

Koar the stalwart dragon, is always at my side, a permanent protector and so very easy on the eyes. He's suddenly interested in a relationship, which he hadn't been before, and I can't say I mind. I could use all the sexy distractions I can get.

And speaking of sexy distractions, Myel, my perfect Goth shifter-vampire, is everything I need, but he doesn't seem to think so. And when he's sent on a dangerous mission, our bond is once again pulled tight which always makes me feel awful.

Then, along comes Bayn, the titan who helped me and my friends defeat Saldrea's minions. And though we barely know each other, he's demanding we get married. If we do, he'll bring the might of the titans to fight on my side. Like I don't already have enough to deal with.

And time is running out. If we don't find allies soon, all of us will be crushed by the ruthless elves. All those I'd hoped to protect... will die.

OTHER BOOKS BY CLARA WILS

Fantasy Reverse Harem

THE MISTS OF ELISTA TRILOGY

Bonds and Blood, book 1

Shape and Shadows, book 2

Form and Fury, book 3

THE SISTER SPIRITS SERIES

Double Discover, book 1

Double Danger, book 2

Double Disaster, book 3

Double Doom, book 4

Double Destiny, book 5

THE LADY BLADE TRILOGY

Mistress Guard, book 1

Sword Skirt, book 2

Mystic Knight, book 3

THE VEILBLOOD ACADEMY TRILOGY

Blood of the Veil, book 1

Test of Tyrants, book 2

Clash of Queens, book 3

Portal Fantasy Reverse Harem

THE GRECIAN GODDESS TRILOGY

Kiss of the Goddess, book 1

Power of the Goddess, book 2

Bonds of the Goddess, book 3

Paranormal Reverse Harem

THE SECRETS GODS KEEP TRILOGY

Craving Demons, book 1

Chaos Demons, book 2

Claiming Demons, book 3

HER BAD BOY WOLVE TRILOGY

Pack To The Wall, book 1

Want You Pack, book 2

Pack In Business, book 3

www.ingramcontent.com/pod-product-compliance
Lightning Source LLC
LaVergne TN
LVHW050927080826
845145LV00001B/241

* 9 7 8 1 9 9 0 5 8 7 7 3 3 *